FANTÔMAS

The Daughter of Fantômas

The Daughter of Fantômas

by
Marcel Allain
and
Pierre Souvestre

adapted by
Mark P. Steele

A Black Coat Press Book

Acknowledgements: Special thanks to the following for this book: Jack at ildado.com for information on Baccarat; Drach Birch for reading and commenting on the translated text; David Woodhouse of the Heritage Railway Association in the UK at http://ukhrail.uel.ac.uk/ for information on old steam locomotives; of course, Jean-Marc Lofficier, my editor and publisher at BlackCoatPress.com; the folks at the Friends of Fantômas web site for their continuing love and support of the French master criminal; Robin Walz and Elliott Smith, authors of *L'Encyclopedie de Fantômas*, for information on the various editions and movies, and the plot synopses of some of the novels at www.Fantômas-lives.com; www.audiobooks forfree.com for the online audio versions of the 1st 2 books available at their web site; and, of course, to Cor, for sharing me with Fantômas, and putting up with him for these months (not an easy task!); and to David McDonnell for proofreading the typescript.

Mark P. Steele
Eye-n-Apple Prods.
www.anerispress.com/ena

CHAQUE VOLUME FORME UN RÉCIT COMPLET

Pierre Souvestre et Marcel Allain

FANTÔMAS

LA FILLE de FANTÔMAS

COLLECTION REX

100 FRS

Introduction
Who is Fantômas?

People around the world over have been asking this question for nearly a century. To find the answer, we must start by looking at the character's history...

In February 1911, French publisher Arthème Fayard released the first of a monthly series of pulp magazines featuring Pierre Souvestre and Marcel Allain's master criminal. For the next two and a half years, until September 1913, the reading public was treated to the lurid chronicles of one of the earliest continuing crime figures of the 20th century—predating even the insidious Dr. Fu-Manchu.

Fantômas—the "Lord of Terror"—took the reading public by storm and was soon adopted by the Surrealist Movement, affecting the art and literature of the pre-World War I generation. Painter René Magritte, a friend of André Breton, was particularly influenced by the character, but many others of that circle were also taken by the striking figure of the contemplative masked man, dressed in a dinner jacket, boldly stepping over Paris, bloody dagger in hand, as depicted by artist Gino Starace on the cover of the first issue. The first Fantômas "bootleg" appeared as early as 1912, when an unauthorized stage play was performed in Naples.

Soon, Fantômas became the subject of silent movies, starting in April 1913. Louis Feuillade filmed the first three books and an additional two later stories. Feuillade is credited with developing many of the thriller techniques later used by directors such as Fritz Lang and Alfred Hitchcock.

René Navarre, who would later team up with writer Gaston Leroux, creator of *The Phantom of the Opera*, in his own production company, played Fantômas. The final episodes of the Fantômas movie serials were released in May 1914.[1]

Souvestre died in February 1914 of the Spanish Flu, popularly known at the time as "The Plague"—a disease that would wipe out many soldiers during the coming global conflict before it was through.

By 1915, English, Spanish and other translated editions of the Fantômas books were quickly prepared and released around the globe. The first seven books of the original series were eventually translated into English, ending in 1924.[2]

Allain also wrote a book called *The Yellow Document, or The Fantômas of Berlin*, published in 1919 by Brentano's in the US and in 1920 by Stanley, Paul & Co. in England, but Fantômas never appeared in it. No French version of this book was ever released.

An unauthorized American film version of Fantômas was produced in 1920—unfortunately, it is now apparently lost, though Black Coat Press is preparing a special novelization of this early classic, courtesy of David White.

In 1921, the first authorized stage version of Fantômas was performed in France. An Italian version was performed soon after in Italy in 1922.

In 1925, Allain began a series of new adventures of Fantômas, at first serialized in magazines, and later reprinted and expanded into five additional volumes, also released by Arthème Fayard. These books were translated into English and published between 1925 and 1928 by David Mac Kay and Stanley, Paul & Co.—the last Fantômas books ever translated into English, until the publication of this volume.

In 1931, the first sound feature film of Fantômas was released, directed by Paul Fejos, featuring Jean Galland as the

---

[1] More information about Fantômas in the movies and other media can be found in Jean-Marc & Randy Lofficier's *Shadowmen: Heroes and Villains of French Pulp Fiction*, ISBN 0-9740711-3-7, Black Coat Press, 2003.

[2] See *Bibliography* at the end of this book.

eponymous anti-hero. Unfortunately, Marcel Allain was quite critical of this version and, though sequels were planned, they were never released.

Allain then helped prepare a series of edited reprints of the original book series, released from April 1932 to November 1934. Some of these were renamed to include the name of Fantômas in every title.

During this time, Allain also wrote several new *Fantômas* adventures that were published in serial form from 1933 to 1938, but never collected in book form. These were virtually the last original Fantômas works by its co-creator, though Allain lived until 1970. He wrote well over 500 books in his career and created many other characters such as Tigris (1928), Fatala (1930), Miss Téria (1931) and Férocias (1933)—but none ever rivaled Fantômas' fame.

Since then, Fantômas has appeared in an unending stream of movies, television shows and comics. Among these are:

• In 1937, the first Mexican comic version of Fantômas appeared, though this would not significantly affect the history of the character for 25 more years.

• In 1941, the first French comics version of Fantômas appeared in *Gavroche*, but quickly faded due to censorship.

• In 1946 and 1948, two French movies adapting and drawing from the first two books were released, the first directed by Jean Sacha and written by renowned fantasy writer Jean-Louis Bouquet starred Marcel Herrand as Fantômas and Simone Signoret as Hélène, his daughter; the second, directed by Robert Vernay, featured Maurice Teynac as the title character.

• During this time, a radio series of Fantômas was also released, lasting into 1947.

• In 1957 and 1958, a syndicated newspaper strip adapted the first two novels.

• In 1962, in Mexico, a new comic book version appeared, published by Editorial Novaro, which began as straight adaptations of the original stories, but soon created original tales of Fantômas, suddenly turned into a masked crime fighter. Fantômas' black mask was eventually traded in for a white model and he donned a super-heroic uniform. The "Elegant Menace" (as he was dubbed) fought such threats as Hitler's son. This version of Fantômas was assisted by a crew of beautiful women named after the Zodiac, and earned a spot in Jeff Rovin's *Encyclopedia of Super Heroes*. This incarnation of Fantômas lasted around 20 years—a healthy run for a comic book character in any country. A number of writers contributed to this; the art was by the Rubens Studio.

• In 1962 and 1963, a *fumetti* (photo-novel) magazine published by Del Duca adapted books 1-3 and 5 of the series over the course of 17 issues,.

• In 1964, during the Bond film craze, a new movie was made. Though it had its detractors, it did become popular in, of all places, Cuba! One wonder what Castro thought of this foreign import... The infamous blue-green mask of this version is the image that many people to this day have when they think of Fantômas. Two sequels were made. In all three films, famous French heartthrob Jean Marais (of *Beauty and the Beast* fame) starred as both the arch-criminal and his nemesis, Jérôme Fandor, and comic legend Louis de Funès was Juve.

• In 1977, Argentinian novelist Julio Cortazar, incorporated the Spanish comic book Fantômas into a neo-surrealist novel, *Fantômas Contra Los Vampiros Multinacionales*, where the hero/writer, investigating a multinational conspiracy, reads the Fantômas comics and soon finds himself fighting side by side with the Elegant Menace against the Conspiracy. Art from the Spanish studio that produced the comic was incorporated into the novel.

• In 1979, a series of four made-for-television movies directed by Claude Chabrol and Juan Luis Buñuel (the Spanish director's son), adapting the earlier books were made in France and Germany. They starred Helmut Berger as Fantômas and Gayle Hunnicutt as Lady Beltham.

• In 1986 and 1987, a new, English-language version of the first two Fantômas novels were reissued in an American market. Regrettably, the other six language translations were not...

• In 1990-1995, three graphic novel adaptations were published by Belgian publisher Claude Lefrancq, with stylish art by Claude Laverdure.

• Editorial Vid in Mexico briefly revived the original comic in the 1990s and Fantômas found himself fighting against the terrorists responsible for the bombing of the World Trade Center.

• In 2002, we learned in Alan Moore and Kevin O'Neill's *League of Extraordinary Gentlemen* Vol. 2 that Fantômas had been a member of a French organization group called *Les Hommes Mystérieux* who had fought the League in the sewers of Paris in 1913. Parallel to this, in Jean-Marc & Randy Lofficier and Gil Formosa's French comic book series *Robur* (2003-2005),[3] Gurn, a.k.a. Fantômas, is first the merciless enemy, then the cunning ally, of hero Robur.

• Most recently, a 2005 French play featured Fantômas attempting to kill off the world's population, to replace it with clones of his daughter.

In music, Fantômas' name has also been used by a Heavy Metal band of note, fronted by Michael Allan Patton, formerly of *Faith No More*, beginning in 1999. The character also inspired Marc Ellis'[4] haunting *Fantômas Waltz*, composed for the virtually unknown Hollywood movie, *F*, by Clementine Productions, written and directed by Howard A. Rodman and starring Terrence Stamp as Fantômas.

Why has it taken so long for the English-speaking world to catch on to Fantômas?

---

[3] The first two volumes were translated in *Heavy Metal* December 2003 and Fall 2005 issues.

[4] A New Orleans-based composer that, thankfully, survived Katrina's outburst.

Why, after seven stories, did the publishing world cease its efforts to keep us informed about the Lord of Terror's dastardly plots? Was the portrayal of Scotland Yard as unwitting, but willing, accomplices of Fantômas in Volume 7 too much for the English-reading public to accept? Was the portrayal of Natal in this book, with its opium-addicted public, its incompetent British soldiers, administrators, medical personnel, and its bigoted lynch mobs, too much for the World War I generation in England to consider? Opium dens, as portrayed in this book, were also featured in the Fu-Manchu stories of the time, but as a scheme of the Yellow Peril, rather than as a fixture of the British Empire...

Regardless of why previous generations may have lost out to Fantômas in English, we, today, have this "new" tale—and plan on having more!

Fantômas' roots were many: Paul Féval's John Devil, the first master criminal in the history of popular literature, as well as his notorious *Black Coats* saga.[5] Isidore Ducasse a.k.a. Comte de Lautreamont's *Chants de Maldoror*. Pierre-Alexis Ponson du Terrail's Rocambole.[6] Maurice Leblanc's Arsène Lupin.[7] Souvestre and Allain combined various past mystery men in the French tradition to create their picture of their master criminal.

Most of Fantômas' past remains unknown—and rightfully so. Like many other crime novel figures, though we

---

[5] *John Devil* (ISBN 1-932983-15-5) and *The Black Coats: 'Salem Street* (ISBN 1-932983-46-5) are available from Black Coat Press.

[6] *Rocambole* (ISBN 1-932983-57-0) is available from Black Coat Press in 2006.

[7] Three Arsène Lupin vs. Sherlock Holmes titles, *The Hollow Needle* (ISBN 0-9740711-9-6), *The Blonde Phantom* (ISBN 1-932983-14-7) and *The Stage Play* (ISBN 1-932983-16-3), are available from Black Coat Press.

might discover *some* of Fantômas' past and background, we will never know *all*.

Juve obviously owes much, including his name, to Victor Hugo's Inspector Javert of *Les Misérables*, but he follows in the tradition of a number of steadfast and relentless French policemen such as Emile Gaboriau's Monsieur Lecoq and Leblanc's Chief Inspector Ganimard.

Similarly, Fantômas' influence has cast a wide and diverse net. From Fantômas and Juve sprang Judex, a serial crime fighter also directed by Feuillade that was visually virtually identical to the later Shadow in the US.

Just as Sherlock Holmes was the archetypal modern detective, Fantômas became that of the archetypal modern arch-villain. Among his better-known literary descendants are Arnould Galopin's Tenebras (1911), Gaston René's Masque Rouge (1912), Feuillade's gang of the Vampires (1915), Fascinax (1921), Roger-Henri Jacquart's Démonios, René Collard's Démonax, Arthur Bernède's Belphégor (1927) and many more, including Allain's own creations, mentioned above.

In 1962, the Italian Diabolik, arguably the most influential of the Fantômas "clones" was created by two sisters, Angela and Giuliana Giussani. He, in turn, spawned his own wave of imitators and homages: Kriminal, Satanik, Killing, etc.

In June 1969, a series of Italian-made Donald Duck strips were published wherein Donald found the first of the diaries of Fantomius (Fantomiald in French and Paperinik in Italian), the secret identity of Lord Quackett, a notorious gentleman burglar and sometime vigilante that lived around the turn of the century.

In 2002, Grant Morrison introduced Fantomex into the new X-Men, a character that combined aspects of both Fantômas and Diabolik who turned out to be Weapon XIII, three experimental generations after the notorious Wolverine.

Finally, we must return to our original question: Who *is* Fantômas?

Here is what we have learned about him in the seven novels preceding *The Daughter of Fantômas*, all of which have been translated, but only the first two being currently readily accessible.

Fantômas' story began in South Africa during the Boer War (1899-1902), when the British waged war against the natives of mixed Dutch and German ancestry who had settled in tribal lands once belonging to the Zulus. There, a man named Gurn, then in his early 20s, fought on the side of the British. Where he came from was, and still remains, a mystery. We only know that he was an artillery sergeant under the command of Lord Roberts in the Western Transvaal. He also served under Lord Edward Beltham of Scottwell Hill and returned with him, and his much younger wife, Lady Maud Beltham, to England. (The Belthams are apparently connected to the British Royal Family in some fashion.)

During the journey back, Gurn fell in love with Lady Beltham. Their affair continued in England. One presumes that it is during that time that Gurn began embarking on a secret criminal career in France, using the name "Fantômas."

Some time later,[8] Gurn and Lady Beltham were surprised by Lord Beltham in their Paris love nest located in Rue Levert. The jealous husband was about to shoot his wife when Gurn hit him with a hammer, then strangled him.

Until that point, Gurn had hidden his criminal activities from Lady Beltham, but after her husband's death, he began to involve her as an accomplice in his schemes.

---

[8] The first Fantômas novel takes place over the course of about a year. The second claims to start a couple of years after the first, even though it was published only two months later. The dating in the novels is extremely unreliable. For instance, in Volume 9, Juve tells Fandor they have been fighting Fantômas for ten years, which is physically impossible.

Meanwhile, Inspector Juve of the French Sûreté had begun to detect the mysterious hand of "Fantômas" in a series of unsolved crimes that he had been investigating.

In the first novel, *Fantômas*, the Marquise de Langrune is found murdered in her chateau in the Dordogne. Young Charles Rambert is accused of the murder by his own father, Etienne Rambert. Soon afterward, Charles is forced to flee to escape being framed for a crime he did not commit.

A body, believed to be Charles', is eventually fished from the Dordogne River and Etienne Rambert identifies it as that of his son. Juve's investigation indicates Fantômas' involvement, but the only hard clue he finds is a map fragment showing the surrounding area.

Later, investigating Lord Beltham's disappearance, Juve finds the Lord's body in a steamer trunk in an apartment belonging to a man named Gurn.

Meanwhile, a masked man steals jewels and 120,000 francs from the Princess Sonia Danidoff while she bathes. Investigating, Juve soon discovers that Charles Rambert is still alive. He later captures him and determines to his own satisfaction that Charles cannot have killed the Marquise de Langrune. Juve helps him assume a new identity—that of crime reporter Jérôme Fandor, now working for *La Capitale*.

Eventually, Juve captures Gurn, who stands trial for Lord Beltham's murder. During the trial, Juve reveals that Gurn, or "Fantômas," is also responsible for the Danidoff robbery and the Marquise's murder. He also reveals that Gurn was impersonating Etienne Rambert, whose death Fantômas had manufactured; blowing up an ocean liner merely to cover his own trail.

Though Juve's deductions about Fantômas' crimes, and indeed, his very existence, are not widely believed, Gurn is nevertheless convicted for Lord Beltham's murder and sentenced to die on the guillotine.

However, thanks to Lady Beltham's assistance, at the last minute Gurn trades places with an actor made up to look like him, and who is executed in his stead. Fantômas is now free, since he's assumed to be dead. Only Juve and Fandor know that the beheaded Gurn was not the real Fantômas...

After some time spent chasing Fantômas and thwarting his various schemes in France, as chronicled in Volumes 2 to 6 of the series, Juve and Fandor eventually trace their enemy's trail back to England.

As the sixth novel, *Le Policier Apache* [*The Apache Policeman*],[9] opens, Fantômas has taken on the identity of Tom Bob, one of Scotland Yard's top five detectives known as the Council of Five. The other members of the Council are Shepard, French, Reverend Hope and Miss Davis. Fantômas is also posing as Dr. Garrick, and Lady Beltham as his wife.

In Volume 7, *Le Pendu de Londres* [*The Hanged Man of London*], Fantômas plots to replace Jack, Lord Duncan's recently deceased son, with Daniel, the child of Françoise Lemercier, another of his lovers. But Fandor discovers the scheme—and Tom Bob's other identity! However, Fantômas captures him just as the young reporter is writing a letter to Juve detailing his findings. The villain places his victim in a large crate with food, water and ventilation, planning on keeping him prisoner for about a month.

Meanwhile, Detective Shepard has staked out Dr. Garrick's house. Garrick's wife has disappeared and the fact that the Doctor keeps a mistress is known to the Policeman. Garrick (Fantômas) is planning to flee with Françoise to Canada, where she believes her companion has taken her son.

However, Shepard manages to arrest Garrick, whom he then recognizes as Tom Bob. By then, pieces of skin and bones have been found in Garrick's cellar, supporting the theory that the Doctor murdered his wife. Fantômas, still posing as Tom Bob, admits to being Garrick, and Scotland Yard charges him with Mrs. Garrick's murder.

---

[9] In France, at that time, "Apache" was a slang term for street gangs, taking their name from the North American tribe of that name due to their fierce reputation.

But, in France, Lady Beltham, still posing as Mrs. Garrick, has fled to the village of Bonnières. The Council of Five, discovering that Mrs. Garrick is not dead but is in hiding in France, then dispatches Detective French in an effort to prove Tom Bob's innocence.

Juve, worried about Fandor's failure to respond to his recent telegrams, decides to go to London. French contacts him and enlists his assistance in locating Lady Beltham—Mrs. Garrick. Juve realizes then that, if he takes her back to London, his archenemy will be cleared of the murder charge and set free. But his sense of justice will not allow him to lie—Fantômas must not be executed for a crime he has not committed but must pay for his own crimes instead!

Together, Juve and French trace Mrs. Garrick to Bonnières. There, Juve convinces Lady Beltham to return to London with him. But during the trip across the Channel, French is stabbed and tossed overboard by British "Apaches" who have reasons to hate Tom Bob. Lady Beltham is forced to vanish again.

In London, Tom Bob is found guilty of Mrs. Garrick's murder and is sentenced to hang.

Juve, now operating in England under the guise of "Policeman 416," teams up with the remaining members of the Council of Five. Reverend Hope visits Fantômas in his cell. He tells him that there is little that they can do to clear him—the execution is scheduled to take place in two days. Later, Juve also visits Fantômas, and discovers that they need each other's help. Only Juve can find Lady Beltham and prove that Mrs. Garrick is still alive, and only Fantômas can reveal Fandor's whereabouts before the journalist runs out of food and water. The two adversaries agree to a trade.

After a frantic investigation, Juve tracks down Lady Beltham. Though she is jealous of Fantômas' affair with François, she eventually agrees to help Juve in order to rescue Fandor.

Juve has arranged to buy Tom Bob's corpse after the hanging. Reverend Hope tells Fantômas that they have rigged the rope so that he will fall to the ground rather than hang at his execution. He gives him a length of hard rubber hose to put down his airway in case something goes wrong.

On the scaffold, the rope is placed around Fantômas' neck, the trapdoor is released and the Lord of Terror plunges into darkness...

Later, Juve and Lady Beltham revive Fantômas in a safehouse located in the Waterloo district. But when Juve presses Fantômas to keep his end of the bargain, the King of Crime now claims that he doesn't know where Fandor is—he shipped his crate out to sea. The reporter could be anywhere.

Suddenly, Police surround the—insurance against the villain escaping again. Once more Fantômas tries to enlist Juve's help, promising he will help to locate Fandor, but the Policeman rejects his offer.

An Inspector arrives with a telegram for Juve—from Fandor! It was sent from Durban in South Africa and begs Juve to come to his rescue...

At that moment, Fantômas opens a secret compartment in his ring and swallows poison. Before he dies, and Lady Beltham flees, he utters his final words to Juve:

"In three days..."

Mark P. Steele

Chapter I
The Skull

Spotlights probed the surroundings from the tops of their respective pylons, emitting pallid, trembling beams. They illuminated a vast expanse of low, glazed roofs, supported only by high, thin metal frames. Within the area where these roofs were located were vast courses of paved, even ground, designed according to a uniform geometric model, and separated at regular intervals by deep canals filled with heavy, motionless water.

Underneath these vast hangars was an assortment of goods of every kind, of an extraordinary variety: wrapped fabric bundles, various objects displayed in plain or clear cases, pieces of machinery scattered here and there, all in apparent disorder within the rigid and sturdy metal frames.

Still further on were baskets filled with comestibles, the contents of which emitted strong odors.

Elsewhere, within areas that were like pens, tramped innumerable herds of cattle pressed one against another.

The same anarchy reigned within the spaces that were not covered by the glazed roofs, where one could confusedly see a forest of masts and smoking chimneys standing tall toward the Heavens all the way out to the horizon.

What these spotlights lit, during this gloomy night, were the wharves of a seaport, the docks where, during the day, an unusual animation ruled.

This night, however, despite the storm's din, the greatest calm reigned; no one ventured there.

At the edge of the docks, next to massive doors that separated the fences, were security guards, obviously asleep, whose mission it was to not allow access to the premises except during hours permitted by the regulations.

Somebody, however, intended to infringe on these regulations.

About 11 p.m., where a small footwall, no more than five feet tall, bordered the boulevard's stores along the outside edge, an observer could have seen a shadow suddenly stand out. It become clear and manifest, then moved forward cautiously down the middle of one of the paved courses that bordered, without the slightest guardrail, the deep channels filled with black water.

A rider, in fact, had just jumped over the wall—a rider who, henceforth, guided his mount with precaution, directing it with remarkable skill, avoiding all the open spaces, affecting, on the contrary, to follow the walls, naturally seeking to remain in the shadows and taking the greatest care to not show himself in the spotlights' radiance.

After about a half-hour of hesitation, marches and countermarches, the rider arrived at the dock that was the most encumbered with merchandise. There, he dismounted and tied his horse to a nearby post.

He was a young man with an elegant profile and determined bearing. He was short, but solidly built, 16-years-old at most. His face, though tanned by the Sun, sported features that were both delicate and juvenile. On top of his naturally curly and rather long, dark hair, he wore a large, stylish grey felt hat. The left side of the belt around his trim waist held a holstered revolver.

The youth advanced.

Suddenly, he noticed a large bundle wrapped in grey canvas, from which stuck out some wisps of straw. He couldn't hold back a wave of emotion. He drew a knife and appeared to want to disembowel the bundle. He stopped, however, straining his ears, as if he feared someone's arrival—perhaps a dock supervisor—an embarrassing, fearsome witness! Nevertheless, as soon as he believed himself alone, he returned to his first intention, and set about the execution of his initial project.

With a sharp blow of his weapon, he cut the grey canvas, which released a flood of straw from its gaping wound.

A sudden cry escaped from the youth's lips—a joyous cry!

Then, his muscles tightened and his shoulders curved. Making a supreme effort, this mysterious figure tore something dark, hard and resistant out from the bundle. He put his discovery on the ground and considered it for an instant with deep emotion.

It was a metal box, a kind of casket in the shape of a cube of equal dimensions, around 12 inches to a side.

The young horseman feverishly seized the box as if he had just made an extraordinary discovery, grabbing it by a handle fastened to the lid.

Then, unconcerned with the disorder he'd created, without in the least seeking to hide the traces of his passage, the youth left the place as it was, in a great hurry. He retraced his steps to his horse, taking great care not to let go of the box that he had just extracted from its mysterious packaging.

The horse, despite its master's urgent commands, forcefully refused to move. All of its members shook. Its ears flattened, its clear nose trembled and quivered.

Alas, it was not difficult to understand what terrified the poor beast.

An acrid and powerful smell was all around them; it had manifested itself with a light, white plume of smoke and insignificant flakes when it had first appeared, but now, had swelled to worrisome proportions.

There was no doubt—it was fire! A fire that had just begun!

A terrible misfortune, an appalling disaster, not just threatened, but had suddenly struck the vast warehouses stuffed with goods!

The horse still refused to move, notwithstanding the imperative invitation of the person on its back, manifested by the rider's violent blows with his crop.

Finally, a burst of flame shooting towards the sky convinced the horse to run toward a nearby open area. However, as the rider and his mount emerged from the docks and came into the full light of a seemingly deserted courtyard, a gunshot sounded!

At the very same moment, a man, almost a human wraith, suffocating, nearly dead, eyes filled with tears, hands bloody, knees torn, chest gasping, was trying, with great difficulty, to extricate himself from a huge—and swiftly burning—crate

He took in huge breaths of dust and smoke saturated air. Making another supreme effort, he leapt out of the crate in which he had been imprisoned.

This unfortunate man, this human wreck, this frightful being with a gaunt, spectral look, this survivor of fire, this near-corpse who had just escaped from a quasi-coffin, was none other than—Jérôme Fandor.[10]

Less than a month before, Jérôme Fandor had been in London, in his modest French Quarter hotel room. It was an evening in April. Fandor had just cabled his friend Juve in Paris, that he had made a sensational discovery, that he had rediscovered the trail of Fantômas! While he was writing a letter to his friend confirming and detailing the information contained in his telegram, he was suddenly attacked and tightly bound by a daring bandit who, then, revealed himself to be—Fantômas!

The terrible Fantômas had taken Fandor prisoner!

The young reporter had soon found himself in a cell with no windows.

Violent jolts were succeeded by complete stillness. Then came swaying, long, nauseating, rocking swings that made him sick, leading him to understand that he was undergoing a long sea journey.

Before that realization, Fandor had believed that his prison had been fastened to an automobile, or mounted on a railway car.

---

[10] Fandor's plight was detailed in the previous volume, *Le Pendu de Londres* [*The Hanged Man of London*].

In this crate, Fandor had the necessary provisions to survive. Ventilation and light were so well engineered that the journalist did not suffer from either darkness or a lack of air.

Sudden jolts were succeeded by complete immobility. However, little by little, the light had faded. Fandor had seen his provisions exhaust themselves. It was necessary for him to ration his food. And finally, much more seriously, the air inside his prison had begun to grow heavy.

Although exhausted and weakened, depressed by the appalling long days that had passed since his imprisonment, he had minutely studied every inch of his prison.

Fandor had striven with patience and extraordinary energy to produce an exit from the crate, which was heavily reinforced on all sides.

He swore to himself that he would succeed in creating an opening, and indeed, after days of intense labor, he had begun to see the spotlights' glare through the cracks that he had made—but, suddenly, the same openings let in burning, unbreathable air!

Marshalling near-superhuman energy, Fandor triumphed over this final obstacle. He knocked down the weakest wall of his dreadful prison and, as he broke through to the other side, cast his eyes in every direction...

Stunned, Fandor saw flames surrounding him.

Instinctively, he leapt out of the crate.

Barely had the journalist left the temporary shelter afforded to him by his strange prison than he had to avoid being crushed by other falling, charred, semi-consumed containers.

It was at that very moment that the gunshot had resounded.

Fandor had just stepped off of the dock and onto the paved courtyard.

At the same time, the horse bucked at top speed, its pace came to a dead halt, its nose pricked up, its nostrils completely flared, giving up all its energy.

The horseman was ejected from his stirrups, and fortunately, wasn't thrown under the beast, but cast forward. He dropped to the ground with a loud noise, barely two meters from the canal's waters. He almost dropped into the water at Fandor's feet.

Nearby, the horse, losing blood in abundance through its nose, a wound in its temple, trembled in its final convulsions.

Fandor turned away from this sickening spectacle, and dazedly looked at the box that had come half-open due to the violence of the crash. Its contents were revealed to him, glistening in the spotlights' pallid glimmer.

Fandor instinctively dropped his gaze to look, and let out a cry of horror. A death's-head, a skull white like ivory, had been released from the coffer!

Fandor automatically threw his jacket, which he had removed to put the fire consuming it out, over the top of this macabre and assuredly strange discovery.

A moan came from a few steps away. The unfortunate horseman lay unmoving, very pale.

"It's a kid," Fandor thought. "The poor guy—he nearly killed himself!"

The journalist dipped his handkerchief into the nearby water. He dampened the unconscious rider's lips and rubbed his temples.

The youth quickly opened his eyes.

First, he looked at the person in front of him; if he didn't display any amazement, surely it was because he was in good control of his emotions. For Fandor, with his tousled hair, his clothing in rags and his long beard definitely had a most startling appearance!

The youth, as if he were ashamed of his weakness, moved back. Fandor consequently offered him his arm, but the young rider ignored it and abruptly raised himself.

Without dealing with the journalist, the stranger went to check his mount.

He considered it some seconds—the unfortunate beast was dead; there was nothing else to do.

The horseman clenched his fists; then, turning to Fandor, he offered his outstretched hand.

"You saved my life," he said. "Thank you!"

This young man spoke in English, however, with a trace of an accent, which betrayed a foreign origin.

Fandor, nevertheless, understood what he said.

"It was nothing," said the journalist. Then, he indicated the docks with his hand, adding in a worried voice: "If no one comes... if this disaster isn't stopped, all of London is going to burn. I'm sure that this is another of Fantômas' schemes! The monster must want..."

Fandor stopped; the rider had just pulled his sleeve.

"Excuse me," he asked him with concern in his voice. "What did you just say? London?"

"Yes. London might burn! All of London! Look—the fire's raging everywhere... It's Fantômas' doing! Good Lord! He had me locked inside a crate, in the middle of these docks, the better to kill me..."

"Excuse me," said the young man again, increasingly intrigued, yet surprisingly calm. "Would you tell me who you are, please?"

"Who I am? His victim! His victim, whom he condemned to die, but who, despite it all, still managed to escape! Ah! Ah! We'll see who'll win in the end, between the two of us, Fantômas! Fandor's still alive, you hear me? Safe and away from you!"

He staggered like a drunken man, shaking his fist at the flames, his eyes glaring, his lips foaming; instinctively, like in a dream, he ran towards the inferno!

The young man held him back, taking Fandor's two hands in his own.

"You speak of London, sir. Are you truly ignorant of where you are?"

"Why? Yes... no..." replied Fandor, with a wild-eyed look. "These docks, these boats, the river... Is this not London?"

"No. You're in Durban," said the horseman slowly.

"Durban! What? Durban..."

"Yes, Durban," insisted the young man. "Durban, in the region of Natal, in South Africa."

Fandor looked at the youth who stood in front of him, still in a daze.

Then, suddenly, two heavy hands clapped down upon his shoulders. He was pulled at from all sides. Much to his surprise, he found himself in the middle of a troop of men, all dressed in brown uniforms and armed with rifles.

They questioned him at the same time that they threatened him with wild gestures and words!

How did he get here? Where did he come from? How did he explain his presence on docks forbidden to the public? Had he set the fire?

Completely distraught, emotionally weak, failing in strength and morale, Fandor considered these men with bewildered eyes, not able to formulate a single thought, not finding a reply.

One of the men, undoubtedly the leader, had just said to his subordinates: "He doesn't want to answer. He's a miserable wretch. I give him three minutes... After which—well, you know the law. We'll put him up against a wall and fire!"

Fandor had the vague notion that they had mistaken him for a criminal. Hadn't there been a mention of a firing squad?

Nevertheless, he was still so bewildered that, despite his will to live, he barely managed to sputter out some broken sentences.

"The fire... Fantômas... Juve... The burning crate..." he mechanically repeated. "Where am I? London? Durban?"

The men who stood guard around him considered him with fierce looks.

They weren't fooled by what they thought was play-acting. One read in their black eyes that, trembling with impatience and indignation, they awaited only a sign from their chief to execute the suspect whom they blamed for the fire.

In the distance, however, there was already more clamoring.

The city, or at least the population bordering the docks, had awakened. The firefighters had been alerted and were rushing from all parts of the city towards the docks.

The men still waited for the order, but the anticipated execution was suddenly postponed.

The chief—he was an officer according to the two white braids that encircled his brown overcoat's wrists—had just noticed the young horseman whom Fandor had rescued.

"Teddy!" he cried. "What are you doing here?"

"Lieutenant Dragg! I'm happy to see you. What a terrible tragedy! What are we going to do?"

"The firemen have been alerted," replied the officer. "My company was on guard duty at a neighboring post... That's why we arrived before everyone else... Before everyone else," he suddenly repeated, "but, in fact, that's not the case... You must have been here before us?"

"Er, I don't know. Pretty much at the same time, I suppose. I was riding alongside the docks when I saw the flames... I crossed the wall, I came here... and then..."

"And then what?" questioned the Lieutenant.

Young Teddy was obviously troubled, but the officer was too disturbed himself to notice his state.

"And then," continued Teddy, making an effort to regain his self-control, "someone killed my horse... A bandit... A murderer... Killed it with one shot. That's when I was thrown over..."

The officer turned back toward his men and pointed at Fandor.

"Did he speak?" he inquired.

"No. He's got nothing to say, it seems."

"Then, stand him against that wall, form ranks, make the three summations, and then, fire."

When Teddy heard this command, he literally leaped on the officer.

"What are you going to do?" he howled, face contracted.

27

"Only my duty," retorted Lieutenant Dragg. "This man was inside the docks, contrary to regulations. You're not unaware, Teddy, that two weeks ago, the city government, alarmed by the thefts and crimes that happen here, transferred its policing powers to the military authorities. We're therefore under martial law. I questioned this man, but he's unable to answer—or rather, he refuses to answer. I'm convinced that he started the fire—whether by accident or design doesn't matter—it's obvious... You've said to me that someone shot your horse, it must be him, too."

"Go ahead, Sergeant, the summations..." the officer commanded, raising his voice.

The designated subordinate detached himself from the platoon that had been assembled before the unfortunate Fandor, and was going to execute him. If the journalist did not establish his innocence in that very instant, then his life would soon be over.

But only one word, one name, escaped from his lips:

"Fantômas! Fantômas!"

At the second summation, Teddy, who at first had moved away to not behold the ghastly execution, returned running.

He broke through the soldiers' tight ranks, then addressed the officer again.

"Lieutenant Dragg," he begged, "please, don't do this! He's not guilty, he's innocent! I'm sure of it! That man had no weapons; he didn't shoot my horse... I was unconscious after my fall and he revived me... Please, Lieutenant, I beseech you, don't shoot him so quickly... Question him again yourself."

The officer hesitated for an instant, then nodded. He began to question Fandor. The young horseman, Teddy, seemed very interested in the following exchange:

"What's your name?"

"Jérôme Fandor."

"Your nationality?"

"French."

"Why did you enter these docks? Didn't you know that they were guarded?"

"I knew nothing. I was prisoner inside a case, a prisoner of Fantômas..."

"Where were you before?"

"In London."

"And you believe that you're still there?"

"I don't know where I am anymore. I'm here at Fantômas' pleasure... But now that I've escaped, I'll have my vengeance!"

With extraordinary effort, Fandor had succeeded in making these responses in an almost intelligible voice.

Turning away from the journalist, the Lieutenant and the young rider spoke in hushed voices.

Taking advantage of this, Fandor, slowly, staggering like a drunkard, walked towards the dead horse. He found his charred jacket at the beast's feet, and instinctively bent down to pick it up.

However, as he grabbed it, he found it unusually heavy. The journalist then remembered that, a few moments before. he had concealed under the fabric the extraordinary thing that he had found after the rider had fallen: the shining object that had escaped from the metal box, the gleaming, white skull, the skull!

A quick glance around told him that he was still being watched.

Cautiously, the journalist didn't unfold the jacket. Quite naturally, he placed it under his arm, and thereby concealed the skull!

Finally, the officer made a new gesture and the soldiers once more surrounded Fandor.

"I agree with you, Lieutenant Dragg," declared the young man, while taking leave of the officer. "This man's sick, he's mad... You should take him to the Lunatic Asylum..."

"To the Lunatic Asylum!" repeated Fandor, while he left the dock escorted by four guards. "They mean to lock me up among madmen!"

Chapter II
A Mysterious Theft

"Severe but just, impartial but good, and especially profoundly honest... Such is my motto, and this policy works perfectly for me... Some orangeade, my dear Fraulein Grosschen?"

"There's no way I could refuse, Mr. Elders, especially since this afternoon's temperature is truly torrid!"

The pair moved toward an elegant buffet set up at the veranda's far end, attended by an entire army of servants, attentive to the least wishes of the guests who desired refreshment during this elegant reception.

Mr. Hans Elders, director of an important diamond mine located in the country, a few miles from Durban, was celebrating the 18th birthday of his only daughter, Winnifred.

"Yes," continued Hans Elders. "Scrupulous honesty is still the best means of succeeding in life. You might be able to see that in me."

"I do," replied the parched German woman, with a piqued air. She was a tall woman of 45 or so years, and looked prematurely aged.

Hans Elders was referring to a theft that had occurred only a few weeks before and the victim of which had been Fraulein Grosschen. One night, a hotel thief had robbed her of her purse and a gold chain. The woman now held it against the entire nation of South Africa.

Fraulein Grosschen, an eternally single woman, had been in South Africa for several months. She had come to write an economic and social study for a Berlin newspaper. It was quite evident her work would now reflect the already unfavorable opinion that she had formed of Natal's inhabitants.

Wishing to improve her disposition, Hans Elders explained to her in great detail the business organization that he had built.

Having come to this new country 15 years ago, he had been lucky to discover a few, small diamonds in a riverbed, which had led him to believe he had found a deposit of the first order.

Hans Elders had kept his discovery secret and had bought several land parcels all around it. He had then hired a sizeable staff and announced his marvelous find only after everything was organized and ready.

At first, no one had wanted to believe him, because never in man's memory had anyone found diamonds in Natal.

"Isn't it true," asked Fraulein Grosschen, who was scrupulously taking notes, "that you have since improved your operations?"

"Indeed, I have" replied Hans Elders. "In order to lower my costs, I eliminated the middleman and imported a gem cutter, just as good as the ones who operate in Amsterdam. I knew his performance, truly unique in the world..."

Fraulein Grosschen was going to ask some more questions of her host, but suddenly, he left her to go and greet a new couple who had just made their entrance on the veranda. They were undoubtedly important, for, upon their arrival, all conversations had stopped.

The new arrivals were none other than Sir Houston, Durban's Governor, and his wife. Sir Houston represented Her Majesty's Government with the traditional decorum and gravitas.

Hans Elders rushed to greet his famous guests.

"Mrs. Houston," he said, gallantly kissing the beautiful Englishwoman's hand, "please excuse the frugality of this small, intimate gathering, a far cry, I'm sure, from the splendor of your grand receptions at the Resident's Palace."

Sir Houston congratulated Hans Elders.

"You employ many workers in your diamond business," he inquired. "I suppose the majority of them are British?"

"Oh! Certainly, they are," affirmed Hans Elders. "British workers are the best in the world. And this has the advantage of reaffirming the Empire's presence in the colonies."

Hans Elders then introduced his daughter Winnifred to the Governor and his wife.

Out of respect for the Governor, in their discussions, the guests minimized the impact of the recent fire at the docks, the damages of which would fortunately be covered by insurance.

With charm and grace, Winnifred Elders gave the Governor's wife a tour of her father's house.

Soon, Sir Houston, having noticed a group of officers smoking in the garden in the shade of a large tree, went to mingle with them.

Hans Elders was now alone. He was quietly slipping out of the room where the dancers were resuming their waltzes when he collided with a young man.

"What are you doing here, young savage!" cried Hans Elders. "How is it that I should run into you at this fashionable party?"

The youth whom Hans Elders had called a "young savage" turned slightly pale.

"It took an effort on my part, sir," he murmured. "But I do believe that I find your reception charming."

Hans Elders had already moved away, but the young man continued:

"An effort on my part to shake hands... to show a pleasant face to this monster, this bandit! Such are the cruel necessities of life... But at least, he suspects nothing..."

From different sides of the room, several young men and women shouted at the new arrival.

"Teddy! Teddy!"

Teddy, for it was he, smiled at them.

"We're going to play golf," said a robust, sturdy fellow. "Will you join us?"

However, a sensational new attraction suddenly competed with the golf party. Led on by the crowd, Teddy found himself on the veranda, in a group of young men and women surrounding a truly remarkable black man.

His name was Jupiter.

For five or six years, he had been the most devoted of all the workers at the diamond mine.

Normally, it would have been unusual to meet him at this elegant and fashionable reception. In the region, most black men were obliged to earn their living by excavating the soft earth to extract diamonds. However, Jupiter, making the most of his Herculean strength, had trained as a boxer. Quickly, he had excelled at the sport, and before long, had become the region's champion.

During a sensational match, he had knocked out and beaten the Australian champ, the famous Bully Stone, and had won the sum of 100,000 pounds.

Those who followed Jupiter's career were divided into two groups: there were his unconditional admirers, people in love with the noble sport, who respected the power of his fists, which had demolished a man widely considered invincible until then. But there were also those who could not accept that a man of color should be received into white society—even one as diverse as that of Durban.

Jupiter, however, did not seem affected. Someone had given him a superb gold bracelet, which he wore on his wrist and showed to everyone, when he tapped with his broad hand on his jacket's inside pocket where he kept his fortune in bank notes.

Noting Hans Elders, who was walking by, Jupiter called out to him.

"Mr. Elders," he said, "I don't want to keep all this money on me... I don't need it... Could I give it to you to keep in your big safe? I'll get take it back when I get myself a wife."

Hans Elders smiled at the man's trust. At first, he refused to take the deposit, but—like a child—Jupiter wore him down by looking so upset that the director did not have the heart to refuse.

Later, Mr. Elders went into his study with some close friends and temporarily dropped Jupiter's bank notes into a drawer, which he locked, reminding himself to put them inside the company's safe the next day.

Meanwhile, young Teddy had not stayed in Jupiter's company for long. He felt a sincere and cordial affection for the boxer, but he had more pressing concerns.

With clever and inquisitive eyes, he searched the shade of the massive woods and the wide avenues of the park.

A couple looking for solitude walked there.

"Oh! Oh!" thought the young man. "Winnifred and Lieutenant Dragg! My word, they make a handsome couple... But that old gangster, Hans, will never stand for it..."

What could possibly compel a pleasant young man with gentle, elegant manners to feel such hatred for a man already of a ripe age, who seemed to have won public esteem and consideration by his work?

All conversation suddenly stopped on the arrival of a man completely covered in dust. The unusual apparition only stayed for a moment, then prepared to leave.

But Hans Elders had seen him. He ran to him and pulled him into the middle of the guests, striving with all his strength to introduce him to the Governor.

"Sir Houston," said the director, "please allow me to introduce you to my collaborator and friend: Monsieur Ribonnard, a Frenchman who's very active in the sales of our diamonds."

"Surely that must be an easy job?"

"Not altogether," said the Frenchman. "It depends on the demand... The markets can be very volatile, as they've been these past few years. Brazil's our big competitor. Nevertheless, business isn't going too badly at the moment! I've just arrived from Pretoria where the Stock Market is going strong..."

The diamond broker and the Governor continued their discussion; little by little, the salons emptied.

Teddy slipped away among the last guests, more sullen than he had been earlier. It now seemed as if the young man would have liked to stay at the rich diamond magnate's villa.

What were his reasons? Whatever they might have been, he did not follow them. Jumping on his horse, he raced across the countryside, galloping in the direction of a large forest at the edge of which, six miles from Hans Elders' residence, was the picturesque farm where he had been raised.

The silent sadness that often follows a successful party now settled upon Hans Elders' villa.

In the disorderly living room, which the guests had just left, Winnifred, her father and Jupiter had reunited.

"Miss Winnifred," said the kind-hearted boxer, "I don't need all that money... If your papa don't mind, I'd be happy to give you some so that you can marry the man you love."

The girl smiled wanly, but Hans Elders, in a foul mood, scolded his former worker.

"You're too naïve, Jupiter! I appreciate your good intentions, I do, but Winnifred can't accept your offer... The Devil! To each that which belongs to them! You earned that money fair and square—now, you should enjoy it to the fullest. Honestly. Honesty, you see, is always my motto!"

Jupiter listened for a while, day-dreaming about what uses he might have for his bonanza. He could, he thought, acquire a vast estate, almost an entire province, and search for gold. The notion made him consider exchanging his bank notes for some beautiful, gold coins.

While pondering his fortune, the boxer repeatedly drank copious gulps of whisky.

Hans Elders had stopped paying attention to the awesome Jupiter. His daughter had left the room and his attention was now back on the problem at hand.

For, a good half-hour before, words had been passed between father and daughter, words that had left Hans Elders very anxious.

He and his daughter had a disagreement: Winnifred had declared that she wanted to marry Lieutenant Wilson Dragg.

The two young people had loved each other for several years. But when Winnifred, blushing, had told her father the news, during the course of the party, which was intended to celebrate her 18th birthday, the diamond merchant had unambiguously replied that he would never consent to her marriage to an impecunious officer.

After a protracted scene, Winnifred had quickly returned to her rooms.

Suddenly, Hans Elders stood up and looked at his watch.

"How late it is!" he said. "Jupiter! Jupiter! Wake up! It's time for you to go home..."

The boxer didn't budge. He was half-sprawled on the ground, snoring, sleeping the sleep of the just, especially if by "just" we mean a drunken man.

At his side, still within his reach, was a whiskey bottle, now almost entirely empty.

Hans Elders considered the sleeping giant for a moment; then, making a sudden decision, he left to go to his own rooms.

"Bah!" he said, "if Jupiter awakes, he'll find his own way out, and if he wants to sleep here until morning, well, he's free to do so!"

Outside, the clear, starry night was not disturbed by any sounds; one could have heard a fly buzzing.

That is why when a door slowly creaked open in the middle of the night, those who had just pushed it were startled!

Two shadows stood out, lit by the moon, and soon merged in a mutual embrace.

"Darling Winnie!"

"Dearest Wilson!"

Winnifred cried on the young officer's shoulder.

"I'm lost," she sputtered. "I'm disgraced... My father's opposed to our marriage... I'll never be able to tell him that I'm your lover!"

Moved, the officer strove to console Winnifred.

"My dearest love," he said, covering her with tender kisses, "you may not yet be my wife in the eyes of men, but you are in those of God."

36

"Ah!" moaned Winnifred, "may the Lord hear you, my love!"

The two lovers embraced again.

"Do you want me to go and talk to your father?" asked the Lieutenant. "Man to man."

"No, no, never! My father is not a man who compromises easily. He won't listen. You must leave... Tomorrow, we'll see each other again. I'll send you a note..."

They remained silent and motionless for a moment. No sounds broke the silence that reigned around them.

In the living room, Jupiter was snoring like a smithy's bellows. Then, suddenly, the boxer woke up; someone was shaking him.

It was Hans Elders, clad in pajamas, his bare feet in leather sandals.

"Jupiter," Hans asked in an alarmed voice, "did you hear anything?"

"Hear what?" said Jupiter. "What's happening?"

"There's someone here... I heard walking on the first floor, just above us!"

"Someone walking on the first floor?" Jupiter repeated. "In the middle of the night? You want me to check it out?"

The diamond merchant nodded. He was armed with a revolver. As he was about to leave the living room, he asked:

"Are you armed, Jupiter?"

The giant smiled and showed his enormous fists.

"I'm always armed," he replied with a stifled laugh. "I carry clubs at the ends of my arms!"

As they crossed Hans Elder's office, walking stealthily towards the grand staircase that would take them to the first floor, the black man, who led the march, uttered a cry.

The director's desk had been broken into; the drawers were wide open, papers were scattered about, as if someone had just searched it and fled.

"Mr. Elders!" sputtered the boxer in panic. "Look! You've been robbed! My money's gone!"

Huge tears rolled down the giant's cheeks.

But Hans Elders leaped towards the staircase gun in hand. He had again heard the stealthy sound of footsteps.

"Who goes there?" he shouted into the darkness.

The noise suddenly ceased.

Hearing Hans Elders' cry, Jupiter overcame his despair and rushed to defend his friend.

Hans Elders turned on the lights.

The chandelier abruptly dazzled their eyes, flooding the entire hall, lighting up the stairway.

The boxer ran up the steps in pursuit of a shadowy fugitive.

"Someone's running away," he howled. "It must be the thief! Thief! Thief!"

Hans Elders, less agile than Jupiter, ran after him. When he reached the landing, he saw that the black man had already caught up the fugitive and had his hands around his throat.

"Jupiter! What are you doing?" shouted Elders.

The boxer stopped strangling his victim; he raised him as if he weighed nothing and set him upright, still holding him by the collar.

The two men were now face-to-face with the fugitive; two cries escaped from their chests:

"Lieutenant Dragg!"

Hans Elders questioned the officer harshly.

"What are you doing here, Lieutenant? Where were you doing? Where did you come from?"

Jupiter, who could hardly contain his anger, shook the young officer. He tried searching his pockets, but the other man resisted.

The Lieutenant addressed Hans Elders:

"Sir," he said, "I implore you. Please order your man to leave me alone. I'm not a robber. I'll explain everything to you. I'll justify my presence here..."

"Do so immediately, sir!" Hans Elders threatened the officer with his revolver.

The Lieutenant did not raise an eyebrow.

"If it's necessary to clear my name, I'll do it."

But just then, at the end of the hall, Winnifred's exquisite and delicate silhouette appeared.

Lieutenant Dragg understood that the girl was begging for him to remain silent about their affair.

Alas! It was necessary for him to obey her; hadn't he promised? On his honor as an officer and a gentleman!

Hans Elders had barely seen his daughter come into the hall. He did not suspect the silent drama that had just been played between the two lovers.

Lieutenant Dragg, panicking, realized that it was necessary nonetheless to clear himself of the monstrous charges being leveled against him.

Winnifred Elders had gotten closer to her father. In a few words, the diamond merchant appraised her of what he believed had taken place.

Hans Elders pointed at the unfortunate officer, accusing him of stealing Jupiter's money.

Dragg silently beseeched Winnifred to release him from his word, but to his utter dismay, she merely avoided his eyes.

In panic, the Lieutenant feverishly turned out his pockets, one by one. He made Jupiter feel his clothes and check his wallet.

"You can all see that I have nothing," he howled. "I am not a thief!" Then, proudly, he added: "I am an officer in the British Army, sir! You'll give me satisfaction for this slanderous accusation."

Hans Elders didn't raise an eyebrow.

"Not so fast, my good sir," he uttered. "I'll give you satisfaction, yes, but only when you've returned the money you stole from poor Jupiter... Yes, I know that your pockets are empty! Good Lord, man, do you expect me to be naïve enough not to believe that you've gotten rid of your loot? You've been in this house for an hour—enough time for you to carry out your plan. Unfortunately for you, you've only succeeded halfway. We caught you before you could run

39

away. Confess your crime, give the money back, and I swear, that will be the end of it."

Lieutenant Drag crossed his arms on his chest, his face became impassive, and he appeared now both resigned, resolute.

"Mr. Elders," he declared, "I've already told you twice that I'm not the thief, that I'm innocent. That's once too many. I won't repeat myself again. Do with me what you will!"

"Well, if you're not the thief," insisted Hans Elders, "what were you doing in my house?"

The officer remained silent.

This time, his eyes did not even turn to look at Winnifred. He avoided looking at his lover, to be certain of not betraying her.

After some moments of reflection, Hans Elders passed his sentence with the solemnity of a magistrate.

"Let him go," he ordered Jupiter. "I want him gone, far from here. I cast him out like an evil being!"

Winnifred fainted in her father's arms.

Lieutenant Dragg found himself forced into the night, banished, condemned under the most odious of accusations.

He fled far from the house where he had left the woman to whom he had sworn his heart, his life and his honor, but he was by no means defeated. On the contrary, he was ready to fight!

Chapter III
At The Lunatic Asylum

"Well? What's your problem? Or are you just being stupid? Come on! Move!"

The hand on Fandor's shoulder was that of the Lunatic Asylum's chief orderly, whose main duty was to supervise the most dangerous patients. With some force, he pushed Fandor into the large cafeteria where the patients took their meals.

"You don't need fresh air every day... I've already told you not to make my life difficult! I know your type; you're always hiding things, but I wasn't born yesterday! Straighten up and behave! Or else!"

Upon his arrival at the Lunatic Asylum, a doctor had questioned Fandor in the presence of two orderlies. One had tried to take the skull that he still carried under his arm. When he had made a defensive gesture, the doctor had intervened.

"Let him keep it! It might help him stay calm... Place him under observation."

They led him to a room containing two beds.

"Undress yourself and make it quick!" ordered one of the orderlies. "You'll be sleeping here... No funny stuff!"

Fandor was careful not to protest.

"What about your skull?" questioned the orderly. "Are you keeping it with you?"

When he heard the attendant mentioning the skull, Fandor couldn't help smiling. He thought about his "find" that he had just put down on the bed.

The journalist felt it was important not to be separated from the macabre artifact. It was a mysterious and strange acquisition that he had made in the midst of the flames. It was worth keeping...

Fandor had a bad night. And the next morning was no more pleasant.

At 7:00 a.m., someone shook him awake. Still numb with sleep, he wondered briefly, with surprise mixed with panic, who this person in a blue uniform was, and why he was ordering him about.

Then, he remembered where he was.

"Get up! Put on your shirt! Your trousers! Off to the showers!"

The orderly scolded him. He had to dress hastily, then take a short walk down paved halls which oozed with damp. Following his guide, he came to a small room filled with showers. Two men took him by the shoulders, buckled his arms and legs against a wall and opened a jet.

When the orderlies finally stopped the jet, Fandor, heard another command:

"On the double! Get dressed! You're going to the garden now..."

Fandor did not bother replying. He did not want to start an argument on the legality of his incarceration. Not yet anyway...

With some concern, he heard one attendant say to another:

"You see the new patient? No one can get a word out of him! He's a wise guy. Sneaky. We'll have to watch him!"

When he was ready, they led him into the garden.

Fandor expected to meet some genuine mental patients there, but when he arrived at the lawn-covered grounds that constituted the Asylum's courtyard—a courtyard surrounded on all sides by high walls, barely enlivened by a few thin trees, the trunks of which were wrapped with mattresses up to a man's height—he saw no one.

"Take a walk," ordered the attendant. "It's visiting day today. Your new pals aren't allowed out. But you'll meet them at noon."

It was strange to walk alone in the melancholy garden, between thee padded walls, where even the trees were wrapped with padding.

The orderly lazily stretched out on the grass to read a newspaper. Fandor had long minutes to think about his predicament.

At noon, the journalist still had not reached any decision on how he should behave to quickly extricate himself from the Asylum. Then, another orderly called him:

"Hey, you! Over there! Didn't you hear the bell? Come on! Follow me! I'll introduce you to your new group of friends..."

Fandor had to leave the garden; his heart tightened. He was led to the cafeteria. It was a large room divided down the middle by two long parallel tables.

When Fandor entered the room, shoved forward by the attendant, he examined the faces of those who would be his companions.

"Sit down," ordered the attendant.

Fandor noticed an empty place and was about to settle there when he was shoved again.

"Not there, you idiot! You belong over there, not with the violent ones!"

Fandor had nearly sat down next to a group of patients dressed in chestnut-colored smocks. He quickly got up, feeling agitated despite his efforts to stay calm.

"Where do I sit?"

"With the others under observation! Good Lord!"

A new shove pushed Fandor towards another group of patients who, like him, were not wearing uniforms.

Fandor, resigned to his fate, sat down where the attendant ordered him. On his right was an old man, on his left, a man dressed as an Afrikaner horseman.

Long minutes passed in strict silence.

When Fandor had entered the room, the patients had raised their heads and looked at him with fixed, distrustful, frightened eyes.

He had barely sat down at the table when a deafening din filled the room, occasionally interrupted by the attendants' orders.

"Eat, you animal!"

"I'll teach you to break plates!"

"If you keep laughing like that, it's the cold shower for you!"

An orderly poured some kind of gruel mixed with pieces of meat in Fandor's plate.

"Eat!"

With a surreptitious glance, the journalist watched his neighbors' manners. They showed no hesitation. As a precaution, the patients were not allowed to use any cutlery, so they used only their fingers.

Fandor took the skull from under his arm and put it on his knees so as to not lose sight of his precious possession. He was ready to eat, when his neighbor addressed him:

"Sir, would you answer me a question?"

"Of course," replied Fandor, anxious to not offend his companion. "I'll be happy to. What is it?"

"But you already know the question, since I'm waiting for an answer. Or are you making fun of me?"

"Far be it from me! But I didn't hear your question. What was it?"

"The answer!"

"The answer to what?"

A violent blow shook the table.

The once-peaceful-looking old man now stood up and shook Fandor by his collar.

"Ah! You too mock me!" he howled. "You think I'm mad, eh? You think that because of my gentle appearance, I'm so weak that I can't fend for myself? You're in league with my persecutors! But I'll have my revenge!"

As the madman shook Fandor and threatened to strangle him, the journalist grabbed him by the shoulders and tried to free himself.

"Let me go!" he yelled. "Help! Attendants! Help!"

Suddenly, the journalist received a sharp blow to the kidneys. Two hands pressed him onto the bench.

"Stop making that ruckus or we'll be stick you back in the showers! Ah! It's the sneaky new patient! Already a problem!"

Fandor had no time to protest.

The old man had quieted down.

Finally the journalist was ready to begin his lunch.

Alas, he had not foreseen the mental patients' duplicity!

While he fought with the old man, his neighbor on the left, the man with the hunter's face, had not raised his head. But he had not wasted any time...

The journalist now noticed that the horseman's greedy hand had fished in his plate, robbing Fandor of virtually his entire ration of food!

Slowly, but forcefully, he removed his neighbor's left hand from his bowl, where it still was, and began eating.

Unfortunately, Fandor had barely swallowed a few mouthfuls—still holding his rapacious neighbor's hand immobilized—when another orderly intervened again.

"Let him go! Unhand him at once!"

"But he was digging in my plate!" protested Fandor.

The journalist did not have time to finish.

An unbearably long electric bell blared in the cafeteria.

"Go! Get up! To the garden!" screamed the orderlies.

Willing or not, Fandor had to obey!

The lunch hour was now over. The unfortunate Fandor had barely had time to suck a bone.

"George?" asked the director.

"Yes, sir?" replied the orderly.

"Where's the new patient admitted here after the fire on the docks?"

"I'll bring him to you, sir."

Fandor was daydreaming, sitting on the ground at one end of the garden. He had started to seriously worry.

The scenes he had witnessed during lunch left him no doubt. Jail would be better than the Asylum. Besides, if he was charged with setting fire to the docks, he could defend himself, hire a lawyer, cable Juve... Anything would be better than remaining trapped inside the Lunatic Asylum!

Fandor still had the mysterious skull. He considered trying to talk to the director, or one of the doctors, and explain who he was and how had had found himself in Durban. At that moment, he heard a call:

"You, over there! Let's go! Stand up! The director wants to see you!"

Fandor heard the orderly and trembled with anticipation.

"I'll tell him my story," he thought. "He must be well-read man. He will have heard of Fantômas. Perhaps even of Juve, and me..."

The Lunatic Asylum's director, Gerard Herbert, seemed sympathetic and the journalist breathed a sigh of relief when he heard him speak in a pleasant, almost avuncular tone.

"Well, my friend," said the director, "now that you're a patient in this establishment, how do you feel?"

Fandor smiled and decided to tell his story.

"Do I have the pleasure of speaking to the director of this institution?"

"Yes, you do. I am Dr. Herbert. How are you doing?"

"Very well, Doctor."

"You don't intend to misbehave anymore?"

"No, Doctor, I don't, as you put it, intend to misbehave anymore. When you called for me, I was thinking of asking to speak to you... I'd like to inquire about my fate here?"

"I see. That interests you, then?"

"Of course," said Fandor. "Don't you think it's natural for me to be concerned about what's going to happen to me?"

The Doctor suddenly fixed him with piercing eyes.

"You don't appear to behave like a lunatic," he declared abruptly. "Are you sane or insane?"

Anyone else but Fandor might have been taken in by this question, asked so suddenly. However, Fandor was wary and saw the trap.

"Doctor," he declared, "if I tell you that I'm not mad, I know you will immediately conclude that I'm incurably so...

46

I'm not entirely unaware that one of the most obvious signs of insanity is to claim loudly that one is perfectly sane."

"Not bad, not bad at all," said the doctor. "You intrigue me. Let us go into my private office. It'll be quieter to talk..."

Fandor followed the director into a small, well-lit visiting room, whose French windows opened onto the courtyard where the lunatics were now playing.

Chapter IV
Sane or Insane?

The director, who had preceded the journalist, sat and turned towards the young man.

"I suppose you won't give me a straight answer and tell me if you're sane or insane, am I right?" he asked.

"I don't think I'll answer that either, Doctor," said Fandor.

"Very well! After all, it's entirely up to you. However, if that is the case, would you mind subjecting yourself to a more detailed examination? Because, all things considered, if I understand your answer—which really isn't one—you don't want to tell me whether you're sane or insane, you'd rather that I find out for myself. Let's see, then... could you define a tree for me?"

"A thorough exam, it is. You'd like me to define a tree, I assume to verify that I'm in control of my discursive faculties. So be it! A tree is a plant of considerable height, primarily characterized by three distinct parts: the foliage, the trunk and the roots. Further..."

"That's enough! Your answer's quite clear and pertinent. And I see that you've guessed the reason for my question. You do intrigue me, my friend! I've just seen, this morning, a note telling me that the police admitted you here after you'd set fire, or took part in setting fire, to the docks. Is that true? Do you deny it? Tell me your story, in confidence of course. Who are you really?"

This time, Fandor did not hesitate.

"Doctor," he began, "have you heard of Fantômas?"

"Fantômas? Yes, I think I have. I've read newspaper reports of crimes that elusive criminal committed in Europe..."

"And in these reports, did you come across the name of Jérôme Fandor?"

"Jérôme Fandor? Isn't he the journalist who writes for *La Capitale*?"

"Yes, he is. Doctor, I am Jérôme Fandor!"

Immediately, an incredulous expression spread across the director's face.

"You're Jérôme Fandor? I see. Let's pursue that! Jérôme Fandor is a famous figure, a crime-fighter who lives in Paris, or London... Not Durban. Only last month, if I recall correctly, he published an article in which..."

"Doctor, please, don't ignore my evidence before you know what it is! I will prove my identity to you..."

"Of course. Do you have papers?"

"No," the young man acknowledged, "I don't have any papers. But I'll explain why. Please, Doctor, listen to my story before you make up your mind..."

Jérôme Fandor then proceeded to relate the tale of his diabolical imprisonment by Fantômas in London; his desperate escape from the fire that he believed was set to kill him, his finding of the mysterious ivory-colored skull and his subsequent arrest and incarceration.

The journalist concluded:

"That is exactly who I am and how I came to be here. As for the strange skull, which I carry with me, I don't yet know why it is important, but I know that it is! I realize that my clinging to it makes me look crazy in your eyes, but you, too, must realize its importance on some level, because you didn't force me to part with it."

During the entire time that Fandor spoke, Dr. Herbert watched the young man attentively, staring at him with growing surprise.

"So," he finally said, "that is your story: You're Jérôme Fandor, the journalist, following the trail of Fantômas?"

"Yes, that's it!"

Fandor replied calmly, but could not prevent himself from shaking when he saw the doctor get up and press on a bell to summon an orderly.

George, the chief orderly, came in.

"Did you call me, sir?"

The director scrawled a few words in his notebook.

"Yes," he said. "Take this man to the violent ward at once! Let him keep his skull—he could become dangerous if we tried to take it away... He's to have cold showers morning and evening. That will be all."

Back in his cell, Fandor thought that his best course of action was to remain quiet and accept his imprisonment without rebelling. Then, if he could to talk to the director again, but this time deny that he was Jérôme Fandor, perhaps, out of kindness, the man might grant him his release...

Left to himself, Fandor again began to think of the terrible sequence of events that had brought him to Durban. Why had Fantômas shipped the crate to South Africa? What was the story behind the fire on the docks? Who was the mysterious Teddy?

And, especially, what was the secret of that skull which he held carefully pressed against his chest, at which he occasionally stared, as if he could wrest from it its secret...

The young man, weary of pacing in the courtyard where the lunatics played, had appropriated a shady corner of the garden. There, holding the skull in both hands, he became engrossed looking at it...

The death head that looked back at him was, at first glance, like any other. A superficial mind would have drawn no particular conclusions from it.

However, Fandor quickly discovered a number of details that would not have been found on normal human remains. First, the skull was strangely heavy. Then, it seemed in an absolutely perfect state of preservation. And finally, by looking at it closely, Fandor saw faint traces of mysterious signs on the polished bone, microscopic to be sure, but distinct nevertheless...

Suddenly, he heard a voice behind him:

"You know, I do believe our director made a mistake... Look at this wretch with his skull... Clearly not a violent case! He's a paranoid. An obsessive compulsive..."

Quickly, Fandor turned around.

The man who had spoken so casually was a good-looking young man—an intern, obviously... Fandor even thought he recognized the young doctor who had admitted him a few days ago.

Although the director had designated him as a violent case, Fandor was pleased to discover that evening that he had been returned to the more comfortable room he had previously occupied.

That night, Fandor had only just closed his eyes; it was almost midnight.

He slept a restless, feverish sleep, waking at the slightest noise. The orderlies had left the door ajar to make it easier for them to watch him.

Fandor's dream blended the real with the unreal. In a semi-conscious state, he sensed what was happening near him, yet reshaped it into an abominable nightmare...

A man with a murderous face had come into the room.

"I'm dreaming! I'm dreaming!" he told himself.

Then, suddenly, abruptly, consciousness returned to him!

The journalist had just extended his hand out of his bed, to check that the skull of which he was so fond, which he'd put on a chair, was still in its place. However, he was unable to find this skull!

He opened his eyes. Dilated by dread, they saw a man, dressed like an orderly, his orderly, who took the skull and fled through the window!

Fandor, in a rapid movement, threw himself out of bed... He rushed for the window, and screamed:

"Help! Thief!"

However, the young man's dash was such that he abruptly collided with the closed panes. His hand went through a pane... he hurt himself... blood spurted.

Through the bars that trimmed the window, he believed that he saw the orderly's silhouette, fleeing and brandishing the skull.

For the second time, Fandor screamed:

"Help! Thief!"

However, he didn't finish.

For at that moment, two large strapping fellows seized him and applied a gag to his mouth. They had to slip a strait jacket on him: he had his hands held, his legs immobilized. Fandor felt himself brutally thrown to the ground... And before he knew it, there was the hard shock of a heavy water jet on his chest.

Now that he was awake, hurt, broken, terrified, under the water jet that tortured him, they whipped him.

Almost indifferent to his torment, Fandor thought:

"Let's see! Did I just have a nightmare? Am I insane? Will I find the skull in my room? Or was it really stolen? Did the thief really run away?"

Chapter V
Old Laetitia

It was late. The circular flight of the night birds caused Teddy to figure that it was close to 11 p.m.

There was no Moon. It was black, overcast and cold; hardly any stars were visible and there were large clouds that appeared ready to burst into one of the torrential, brutal rains that fall in southern Africa.

The young man was on horseback, and, every so often, he urged on his mount.

It was just as well, because, for a long time, the horse and rider had been following the road to Hell.

Both were exhausted, nearly broken with fatigue. It took all of Teddy's energy and consummate skill to keep them moving forward. Nevertheless, with all the dangers that threaten a man and animal riding across the Veldt's on a dark night, Teddy seemed remarkably unconcerned!

The young man, who dressed like all the Cape's inhabitants, had been raised on these vast plains. He knew every meter of the still savage fields for more than 100 miles around the small farm where he lived.

A marvelous rider, like all the Boers, he was also an extraordinary marksman and was ready to draw if danger should suddenly appear...

However, while Teddy hurried home, Teddy's nurse, Laetitia, was sick at heart. She was his only family, almost his mother—the young man called her "Mama."

The young man's nocturnal outings were, in fact, a subject of perpetual debate between Teddy and Laetitia. During her long life, the old woman had seen many tragic incidents involving riders who ventured out on the Veldt at night. The best she could do was to convince the young man to return to the farm by 10 p.m.

And, although Teddy loved Laetitia dearly, he roamed the deserted plains every evening! Was this fair to Laetitia?

If there were anyone there to watch that evening, they certainly would have wondered.

She was simply dressed, but nevertheless did not appear to lack a thing. She was clearly no pauper—however, just as clearly, she was no great lady!

Laetitia waited on the door's threshold.

"Is it him?" she murmured. "No. Nobody! How dark it is! And he always rides so fast!"

Suddenly, Laetitia stopped. Her ear, striving to seize the most distant noises and identify them, hadn't deceived her.

"Is that you, Teddy?"

"Hello! Mama, it's me!"

Several moments passed.

"Hello, Mama!" he repeated. "You're waiting for me again?"

"It's so late! And you know how worried I am when you don't return for dinner! Where did you come from?"

"Where do I come from? From over there... And I didn't go hunting, since I'm not bringing anything back. But... what is it, Mama?" Teddy questioned. "You seem distracted..."

"I worry about you, even when you're not running the Veldt. What's going on, Teddy? You've been so sad for a long time..."

"I'm sad, Mama, because I'd so like to know..."

"Like to know what?"

"Who I am..."

"But I've told you that so often, Teddy."

"No! No! Tell me again..."

"Listen, little one, it was during the war—a very sad time! All the young folk had enlisted in commando units. They said then that, if the British were victorious, if they beat us, then we, Boers, would be horribly unhappy, almost slaves! And then, you understand, Teddy, it was a matter of defending the farms, to protect the children. It was the Veldt that they had to protect. The men didn't want to hear talk about allowing the British there to command them, or even to let them settle here. We were on our land; it was necessary to drive them out..."

"Yes, Mama! Yes! And then?"

"Then, Teddy, they made war. Ah, the dreadful thing! Every day, one learned of deaths, of destruction. The enemy also took children, and they all died in what they called concentration camps. Farms burned. Both the British and the men of our own commandos set fire to them. One side was just as fierce as the other!"

"And it was on one of those nights, Mama, that someone brought me here?"

"Yes, one night, Teddy. The British had approached nearby; they were holding the hill... My masters and I had been watching the fire that evening, from the barn's roof, because something burned over there—a farm, a field, a forest—who knows? As the night went on, we came down to this room, where we are now. You see, I was sitting there, at the niche, near the fire, when someone knocked..."

"It was me he brought?"

"Yes. Oh! I can still see the scene! As someone pounded the door with heavy blows, we were all here, masters and servants together. And we said: 'Do we have to open it? Is it the enemy? Is it a friend?' In the end, we opened the door. A man stood on the threshold; he carried you in his arms. Oh! You were so small and cute. You were only two or three years old. The man declared: 'I'm an Englishman and I'm your enemy, but that doesn't prevent me from leaving this child with you. A few moments ago, they burned a farm but I was able to save it from the flames. Do you want to keep it and raise it?' "

"And your masters accepted me? Tell me, Laetitia?"

"Yes. You were so sweet; you slept so quietly in that stranger's arms... The master hesitated, but me, I knew that it was good. I stood up and took you, and from that moment on, you were family...."

"And then, Mama? The box?"

55

"The box, Teddy? Well, the man that brought you held that too. When he saw that I kissed you and thought you so nice, he gave me that box. 'Laetitia,' he said to me—for he'd just heard me called so by my master—'I charge you with this child. I'll trust you to raise it. Some day, I'll come looking for it, and on that day...' He didn't finish, Teddy. He handed me the box: 'Keep this also,' he said. 'All that this box contains will be of interest to the child if I don't reappear. It's important that the box does not fall into its possession until its 20th year, not for all the gold in the world, not before then!' "

"Only when I'm 20! And I'm hardly 16! Still four years to wait! No! That's not possible! I have to know sooner..."

Then, Teddy raised his voice.

"But then, Laetitia," he asked, "my dear Mama, then you wanted to know and you opened the box..."

Undoubtedly, the young man was referring to something very serious, deadly serious, for suddenly Laetitia gasped.

"Ah! Quiet! Quiet!" she begged. "No! I don't want to ever speak of it! You should have forgotten about it! Ah! What am I saying? I'm crazy! You should never think of it! Although..."

"Although..."

"Look here, you know that I love you? Since the moment you arrived at this farm, you've been like my child. I've often told you of my life's misfortunes: my masters' sons, two small ones whom I raised, were killed in the war. My masters disappeared shortly after. Their grief brought about the house's ruin. Everyone else went off. Only I stayed with you, who were still so young; my masters loved you and made you heir to this farm. I've raised you on my own, and I love you like my own..."

Tears appeared in Teddy's eyes.

"Ah! I want so much to know who I really am," he murmured, "my birth is so mysterious, Mama! And you know the truth! You could tell me..."

"Yes, I know the secret, I learned it by chance one day," she confessed finally, "but I cannot tell you! No! Teddy, don't ask! The worst misfortunes would result if I did! Besides, what would knowing it do for you? Aren't you happy now? Even if you want to know your family name so badly, and the secret of your birth, don't you have the certainty of knowing the day when you will find all the answers? On your 20th birthday, you'll be able to open the box..."

"Mama," Teddy finally said, seeming to come out of a dream, "do you think that this box is still in the place where you hid it? Over there, buried at the foot of the third tree in the meadow?"

"Teddy! Teddy! What are you trying to say?"

"I mean, Mama, that your box has been stolen! It's been two weeks since I realized that it's not in its hiding place any more..."

"Who could do that? Who dared?"

"Who dared? Who is the thief who took it? I searched a long time, I assure you, before I found out!"

"And now, you know?"

"Yes, Mama. The thief is Hans Elders!"

"Hans Elders! Ah! I understand! Yes, I understand... Teddy! Teddy!" the old woman said. "It's vital that you recover that box at all costs!"

"You can count on it, Mama, calm down! I'll find it!"

He was a strange boy, this Teddy... And doubtless, Laetitia would have been astounded if she had seen Teddy take a measuring stick and, standing in front of a small mirror hung on the wall, carefully, meticulously, taking the measurements of his skull...

Chapter VI
Escape

It had been five days since Jérôme Fandor had been admitted to the insane asylum. Gerard Herbert, the director, after having sanctioned his imprisonment the day after Fandor had arrived, had had no further opportunities to deal with his new patient.

In his interns' morning report, they wrote that this mentally ill man who had the audacity to claim that he was the famous journalist Jérôme Fandor, had become quite calm. His behavior was exemplary, and he had begged them for a new audience with the director.

Soon after, Jérôme Fandor was again brought in to see the director.

"Sit down," Doctor Herbert said. His words had an affectionate, sympathetic tone. "You wanted to speak with me—what is it?"

"Doctor, when I spoke to you the other day..."

"No! Listen! You asked to see me, and I've placed myself at your disposal. However, you do understand that it's necessary to behave well when you're with me? If you intend to tell me lies again, to talk about your arrival, to insist that you're Jérôme Fandor, I might as well send you away at once!"

"Doctor," replied Jérôme Fandor, "I'll leave it up to you to decide, at some time in the future, if I'm crazy. I'm not here to dispute my mental state with you. I'm here to make a complaint."

"To make a complaint—of what? Has someone harmed you or tormented you?"

"Yes, Doctor... An orderly..."

"An orderly tormented you? Is that true? Will you tell me his name? Go ahead, speak in confidence. Don't you know that I don't want my patients abused?"

"Doctor, two days ago, on the same evening when you and I had our discussion, I was lying in my room. Before lying down, I'd put my skull—you know, the skull that I'd been desperately holding onto—on a chair next to my bed. During the night, someone—an attendant, my attendant—entered my room and awakened me. I was half-asleep, and that's why I couldn't call out sooner. This man approached my bed, took the skull and got out by the window..."

"By the window? But, look, aren't there bars on your window?"

"That is true, Doctor, and I realize I'm mistaken. I only *thought* that he went out the window, but it can't possibly have happened like that... Now I think that this man who took the skull opened the window and threw it into the wasteland that surrounds the asylum... That's when I awoke."

"And what did you do then?"

"I ran to the window, to rush at the thief, but he'd already escaped. I collided with the window panes. I even broke one and cut myself on the wrist—see the scar? Then, I called, I screamed—I hoped that a second attendant would come..."

"But nobody came?"

"No, Doctor, the very same attendant arrived, accompanied by one of his assistants. They grabbed me from behind. He told the other man that I was having a fit. Naturally, his colleague believed him. They beat me, put me into a straightjacket and dragged me to the shower! Doctor, I have to find that skull!"

Not only was the director moved by Fandor's story, he was also disturbed.

"They beat you?" he questioned. "Is that true?"

"Look, Doctor, my arm is covered with bruises..."

This time, the Doctor didn't reply. For the first time ever in his career, he was suddenly worried about his position.

"Listen, I believe you, and if things happened as you described, I promise that I'll do everything necessary... But if you've lied to me, I'll punish you severely... So, tell me—did you tell me the truth? Consider carefully! You've complained about an orderly—you must know his name. Will you tell it to me? I will question him here myself, in front of you..."

Fandor didn't hesitate.

"It's George," he said.

"Good, then we shall see!"

A few minutes later, having been summoned urgently, George appeared in the director's office.

"George," the good Doctor Herbert began in a stern voice, "do you remember that, when I hired you, I warned you that I would never tolerate you tormenting my patients? What happened the other day? Did you hide the skull that this man carried with him?"

"Me? Take that wretched thing? Ah! Sir, it hurts to hear myself accused of such a thing!"

"Nevertheless, it has disappeared. You don't deny that?"

"But, sir, if it has disappeared, it's not my fault—since it was the patient himself who threw it out the window..."

"The patient? No, George! He can't have thrown it out the window because he called for someone to help him catch the thief! Therefore, *someone else* took it from him... How do you answer to that?"

"Listen, sir," George asserted, "I don't know what this poor man said to you, but I swear before God—here's what happened: I was in the dormitory, with the supervisor, and all of a sudden, we heard him call 'help' and 'thief!' We burst into his room." George indicated Fandor. "We found him standing in his night clothes, yelling in front of the window—a window that he'd broken while throwing his skull through it... He was furious, his teeth grinding, and made an infernal din!"

"Yes, and then you grabbed him? You beat him?"

"No! We grabbed him, but we didn't beat him!... Well, sir, maybe someone might've grabbed him a little too hard, a little too violently! That, I can't say!"

The orderly paused, then resumed, in the same upset tone:

"Sir, it's hard for me to see why you'd even suspect me of such a thing... Why are you blaming me for taking his skull, when it's all a lunatic's sick joke!"

The orderly had said this in a tone so sincere that Doctor Herbert was suddenly convinced of his innocence.

"You've lied to me again" he said to Fandor. "It was you who threw the skull out the window..."

And Fandor, in a flash, realized all the horror of his predicament. He saw in that minute the way he would always be treated.

As an incurable lunatic!

Whatever he said, no one would believe him; whatever he claimed, someone would deny it, and this attendant, all the other attendants, would always be watching him; and he would never leave the asylum.

The journalist felt a terrible anger wash over him, for he'd been defeated yet again.

"Doctor, doctor," he shouted, "this is despicable! This man is lying! It wasn't me who threw the skull out the window, it was he! I told you the truth!"

However, Doctor Herbert was no longer listening; he turned to the orderly.

"I nearly committed an injustice," he said. "By my faith, George, this poor man almost fooled me, he played his part so perfectly... I'll remember that in deciding his punishment. And, of course, no one is to take any revenge... You'll continue being good to him. He's not responsible for his actions! Only, at night, since it's mostly at night that he seems to cause trouble, tie him to his bed..."

It was very dark in the small room where Fandor lived, on the second floor. It had just turned midnight and no noise could be heard anywhere in the asylum, where all the patients but one were soundly asleep.

Fandor enjoyed this silence, this peaceful hour, and used it to reflect on the day's events.

He thought about a curious thing—during his conversation with Doctor Herbert and the confrontation with George the orderly—that had ended so badly for him—Fandor had gotten two very clear but odd impressions...

First, he realized that, though he had initially believed otherwise, George was honest. When that man had said, "I didn't steal the skull!" he was telling the truth...

"Let's see," he thought, "one fact is certain: the skull disappeared. Therefore, someone took it. Who is that someone? I accused George. However, he appears to be innocent... On the other hand, in my dream, when I awoke, I believed that I saw the thief entering and leaving by the window. Now, George arrived through the door. Therefore, it's quite probable that George did not see the thief and was justified in believing that the skull wasn't stolen..."

Second, the journalist thought of one of the director's observations. "How do you think," Doctor Herbert had said, "that someone got into your room by way of the window, since it's fitted with bars?"

After the evening's supper, Fandor had gone back up to his room, dashed quickly to the window and inspected the four of the bars, each located 15 centimeters apart. They did indeed prevent anyone from getting through the window.

Fandor had examined the bars carefully; they were intact and showed no sign of having been sawed through.

What, then, had he discovered?

"If I remain well-behaved for a week," he thought, that night, "I hope they will no longer tie me to the bed at night... For now, that's all that I ask, for after my recent discovery..."

But what was his discovery?

Time passed. The attendants, convinced that their patient couldn't move, had gone to sleep, relaxing their supervision.

Suddenly, in Fandor's room, a voice murmured:

"Do you hear me, Monsieur Fandor?"

In a second, Fandor was filled with joy and yet tortured by doubt.

"Who's speaking? Who's there?"

"Don't make any noise! Careful! I'm a friend! It's me, Teddy!"

"What do you want?"

"Why, I've come to help you escape, of course!"

Teddy had carefully risen, crossed the room and come to sit near Fandor, on the edge of his bed.

"Isn't it horrible to be here?"

Fandor interrupted him.

"Horrible, yes. But I must thank you. If the other day, on the docks, you hadn't said that I was crazy, I'd have been shot..."

Teddy's hand was pressed on Fandor's mouth. The young man's shoulders shrugged.

"That's fair. I saved you, but you'd also saved me, so we're even. Now, let's not waste time... Tell me, do you have any idea how we can get out of here?"

"Yes, if you can free me! I can't untie myself from this bed. The attendants strapped me down because they think I'm a violent lunatic..."

Teddy pulled a long, sharp knife from his pocket and cut the leather bonds which held Fandor.

"You're free," he said, continuing to speak in a soft voice, and paying great attention not to make the slightest noise, "but that still doesn't get us very far..."

"Don't worry!" said Fandor, who rapidly got up. "In ten minutes, we'll be outside..."

Teddy regarded Fandor with an amazed expression. The journalist crossed the room and went to the window.

"What about the bars?" questioned Teddy, who guessed that Fandor thought to leave by the roof.

"The bars," repeated the journalist ironically, "which made me a liar! Four of them are made of iron, but the fifth is made of wood! Hold on..."

Fandor had just seized one of the bars that formed a latticework over the window and, without effort, caused it to slide. He then pulled it out from the window frame, where a few minutes before, it had appeared to be tightly held.

This was, indeed, the extraordinary discovery that Fandor had made upon his earlier inspection of the window, that had made him so happy. How had he made this discovery? Fandor's reasoning had been as follows:

"If George is innocent of the theft, then clearly it was committed by someone else. That person could only enter through the window. The window is latticed with iron bars. Therefore, if someone entered despite these bars, then it follows that at least one of them is fake..."

All this Fandor briefly explained to Teddy.

Now, having moved the false bar aside, the journalist grabbed one of the real iron bars. With Teddy beside him, he hung from the window ledge, carefully sliding the wooden bar back into its slot.

"Now," he said, "it's child's play for us to leave."

"Child's play, indeed," said Teddy, sliding along a gutter pipe. "But aren't you forgetting your skull?" she added.

"No," Fandor replied, while beginning a dizzy maneuver that enabled him to jump from the shaky gutter onto the top of the outside wall. "No! I'm not taking the skull, Teddy, because someone stole it from me... Someone whom I don't know— but that you might know? He left by the same route we're now taking."

Teddy didn't answer. He was suspended over the void, holding on by a single hand. With a tremendous effort, he followed Fandor.

This was not the time for idle chatter, however; they needed to flee the asylum as quickly as possible, for daylight was beginning to appear...

An hour later, they dropped, exhausted, into the open country and found themselves, at last, in total safety.

Teddy was the first to break the silence.

"Someone stole the skull?" he asked.

"Yes, they did."

"Why did you take it in the first place? Why did you look for it in the fire?"

"It was pure chance. I had no idea it was of interest to you. I believed it was some new taunt of Fantômas..."

Then, he gave his young companion a brief but clear account of the adventures that had led him to Natal. Teddy, with a grave expression and a concerned air, listened to him, shaking his head.

"Fantômas!" he said at last, as Fandor fell silent. "What a character—both tragic and sinister! Ah, Monsieur Fandor, it's frightening just to hear you speak of him!"

After a small silence, he added:

"But you must wonder why I'm so taken by those grimy old bones? I don't have much to tell you. You see, I don't even know who I am... Oh! Don't be astonished—it would seem that I'm a child from around here. Someone saved me during the war. An old woman, whom I love like a mother, raised me. If you saw me trying to make off with that box in the fire, it's because my dear nurse kept that box, and seemed to attach a great value to it! She claimed it contained the secret of my birth! However, I found out, several days ago, that it'd been stolen, so I followed its trail. I'd gone looking for it in the docks. But, on my honor, I swear to you that I was unaware of its sinister contents..."

The young man's declaration seemed extraordinary. Fandor remained silent as he thought about it.

"All these things are mysterious, very mysterious," the young man continued. "You, Monsieur Fandor, seek to catch the elusive Fantômas. I seek to learn the secret of my birth, and then avenge myself on terrible enemies whom I feel hide in the shadows around me. My enemies... Fantômas... After what you've just told me, I wonder if they aren't the same? Perhaps there are forces allied against us? Monsieur Fandor, do you want to turn the tables on them and work together?"

Fandor held out his hand.

"I accept!"

Suddenly, Teddy became concerned.

"Say," he asked, "there's something I didn't think of... Do you have any money? Do you need..."

"No! No! My dear Teddy, I don't want anything from you. But perhaps you could help me find a job?"

Teddy's face lit up.

"Listen," he said, while handing a revolver to Fandor, "you refuse my money, I understand that, but please, do me a favor... Here, in Natal, being armed is a necessity. Take this gun and remember what I've said. I give it to you gladly. As for a job, yes, I have an idea... There's a factory nearby, a diamond refinery... It belongs to a man called Hans Elders—a suspicious person... I could get you inside his place as part of our plan. It will be hard work for you, but it will doubtless be useful... Are you interested?"

Fandor smiled and answered with a single word:

"Certainly!"

Chapter VII
Out Of The Tomb

As events unfolded with frightful rapidity in distant Natal, a series of brief and tragic events occurred thousands of miles from there, in England, right in the heart of London!

During the night of June 18, the habitual silence of the giant cemetery located northeast of the city was disturbed by the sound of stealthy steps and strange comings and goings.

On a dark, narrow path, surrounded by cypresses, which whispered gloomily under the wind's caress, a shadow could be seen, walking slowly.

This shadow was that of a woman; tall, fair, with a distinguished stride. One could have easily said that she had the bearing of a queen.

The woman clearly knew the sinister place that she was visiting. With her delicate hands, she'd tried to open a vault that she undoubtedly had assumed to be unlocked. However, it was closed with a heavy lock. She didn't exhaust herself with useless efforts, but turned to a set of tools, which she hoped would achieve her purpose. When that failed, the woman fell prey to an inexpressible despair.

What was the goal of this strange woman, whose bearing and style unmistakably indicated her aristocratic origin?

In the middle of her attempts, the mysterious woman suddenly stopped, suppressing an anguished cry. Someone was walking not far away...

Who, besides herself, would wander in a cemetery at this late hour?

A thick silhouette was outlined amongst the tombs; it was that of a robust and stocky man who walked slowly, holding a heavy pickaxe in his hand.

The man gave a sudden start when he saw the woman, and stopped in front of her without saying a word, amazed by this apparition. He was dressed all in black, but his clothing was adorned with silver braids and metal buttons.

The woman immediately recognized that she was dealing with an employee of the cemetery, perhaps a night watchman or a gravedigger.

"By God! Madam," said the man, "I'm extremely astonished to find you here, and, as I don't have the honor of your acquaintance, I'd be happy to know—who are you? You can't ignore the regulations that forbid any person from outside the cemetery's staff from being here outside visiting hours. My duty is to take you to the guardhouse where you'll be asked to..."

Was the woman dealing with an intractable civil servant? Or was she in the presence of the type of person who was touched by those who were in pain, and whom a pretty woman's prayers might succeed in moving?

"Forgive me, sir," she murmured, "and don't condemn me... Alas! I know that I'm guilty... But there's an explanation, and I'm sure that, when I've told it to you, you'll reconsider your decision to take me to the guardhouse... I'd prefer to die than undergo such a disgrace."

"It's not a question of dying, lady, but merely of providing me with something that will justify your presence!"

The woman drew a breath. She indicated the vault.

"This gate," she asked. "It's locked. Why isn't it open?"

"It's indeed locked, as coffins were unloaded here yesterday afternoon."

"I know, that's why I came, that's why I'm desperate."

"But why?"

With rapid words, clipping her sentences, moving closer and closer to the gravedigger, as if she wanted to convince him of her sincerity by her sheer presence, the woman recounted her story with barely a breath.

"The last coffin that they took down into that vault is that of a relative, a friend... Someone I love... Whom I loved more than everything in the world! A dreadful mistake has been made. They left a very important document with him inside his coffin and... I want to believe that you'll help me... I came here intending to open the coffin and remove that document!"

The man shrugged his shoulders.

"Impossible," he said simply.

"Oh! Please don't tell me that," she exclaimed. "It would mean my death. It would cause the most horrible tragedy that it's possible to imagine in this world... Please, sir, since it's in your power, unlock this gate, so that I may open that coffin!"

"It's quite forbidden! Anyone infringing this order would be severely punished."

Despite the rather unencouraging words, the woman gave a small, triumphant smile.

Discreetly, she took a small purse from her bag, which she slipped into the gravedigger's hand.

"I swear to you," she said, "that no one will know anything about it."

Assuredly, a struggle was taking place within the gravedigger's conscience. After a long hesitation, he finally gave in to the woman's increasingly passionate pleas.

From a bunch of keys, he took one, which threw back the lock's bolt.

The gate opened and the two entered, descending slowly into the icy vault.

There were several coffins lined up next to each other, deposited there temporarily as they awaited their final burial.

The woman wandered unsteadily step amidst the sinister boxes, until a moonbeam that lit up the vault's inside led her to a large casket, on the lid of which was fixed a metal plate, as large as a visiting card. On it was engraved a simple name:

Tom Bob

She pointed to it.

Resolved to keep his word, the gravedigger used his knife to remove the screws that barely kept the oaken lid shut.

Then Death appeared!

It was a man of about 40, with a calm and rested face, jet-black hair with a mere hint of silver on the temples.

He appeared to be merely asleep, and his limbs didn't have a corpse's usual rigidity.

"Hurry up, Ma'am," said the gravedigger.

The woman threw herself on her knees near the opened casket and, before the gravedigger had recovered from his surprise, she poured the crimson contents of a vial hidden in the hollow of her hand onto the dead man's lips. The gravedigger cried in astonishment.

"What's this, Ma'am?" he asked. "What are you doing?"

He didn't continue. The spectacle which he witnessed was so unexpected, so extraordinary, so terrifying that the poor man fell backward and collapsed with a thud onto another coffin, deprived of all feeling—even his fear had evaporated.

A few seconds after the corpse's lips had been moistened, he appeared to return to life! His eyelids moved, his mouth quivered, his arms shook...

And, finally, he stood up.

"Lady Beltham," whispered Fantômas, "thank you. I waited for you... for more than an hour."

The woman was, indeed, Lady Beltham, who'd undertaken the fearsome task of opening Tom Bob's coffin.

"You were already awake?" she asked.

"For an hour," said the man who had returned from the dead. "I heard you, but I couldn't make the slightest movement! If my mind lived, my body was still trapped in the most appalling catalepsy."

"Tom," begged Lady Beltham, "let's go... Let's flee this terrible place!"

The man whose coffin had been labeled with the celebrated name of "Tom Bob" slowly raised himself. Suddenly, he noticed the unconscious gravedigger.

"What's he doing here?" he asked harshly.

Lady Beltham explained the tragic incident of the locked gate and the fortunate fate that had sent the gravedigger. She stressed the irreparable misfortune that would have resulted if he had refused to unlock the vault.

Fantômas, however, who slowly felt his strength and power returning, said nothing, but remained thoughtful.

"The gravedigger," he finally said slowly, "is an unfortunate witness to my resurrection..."

Lady Beltham interrupted him. She had an alarmed look. She knew his intentions.

"Mercy, Tom," she pleaded. "Mercy for him!"

However, Fantômas wasn't listening.

With appalling cold-bloodedness and indomitable will, he leaned over the unfortunate gravedigger's body. The concussion had been violent; the man hadn't yet regained consciousness.

Fantômas smiled. His strong, muscular hands fastened around the gravedigger's neck. Then, for a very long time, his fingers tightened, his thumbs squeezing the carotid and tracheal arteries.

The unfortunate gravedigger didn't make a movement in revolt. A slight death rattle could barely be heard escaping from his throat. His head fell backwards, while his lips turned white and his eyes rolled into his head.

Lady Beltham, terrorized by this cruel, wanton act, accomplished with such monstrous coldness, had dropped to the rocky flagstones that made up the floor of the vault.

With her eyes enlarged with terror, she watched her lover mercilessly kill the gravedigger.

Then, Fantômas, his Herculean strength fully restored, grabbed the corpse and, carrying the dead man with both arms, deposited it in the very coffin that he, himself, had just left moments before.

The horrible act accomplished, the villain screwed the lid back onto the casket with fevered haste—and soon, order was restored to the funeral crypt. Not a sound pierced the darkness!

Inside the coffins, lined up against each other, there was henceforth none but the dead... the truly dead!

The night was still not over when Fantômas and Lady Beltham found themselves opposite each other in a small, secluded house in the London suburbs.

However, the blonde woman was still struggling against the emotions that tortured her.

Fantômas, always methodical and careful, had devoted himself to more practical matters; he had meticulously washed and dressed in new, clean clothes, and was now ready to leave.

"Tom," begged Lady Beltham, alarmed at his intentions, "you're leaving me, me, who just saved you?"

"I also saved you," retorted Fantômas, "and I'll save you again, but a man, even a man like me, has only his word... And I've sworn to uphold it!"

"What are you planning to do?" asked Lady Beltham, frightened.

"To see Juve," declared Fantômas, "to whom I made a promise to return Fandor. I made an appointment with Juve for three days after my death." [11]

"You plan to return Fandor to Juve," she said. "But do you only know where he is?"

"Yes, I do, Madame, and I'll be true to my word. Also, by returning Fandor, I might secure from my foes the reprieve I need to accomplish the work I've been planned for now 15 years."

"Tom," exclaimed Lady Beltham again, "is it possible? The secret that you once confided in me... Is it true?"

"It's the truth, Madame... And no matter what happens, never forget that, above all things, all human feelings, all emotions, all dramas, there's no more powerful love than this love..."

"And this love is?" questioned Lady Beltham.

---

[11] Fantômas' bargain with Juve was, of course, made in the conclusion of the previous volume, *Le Pendu de Londres* [*The Hanged Man of London*].

"Paternal love!" replied Fantômas.

The man called "Tom Bob," who had just miraculously escaped from a horrible death, wasn't only, as most people believed, the most well-known of Scotland Yard's detectives and a member of the Council of Five. He was, and had always been, Fantômas!

In the course of his latest adventures, the London Police, who believed him to be a doctor who had murdered his wife, had imprisoned Fantômas—for a crime of which he was actually innocent! Fantômas, under a borrowed name, had been sentenced to death by hanging.

Naturally, the Council of Five had rigged the execution so that Fantômas was able to avoid death. However, even though he had escaped from the gallows, Fantômas had fallen into the hands of his sworn enemy, Inspector Juve of the French Sûreté. Indeed, Fantômas, mistaken for dead, had been led, alive, to Juve's refuge, a London house he had rented expressly to imprison Fantômas.

The outlaw had no desire to remain at the mercy of his formidable enemy. So he had pretended to poison himself before Juve's very eyes. In anticipation, he had taken the precaution of telling his mistress, Lady Beltham, that he would revive in three days, and that she should make sure that someone came to help him escape from the vault where they would confine his body.

Juve, having witnessed the so-called suicide of Fantômas, had nevertheless not been fooled by it.

He knew the madman's subtlety, his extraordinary audacity. He was perfectly aware that, as far as Fantômas was concerned, one could expect anything!

Juve had watched Fantômas on his death's bed, and had not lost sight of him when he had been laid in his coffin, convinced that, at any moment, even as he came ever closer to the grave, Fantômas would find a means to awaken and attempt to flee.

Yet, nothing like that had occurred and Juve had seen Fantômas properly entombed under the name "Tom Bob." He had attended his funeral, forcing him to believe in the reality of Fantômas' death.

But his was still a relative belief, rather than an absolute conviction, because Fantômas' last words had been: "Juve... in three days."

Juve, despite everything he had witnessed, awaited the expiration of his adversary's deadline with tremendous anxiety. And, in truth, Juve hoped that Fantômas would rise from the dead because, if revived, the villain would be able to tell him where Fandor was. Perhaps Fantômas would even help him find the journalist, for whom he seemed to have an incomprehensible sympathy.

Incomprehensible? Not entirely. Juve knew that, if Fantômas had spared Fandor until now, it was because he had a need for him, and perhaps even a need for Juve, because of something that was buried deep in Fantômas' heart.

It was a terrible secret that the outlaw didn't even acknowledge to himself, but that Juve, ever the policeman, had guessed.

So, despite everything, trusting in Fantômas' word, Juve ardently hoped to see him at their rendezvous.

It was for this reason that Juve had not wanted the approaches to the cemetery watched, knowing full well that the one that would save Fantômas, that is to say Lady Beltham, would not intervene if she knew that her lover would rise from the dead only to fall into his opponent's hands. Having counted the days, Juve now counted the hours.

The evening came. With the night nearly over, the third day would soon be over; the deadline fixed by Fantômas would end.

Would Juve see his foe again?

Of course, his decision was made: if Fantômas did not return, Juve would go to the cemetery himself and, after telling Scotland Yard what he knew, would have the coffin opened.

However, Juve wasn't yet ready to say anything, didn't want to act before the deadline's expiration.

It was 7:00 p.m. In one hour, the Sûreté Inspector would be free to act.

Juve paced in the small room he occupied in his London hotel. Gripped by a powerful emotion, he surveyed his surroundings.

Suddenly, his whole body trembled.

He heard a discreet rapping at the door.

In a voice strangled with emotion, he said: "Enter."

The door opened.

Fantômas appeared.

Chapter VIII
Strange Cartridges

"My dear Winnie," said Teddy, "you're absolutely wrong to be upset. First, creating bad blood never serves any purpose. Besides, everything will sort itself out, you'll see..."

"Ah, Teddy, I can see you haven't put yourself in my place. You don't understand the full horror of the situation."

"But nothing's final, Winnie, why not wait and see?"

"Perhaps, Teddy, but what if his innocence is never proven?"

"The man who stole such a sum of money is bound to commit an indiscretion before long... He'll spend excessively. He'll gamble... In short, he'll draw attention to himself."

Winnie shook her head sadly.

"No!" she declared. "You're mistaken. That miserable money was stolen too skillfully. It's obvious that the thief is a clever man. He certainly knows by now that Lieutenant Dragg–Wilson–has been accused in his stead. He'll be careful to do nothing to attract suspicion... It's a common business: an innocent will *pay the law* for him. It happens all the time. Wilson is lost!"

"He can't be!"

"But what do you want him to do? If his colleagues, or his superiors, ever learn of this, imagine the scandal, the terrible dishonor which will fall on him..."

"Your father won't say anything, Winnie."

"Papa, no, undoubtedly. He wouldn't like to shoulder such a responsibility, but Jupiter will talk! Think about that..."

The young man and the young woman had been discussing the subject for over an hour. They were in the vast living room that occupied almost all of Diamond House's ground floor.

Teddy had arrived on horseback around 9:00 a.m., as was his habit. He had returned from a long run and a tiring walk. He didn't have enough time to go home for dinner with Laetitia. He had stopped at Diamond House to solicit hospitality from its owners, the traditional morsel of "*blitong*" that. in all of South Africa, constituted the plain, usual meal of riders and hunters.

Teddy had found Diamond House almost deserted.

Hans Elders wasn't there. The servants had already gone up to bed. Winnifred sat alone in one of the parlor windows, daydreaming.

It was she who had come to meet Teddy, and who had improvised a frugal supper for the young man.

Now, Teddy was trying hard to console her, because she was upset about the terrible charge leveled against Lieutenant Dragg earlier, and about her father's anger.

Winnie's pain was horrible. She loved her Lieutenant, and, for many long weeks, had cherished the tender dream of becoming his wife.

A few days earlier, Teddy had told Laetitia that he was sure that Hans Elders was the man who had stolen the infamous box... Now, Teddy, who liked Winnie a great deal, and who considered her a friend, almost a sister, foresaw the possibility of another terrible scheme...

To him, Hans Elders was a cur; he hadn't hidden that from Fandor.

And what saddened Teddy even more was the thought that, even if Dragg's innocence became clear—and it would—a wedding between he and Winnie would be no less difficult.

In fact, wouldn't Dragg eventually learn, possibly from Teddy himself, the exact nature of Hans Elders' miserable character?

Winnie cried silently. Teddy, out of arguments, was upset by her grief, but had no more idea of what to say. All of a sudden, the two young people were surprised by a brief vision.

"Did you see?" Winnie gasped.

"Yes, it seemed..." Teddy was already up. He went to the window. "Hello! Who goes there?"

The young man's voice resounded, echoing in the evening's quiet silence. But no answer came.

As Winnie rejoined him, looking pale, and visibly trembling, Teddy became persuaded that they had been victims of an illusion.

"We made a mistake," he said. "There isn't anyone."

"No! I'm sure of what I saw. Someone stuck his face to the window, and was spying on us... But who?"

Teddy shrugged his shoulders.

"Perhaps it's your father who came back, and who, seeing the light, looked in while passing... We'll hear him open the door, and..."

"No, if it were papa, he'd answer our calls."

Suddenly, Winnie jumped again.

"There! There!" she said. "Look!"

Teddy's sharp eyes had, like Winnie, seen a shadow that seemed to carefully slip into the back of the garden.

"Yes!" he acknowledged. Opening the iron shutters that closed the window and sheltered the room from any attack, he quickly added: "I'll find out what's going on! Stay here, Winnie, I'll search the garden."

"Oh, no!" cried the girl. "For the love of God, don't go out there! It's certainly a criminal. Convicts have been spotted in the vicinity. Don't go out there, please, Teddy!"

However, as soon as there was a question of running into danger, it was impossible to hold Teddy back.

"Don't be silly!" he said. "If by any chance there's a criminal in your garden, that's just a further reason for me to go after him!"

"Then, arm yourself! Wait! In my father's office, you'll find his gun and there are bullets in the small cupboard against the wall..."

The gun Winnie spoke about was in a rack.

Teddy took it and rushed to the cupboard that Winnie had told him held ammunition.

On the cabinet's shelves were some stacked cartridges. Teddy took a handful of blue shells, similar to those he used himself, and put them in his pocket.

However, as he slipped one of the cartridges into the weapon's chamber, a whole stack of other shells, bound together and of a pink color, fell from the cupboard. One of the cartridges became separated from the others and he pocketed it.

He then rushed to the study's French window, opened it and ran into the garden, the gun under his arm.

"Who goes there?" he cried again, feeling as if he'd just flushed someone out of a thicket, and they were fleeing in front of him.

No one answered.

Teddy listened for a moment, then abruptly pivoted on his heels, aimed and fired in the direction of his target to see if something, whether man or animal, would run out of the darkness.

Instinctively, the young man tipped open his weapon's barrel to replace the shell that he'd just spent. However, the cartridge that he had just tried to load into the gun must have been badly gauged, for he was unable to slip it inside.

Teddy lowered his eyes and, returning to the brightly-lit windows, checked what impeded him. The cartridge that had refused to go into the gun was one of the pink shells. He considered it a minute, then no longer caring about following the creature in the garden at which he had just shot, he retraced his steps. The young man rushed to Hans Elders' study and had his foot on the steps that connected the garden with the room when, quite suddenly, he stopped dead, swearing a silent oath.

What had he just seen?

Hans Elders had employed Jérôme Fandor for three days, acting upon Teddy's recommendation, for the young man had become Fandor's unofficial protector.

Fandor worked in the diamond mine, performing whatever tasks were required of him: hauling earth, carrying tools, helping others, all the while earning a meager salary.

Fandor was, however, perfectly happy. This was far better than life in the lunatic asylum.

After the conversation he had had with Teddy, when the young man had helped him escape, Fandor had come to an agreement with him. It was clearly important to carefully monitor Hans Elders' activities. The journalist was perhaps equally curious to learn more about Teddy as well.

A day after he'd been hired at the *cherchery*, Fandor had already been able to form an informed opinion: there were indeed many small strange and disturbing things happening at the mine.

Some of the workers had the faces of pirates and bandits. The work that they did wasn't well defined—if they actually did any real work. And there was something else that surprised Fandor: the abundance of diamonds that, on some days, were discovered in the washed earth, generally by the same workers...

Yet, Hans Elders appeared to be the most honest, least suspicious, of all who lived in Diamond City.

However, if the proverb *Know the Master, Know the Servant* is often true, Fandor believed the opposite was also true, and thought that *Know the Servant, Know the Master* was just as trustworthy. So, each evening, after work was over, Fandor—a man who knew a overabundance of tricks—strove to remain hidden either in the mine's buildings or in Diamond House's gardens.

On this particular night, Fandor was to encounter a series of surprises...

He had seen Teddy arrive on horseback, greet Winnifred and go with her into the salon.

He thought that it extremely interesting to see how close Teddy and Winnie were, even when Teddy maintained that Hans Elders was a thief.

Skillfully, Fandor had approached the window, stuck his face to the glass and spied on the young people. At first, things went well. But suddenly his luck turned. The journalist had barely time to disappear, having realized that someone had spotted him, when Teddy sprang toward the window.

Fandor chose to flee. However, a detonation resounded, a hail of lead splattered, perforating the leaves next to him.

Fandor had instinctively thrown himself flat on his stomach. "That was a wrong move indeed," he muttered. "And I can't identify myself. What would Teddy say? Is he going to leave?... The Devil! He's reloading his weapon!"

After that, Fandor no longer understood what happened.

He saw Teddy slip a shell into his gun, react in surprise, then run back to Hans Elders' study.

But Fandor wasn't at the end of his confusion!

He then saw Teddy move cautiously away from Hans Elders' office.

The young man went to one end of the garden, then, barely shouldering his weapon, randomly shot two rounds into the air, seemingly without aiming at anything!

The detonations were still echoing when Fandor heard Teddy call at the top of his lungs:

"Help, Hans! Help me! Here!"

Alarmed, Hans Elders left his study and, attracted by the young man's cries, headed in Teddy's direction.

However—and this was what surprised Fandor the most—while Hans was running forward, screaming with all his might: "Don't worry! Hold on! I'm coming!" Teddy was performing a strange maneuver.

Fandor, still concealed on the ground and hidden by a huge tree, realized that the young man, far from awaiting Hans Elders—whom he nevertheless had called—bent down, crept along and, taking care not to make the slightest sound, or let the businessman see him, headed for the study and entered it.

"What the devil is Teddy doing?" thought Fandor. "He deliberately drew Elders from his study, left him to fend for himself in the garden, and then entered back into the house..."

Fandor didn't hesitate. He also ran towards the house, and saw that, unfortunately, thick iron shutters closed the windows of Hans Elder's office. However, there were openwork flower rosettes on the decorative shutters. Fandor was able to peer through the interstices and what he saw made a cold sweat appear on his temples!

Teddy, barely inside the room, had run directly to the small piece of furniture that contained the gunshells. With a fevered hand, he seized one of the pink cartridges, tore it open and drew out the paper padding. He unfolded it, looked at it and turned pale.

The shell was filled with a 10,000-pounds certificate!

He tore open two other pink cartridges, both of which were also stuffed with bank certificates.

Fandor then saw Teddy take the whole box of pink cartridges and put it in his pocket.

Perhaps the journalist, a victim of his own natural impetuosity, would have rushed and leapt on Teddy, but someone else had entered the study. It was Hans Elders, who had returned from the garden, where he hadn't found anyone.

The door was slightly open, so Fandor heard Teddy very calmly reassure the house's master.

"Yes! I shot at someone! That's why I called you. Then, I ran up here because I thought that the thief had come into this room right after you went out..."

Hans Elders, at those words, turned pale.

"A thief! Here!" he said. "But what would he...?"

Alas, Fandor didn't hear any more!

With a kick, Teddy had just closed the door so the journalist had to be satisfied with seeing both men, without being able to listen to what they said.

Nevertheless, remaining at his observation post, seeing Teddy and Hans Elders talk, swiftly but certainly without animosity, Fandor suddenly believed he understood.

"I'll be damned! There's only one outcome to all of this: If Hans Elders is a crook, which is quite possible, then Teddy is another!" After a moment's reflection, the journalist added: "But, if Teddy is a thief, too, am I wrong to confide in him? Who is to say that he doesn't intend to lure me into a trap?"

Chapter IX
An Eventful Crossing

The *British Queen*, a large steamer, sailed through the Atlantic.

She would stop for a few hours in the Cape Verde Islands, to disembark passengers on Africa's west coast. After that, she was to cross the Equator and travel south to her next port of call, the Cape of Good Hope.

Finally, she would again head north, up the Indian Ocean, to Durban, Natal's port, where her great journey would end.

The *British Queen* was one of the superb ships whose passenger service regularly linked the British capital to its South African colonies.

It had been a few hours since the *British Queen* had left Southampton. In the first class passengers' port corridor, on the odd-numbered side, an elegant, distinguished man approached the steward in charge of that section's cabins.

"Is Monsieur Duval settled into 91?" he asked.

"Monsieur Duval hasn't yet returned to his cabin. However, he must be aboard, since his luggage is there. Whom shall I announce when he returns?"

"Tell him that Mr. Smith... In fact, my friend," the man reflected, "it's unnecessary to inform Monsieur Duval of my visit at all. Don't say anything to him."

On the ship's other side, in the starboard section, at the same instant, a similar scene was taking place. A middle-aged man was asking a chambermaid:

"Is Mr. Smith in cabin 92?"

As she answered him in the negative, the visitor poorly concealed a dissatisfied restlessness.

"As soon as he arrives," he said, "tell him that Monsieur Duval asked for him... No, on second thought, don't say anything to him, absolutely nothing."

Clearly, it would not be long before these two passengers met.

A few moments after these incidents, Duval returned to his cabin. He didn't think of questioning the steward, and the latter, faithful to the instructions he had been given, refrained from telling him about Mr. Smith's visit.

Mr. Smith, who had also returned to his cabin, was more concerned about a possible visit and he questioned the chambermaid.

"My faith, sir, it was only a few moments ago that a Monsieur Duval asked for you, but if he mentions it, don't tell him I reported his visit, for he told me not to."

Who were these two travelers who seemed to be seeking each other impatiently, while at the same time, clearly avoiding one another?

The scene was less odd as it seemed if one knew that both Fantômas and Juve were currently on board the *British Queen*.

How and why did these two indomitable foes make the mistake of boarding the same ship?

Was one of them unaware of the other's presence, or had they made a pact where the elusive outlaw and the cunning policeman had agreed to make this trip together?

A few days earlier, Fantômas, faithful to the promise he had made to Juve at the time of his alleged suicide, had returned to see the policeman at his London residence.

Face-to-face, between four walls, the two had had a long conversation, which had ended with no attempt at arrest, no attempt at murder.

Of course, during their discussion, they had acted with great reserve, and had been wary of one another, but in reality, the circumstances were such that they each had been mutually obliged to spare the other.

Fantômas controlled Juve with the secret of Fandor's whereabouts, while Juve controlled Fantômas because the villain needed the policeman's neutrality to find someone who was clearly dear to his heart and who was in the same region as Fandor.

Both men had thus concluded a tacit alliance, and their first act had been to book passage aboard the *British Queen*, where Juve had registered under the name "Duval" and Fantômas under that of "Smith."

But despite it all, the two adversaries were as antagonistic as ever. They had mutually watched each other during boarding. They had not lost sight of each other the whole time the ship had cast off. And it was only when they were out of sight of the British Coast that they had even slightly relaxed their mutual monitoring.

What would their existence be like during their 22 days of constant, confused proximity, while they were living on board the liner?

Despite the promises exchanged, Fantômas feared Juve's wrath, and Juve distrusted Fantômas' word.

It was possible that each had good reason to distrust the other, as both men had virtually vanished the day after departure.

Fantômas had become untraceable, and Juve had disappeared. People in the vicinity of their cabins wondered what could be up with the strange Monsieur Duval and the equally odd Mr. Smith, for it appeared that neither one nor the other occupied their respective apartments.

During the stopover in the Cape Verde islands, Juve had thoroughly watched the movements of the passengers disembarking. He was certain that Fantômas had not left. Yet, since the *British Queen* had resumed its voyage southward, Fantômas was still undetectable as ever.

The *British Queen* no longer presented the elegant and joyous veneer that she had at the journey's beginning in

Southampton. The vibrant accents of the Austrian ladies' orchestra were heard no longer. The laughter of young men and women no longer filled the corridors with their echoes. The passengers looked overly busy, distraught, unceasingly casting anxious, terrified looks about them.

What disaster had caused this change in the superb steamer's inhabitants? It didn't take Juve long to find out.

For it was indeed a disaster that had occurred.

The Plague was on board!

Two cases had been reported that very morning to the sick bay.

By evening, there were 25 cases, and the death toll had risen to ten.

In mournful silence, full of anguish and terror, the *British Queen* advanced along the South African coast.

One day, while passing near Cape Agulhas, a man, likely a passenger, had fallen into the sea! The crew had tried hard to rescue him, but the unfortunate man was never seen again...

They knew that the region was infested with sharks, and the man had surely been devoured by the marine monsters.

Could that mysterious man have been Fantômas?

Chapter X
The Baccarat Game

"Natal," thought Fandor, "is definitely a good state!"

The journalist had found himself on Lord Street, Durban's main street. Durban was a city that combined in its appearance both the quaintness of the exotic cities of the new world and the liveliness of the civilized cities of the old continent.

There were elegant boutiques, marvelously decorated, which sparkled with a thousand points of light in the evening, large buildings with floors containing business offices, and even private apartments, renting for high prices to an elegant and well-off clientele.

As the journalist returned to the small room that he had rented in the suburbs, he reflected upon his situation.

He never failed to ask the concierge, three or four times a day, if there were a telegram or letter for him.

He was invariably answered in the negative. Each time, Fandor expressed his frustration with stifled swear words.

This day, as he dressed, he had again grumbled about his friend's stubborn silence.

If Juve hadn't answered, surely it was because something had happened to him... But what?

Besides, the journalist had other concerns to occupy his mind.

The extraordinary mystery into which he had been thrown since his arrival in Natal was still far from becoming clearer.

Fandor spoke aloud to help clarify his thoughts while he finished putting on his dinner jacket.

"There are three things that worry me: Hans Elders, my friend Teddy, and the missing skull..."

Fandor left his humble apartment with the air of a perfect gentleman and jumped onto the trolley that would take him to the city's center.

By what strange chain of events had Fandor, still employed as a worker in the diamond cherchery when we last saw him, been suddenly transformed into an elegant man about town, ready, it seemed, to enjoy an evening in a fashionable night spot?

Fandor had sworn to solve the mystery of Diamond House the day after he had witnessed Teddy's ambiguous behavior. He had realized that, if he continued to work at his menial job at the diamond cherchery, he would learn nothing. So, the journalist had decided to risk everything he had, to dress as a proper gentleman, to spend the few pounds he had earned pretending to be rich and, at all costs, to get to the heart of Hans Elders' relationships where he thought he would find the answer to his questions.

Having carried out the first part of his plan, in other words, having dressed himself for the part, Fandor went on to carry out the second phase.

"Place your bets, gentlemen! Place your bets, *rien ne va plus*! Seven on the right, eight on the left... Cards with the bank, will you take one? *Rien ne va plus*, gentlemen... Nine in eight..."

In an immense room decorated in gaudy luxury and dazzling light, card games continued endlessly.

Mingling with the men, all immaculately dressed in black dinner jackets, who circulated in the room, and carefully observing what took place around him, was Fandor.

What did the journalist hope to accomplish here?

The National Club, with its concrete reinforced facade, and its entrance guarded by two men in full dress uniform, was, in reality, nothing more than a vulgar gambling den.

Nevertheless, it held a special interest for Fandor. It wasn't simply the haunt of Natal's high society, young people, both chic and extravagant, and of British officers, but also that of a shadier class of business tycoons, foreigners on holiday, gold diggers and the country's big livestock merchants. Moreover, no one there was concerned with anyone's social status, let alone their criminal record.

As soon as he had arrived in the immense room, Fandor had recognized faces that were familiar to him.

Automatically, as if he was irresistibly attracted to him, Fandor approached the man for whom he had been but a modest employee the past week.

For Fandor had noticed Hans Elders sprawled in a broad leather armchair, half-asleep, blissfully smoking an enormous cigar.

Trying to avoid drawing attention, Fandor approached Winnifred's father.

Despite himself, the journalist thought of Fantômas, so expert, so subtle in the art of disguise!

With his perceptive and inquiring eyes, Fandor itemized the slightest details of Elders' face, studied his gestures, his profile.

Could Hans Elders be Fantômas—as Fandor both feared and hoped for?

However, as the journalist continued his examination, he soon convinced himself of his mistake.

No, this strange diamond dealer was definitely no one he had met before.

He was not Fantômas.

Fandor had had to make a rather large dent in his modest savings to acquire the decent and correct appearance required by the National Club's regulations.

He still had a few pounds at the bottom of his pocket, and he automatically stirred them with his hands. He thought that it would be wrong not to take a chance, and to ignore the famous green carpet.

Fandor, who wasn't a gambler, and, indeed, was somewhat superstitious, decided, after some hesitations, to approach a table that seemed less crowded than the others. For a brief while, he attentively watched the players and tried to understand the game. It was a simple game of Baccarat. He risked a pound once... twice... three times!

From that moment, Fandor was taken by the game, especially since he had won.

Luck favored the journalist. At the end of a quarter of an hour, he was already in possession of a small pile of gold coins, mixed with a few bank notes.

While he was still winning, the game suddenly stopped. The bank had just skipped. The man who had held it had got up, very pale, and, without saying a word, left, losing himself in the indifferent crowd. Then, the croupier, with a shrieking voice, began shouting.

"Begin the bidding, gentlemen! The bank with 100 pounds, 200..."

"500!" said a voice.

Precisely at that instant, Fandor had buried his profits in his pockets and was preparing to leave. However, there was a concert of protestations and the other gamblers who surrounded him tried to cause him to change his mind.

"Don't leave," they said. "You have the luck... Stay! We'll win with you... Play and you'll break the bank again."

Fandor, dazed, somewhat intimidated, and fearing to break a local custom, agreed to remain.

He even felt a certain pride when he realized that he was being gently pushed closer to the head of the table, and that the banker would now deal him the cards.

When he raised his eyes to meet the new banker's, Fandor had a start. For his opponent, from now on, would be none other than Teddy, his enigmatic and mysterious friend! This strange and sympathetic boy who had drawn him into this affair, and whom he constantly met when he least expected it!

Fandor was ready to leave abruptly, tearing Teddy away from the gaming table, and demanding an explanation from the young man regarding the theft that he had witnessed, when Teddy had taken the amazing pink cartridges from Hans Elders' office. However, the journalist realized that it was neither the place nor the time for speaking of such things.

Furthermore, Teddy had started the game, pretending not to recognize the player opposite him.

Teddy proceeded to lose everything he had, and even that which he didn't have!

As he won, Fandor felt cold sweat appear on his brow.

How did young Teddy have so much money? Where did all this gold which he was squandering in such an offhand manner come from?

In fact, whenever Teddy lost, the boy smiled with a strange, almost Machiavellian, expression. Moreover, it seemed to Fandor that the young banker, whose pocket emptied themselves as if by magic, felt a deep pleasure at seeing his adversary becoming rich.

The journalist was brusquely interrupted in his reflections.

Someone had put a hand on his shoulder with authority and raised his voice in the midst of the silence.

"Don't continue, gentlemen, this man's cheating!"

Fandor remained quiet for an instant, then, springing up under the insult, he stood up, and looked at his accuser.

The man who had just hurled the defaming charge was Lieutenant Dragg!

The two men stared at each other.

Absolutely stunned, fearing to be the victim a perfidious trap, Fandor didn't know what to say.

He remembered the officer well. He feared that the Lieutenant would recognize him as the man he nearly had had shot the evening of the fire at the docks.

But the officer couldn't imagine for a moment that the poor wretch dressed in rags that he had spared the week before, committing him to an asylum, and the elegant gentleman that he had just accused of cheating, were one and the same.

"Sir," cried Fandor, regaining his composure little by little, "you'll retract what you've just said and apologize."

The officer shook his head.

"I maintain what I said, sir. It's impossible that you didn't cheat... You've won too much..."

The officer didn't continue. A masterful slap had slammed into his cheek.

Fandor had thrown it.

Meanwhile, the game had stopped. Fandor, without thinking to collect his money, faced his accuser.

"You'll give me satisfaction, sir," said the Lieutenant, pale with anger.

"Name the time and place," replied Fandor.

"That would be now," said the officer, putting his hand on his holster.

Lieutenant Dragg was undoubtedly in the habit of duels in the American Western style.

"Where then?' demanded Fandor simply.

"In the Club's garden, sir, if it pleases you..."

However, as Lieutenant Dragg showed the way to Fandor, who had left the gaming table, a young, clear voice, broke the silence.

"Monsieur Fandor," it said. "Jérôme Fandor."

It was Teddy who had spoken.

"Monsieur Fandor," repeated the adolescent, "you can't fight with that man!"

Teddy indicated Lieutenant Dragg.

"Why not?" sputtered Fandor, taken aback.

"Because," Teddy resumed, striving to strengthen his trembling voice, "because that officer has been dishonored."

Lieutenant Dragg became pale in turn.

"What? Is it you, Teddy, my friend," he said in a reproachful tone. "How can you say such a thing? I demand an explanation."

The teenager didn't seem flustered.

"I say that Lieutenant Drag has been dishonored," he replied. "I say that he is, in fact, a thief. He stole the 10,000 pounds earned by the boxer, Jupiter. You understand, gentlemen, that one cannot fight with such a man."

"Prove it!" someone screamed. "Prove it!"

Teddy, increasing his short height by standing on tiptoes, indicated someone who was walking towards the group.

"Ask Mr. Elders here if what I'm saying is true," he said. "The theft was made at his place. Jupiter didn't file a complaint at his request. I believe he granted the Lieutenant 48 hours to make good. However, that time has now passed, the officer hasn't done so and, therefore, he's unworthy and dishonored... One doesn't fight with such a man."

The crowd's emotion turned to a dumb stupor.

Hans Elders advanced slowly, staring at the three persons before him.

Fortunately for Fandor, Elders didn't recognize him. The journalist had just become his employee, but still, he was so menial that his boss was quite unaware of him.

Besides, Hans Elders, without lingering to consider Teddy or Fandor, took a pitiful look at the officer, who was trying hard to stammer some vague protest.

"Our friend Teddy speaks the truth, gentlemen," finally declared Elders, with the air of a man making an overwhelming confession. "I ordered Lieutenant Dragg out of my home, just after he'd committed the theft in question."

"No," the unfortunate officer shouted. "Please, Mr. Elders, I swear to you on my mother's head, as I've already done, that I'm innocent of that hateful crime."

From all sides, the men now questioned Hans Elders, Teddy, and even Fandor.

Alas, with the explanations provided by the first two, there was no doubt left.

Lieutenant Dragg appeared to be guilty. Someone had caught him in the act, so to speak, and it was his prospective father-in-law—since the officer was to marry Winnifred Elders—who had been forced to drive him out.

However, while Hans Elders detailed the scandal, Teddy, who had been the principal author of this accusation, was enormously affected. He increasingly withdrew into a moody silence.

Taking advantage of an instant when he was no longer the focus of anyone's attention, he slipped away from the crowd.

However, without saying a word, without giving the slightest hint that might reveal his thoughts, Fandor had been striving to understand what Teddy's motives in helping him avoid the duel might have been.

Was he Hans Elders' accomplice? Why had the teenager hidden what he knew from Fandor until now? Moreover, why did Teddy, who claimed to be Elders' enemy, ask for the diamond dealer's testimony to prove the guilt of an unfortunate officer who, according to what Fandor had witnessed, was truly innocent?

Fandor, who had not lost sight of Teddy's movements, had seen the young man surreptitiously leave, hugging the gold-paneled walls. The journalist dashed forward in pursuit.

"Hey, there, my friend Teddy! Wait!"

"What can I do for you, Monsieur Fandor?"

"Why are you in such a hurry to leave?"

Teddy, shyly, looked around him but said nothing. The journalist, burning with impatience, would not relent.

"This time, will you explain your actions to me?"

"I helped you out of a dangerous situation," Teddy finally murmured. "Lieutenant Dragg would certainly have shot you dead before you could raise a finger."

"Thank you very much," said Fandor. "I will gladly acknowledge that you're always there to get me out of trouble. But, really, you're too kind, and this exaggerated attention is starting to weigh heavy on me. Besides, if you accused the Lieutenant of this theft, is it because you know for a fact that he's guilty?"

"No. I know for a fact that he's is innocent of that crime."

"But then, why did you accuse him, you rascal! Tell the truth, for once, and don't constantly create mysteries!"

Without noticing Teddy's agitated state, Fandor continued:

"First, I must tell you... If you're sure of Lieutenant Dragg's innocence, I'm certain of your guilt, for last night, I saw you sneak into Hans Elders' office and steal the money he'd hidden inside those pink cartridges... this same money that's burning my fingers right now! If someone's cheated today, it's not me, but you—you who lost the money from your theft to me!"

And Fandor threw the bank notes that he had so easily won in Teddy's face. The teenager became dreadfully pale but then, quickly regained his self-control. He picked up one of the bills that Fandor had thrown around.

"Monsieur Fandor," he said in a soft and earnest voice, "you've earned this money. It belongs to you. Keep it."

Fandor protested with a gesture.

"Then, I'll keep it for you," said Teddy. "At your disposal. And I know you'll soon claim it from me, because it's right that you should have it... Listen, Monsieur Fandor, this money has nothing to do with that you saw me take last night from Hans Elders' cartridges. A funny place to hide money, eh? Yes, I took that money! I don't deny it. I don't regret it, I even boast about it! If I had it to do again I would..."

"Teddy," interrupted Fandor, no longer with contempt, but begging for answers, "Teddy, you've known of the theft from Jupiter. Well, in the name of our friendship, tell me the truth!"

"My friend, you're foolish... If you didn't have me to keep you out of trouble, you'd have embarked on the most hopeless adventures... However, I like you because you're nice to me. We two, we'll solve this mystery... Hans Elders is the true thief. He's a bandit, a monster, an outlaw. He stole Jupiter's money and led the world to believe it was Lieutenant Dragg who robbed him. He played this nasty trick on him because he knew the officer was his daughter Winnifred's lover. He doesn't want a penniless lieutenant to become his son-in-law!"

"But," said Fandor, "that doesn't explain that..."

"That matter of me pocketing the cartridges, right?" continued Teddy. "Well, that's simple, my friend... Elders faked a theft and carefully hid the money stolen from Jupiter. The odd probability of loading a gun with one of the fake shells led me to discover his hiding place. I took the money back to Jupiter and here we are. So, tell me, Monsieur Fandor, was I wrong to rob a robber to return his money to the one who'd been robbed?"

Fandor chuckled in agreement. Undoubtedly, Teddy had been right. He was a brave little fellow, and the journalist regretted having browbeat him and, especially, suspected him.

Fandor, however, returned to the subject of the unfortunate Lieutenant Drag.

"Tell me," he asked frankly. "You could have said nothing a few moments ago. It must have been very hard for you to do what you did... To accuse the Lieutenant of a crime of which he's innocent... Why did you do it?"

"I told you, to stop him from killing you! To save your life!"

"To save my life," repeated Fandor, perplexed. "Why do you want so much to save my life?"

Teddy seemed horribly embarrassed by this question.

"You'll know that when we find the skull!" he replied.

Then, he disappeared.

Chapter XI
A Good Joke

No one seeing the horseman ride by would have been able to refrain from trembling!

His silhouette was strange and unsettling.

Just seeing him made one sure that he had watched something dark and disturbing, someone headed towards some sinister and mysterious task...

Yet, he was only a shadow in a dark, starless night, full of opens. His face was indistinct, his shape difficult to identify... He was cloaked in a cape that flew behind him, so great was his speed. His face was half-hidden by a broad hat's lowered brim and he rode on a black, raging horse that he held back with difficulty. From time to time, he whistled to three huge dogs that accompanied him, tongues hanging, tails low, their whole bodies stretched full-out as they raced along behind him. He appeared to be some figure escaped from legend, a knight of old racing off to war, in quest of harrowing adventure.

A moonbeam that momentarily shined between two clouds glinted on a bronze carbine that the horseman wore slung across his shoulder. Gun butts stuck up from his belt. And if anyone had been able to see his face, they'd have noticed his brow frozen in a deep frown. He wore a grim, evil expression...

"Strange place! Strange race!" the rider said to himself. He seemed in a better mood, and almost smiled. "I wonder if I'm wrong doing what I'm doing, and if I'm using too theatrical a method... I could have left my lucky find at his place, but would that have been prudent? He's constantly sick, no matter what. If by chance he weren't alone tonight, I'd take the risk of returning this to him for someone else's benefit... Besides, the game will be worth a little trouble..."

The rider suddenly interrupted his monologue. He stopped his mount in the bend of a ravine.

After tying his horse, the rider dealt with his dogs. He whistled for them, gathered them together, and, in a flash, passed another rope through their collars, which he also attached to a nearby tree.

"And now we'll have a bit of a laugh!"

The dogs tied, the rider returned to his horse and carefully unwrapped a package that was tied to his saddle.

He then took it over to where the dogs could smell it.

"Smell that, my little friends," he said to them in a low voice, as if the clever animals could understand his words. "It's meat, good meat, and since it's been a whole day since you've eaten, I imagine that you like it..."

Indeed, the rider held a bloody quarter of red meat in his hands!

Moving away from the dogs, which now pulled on their leash and made every effort to rush the prey that they coveted, the horseman headed for a crossroad, where he stopped. As he advanced, he was able to see the outlines of a dwelling in the black shadow of the night. It was a farm perhaps, or rather a hut.

The rider approached this humble abode, taking care not to make the slightest noise.

He showed no hesitancy. With a sure hand, he unhooked the thin wood peg that locked the shutters.

"It's his room!" he said, speaking to himself.

Against the right wall, was a table. There was a chair on which clothing had been hung. Finally, at the far end of the room, was a pallet, low to the ground, with a straw mattress. This was not the home of a rich man.

The regular breathing of the man lying on the pallet indicated that he was deeply asleep.

"What an awakening he'll have!" the rider smiled.

He then did an odd thing.

Taking care not to make the least noise, he threw the meat that he'd been holding into the room through the window. With a soft thud, the object fell on the dirt floor. Inside the room, all remained silent. The sleeper was too deep in his dreams to suspect that a visitor was watching him at the window, and hadn't awakened.

Having thrown his bizarre burden into the room, the rider rubbed his hands in satisfaction, while a mute laugh lit up his face.

"My old friend Jupiter," he scoffed, "in five minutes, you're going to have quite a fright, but in a half-hour, I think you'll be overcome by quite another feeling!"

Jupiter was a good man but he was also a man of contrasts. Nature had bestowed him with Herculean strength and, at the same time, endowed him with a youthful, good nature

For the last few days, Jupiter had, however, felt a violent sorrow. He was suffering greatly over the loss of the money he had won in his final, victorious match.

He hadn't been able to drink or eat since the incident—although, clearly, he hadn't lost his ability to sleep through anything!

Thus, he slept in his bed, in the hut that he had built for himself in an isolated gulch, for reasons no one knew. He slept there, blissful and content, like a man with no other concerns.

Jupiter dreamed .

Suddenly, while he imagined that he was digging into an enormous pie into which a cook had set an entire sheep before baking it in a crispy golden crust, he was startled and abruptly woke up. He began screaming horribly.

Jupiter jumped out of his bed in terror, unable to tell if he was living a nightmare or reality, for just as he had been about to bite into the delicious pie of his dreams, hoarse, inhuman cries had assailed his ears. Then, he had felt something hideous and energetic land right on top of his body.

He had opened his eyes, and in the half-light, made out three black creatures leaping around his room. One sprang up on his table, another was jumping for joy on his bed, and the third was running a circular race on the floor, overturning chairs, scattering clothing, all the while growling hideously.

This was the sight that had caused Jupiter to spring in horror from his bed.

It was the mysterious horseman's three dogs which had leapt inside the hut, looking for the meat, and, in so doing, had awakened Jupiter. It was as unexpected as it was brutal.

Fortunately, the dogs were not fierce!

As Jupiter hurriedly pulled on his trousers, he noticed that the dogs seemed to be much more interested in something other than him, which they were eagerly tearing apart.

Suddenly, his face lit up.

"Some practical joker's played a trick on me!" he said. "He sent these dogs to wake me up!"

But who could that practical joker be?

Because of his good nature, Jupiter was already prepared to laugh the joke off, believing that another boxer was paying him an unexpected visit. He finished dressing, then ran to the door.

"Hello," he cried, "who's there?"

However, he strained his ears in vain. He heard nothing. Then, as if from a great distance, a voice replied:

"Over here, Jupiter! By the hollow path"

The hollow path? Jupiter knew it well. It was a narrow passage that wound between the rocks and that led, 200 meters away small, rocky cape that stuck out into the open sea, overlooking a deep cove.

By the time Jupiter arrived at the cape, he was walking more calmly. He wanted to discover who the trickster was. Then, a piercing whistle broke the night.

As the sound seemed to be coming from some distance ahead, Jupiter quickened his step.

In a sudden beam of moonlight, he noticed fresh hoof prints on the path's soil, damp from recent rains.

The night's adventure was just beginning...

Then, Jupiter heard a new whistle, this time answered by barking... The boxer, who, at first, had believed that this was only a meaningless practical joke, was frightened to see the three dogs that he'd left in his hut galloping towards him along the hollow path.

Jupiter understood his predicament. He was between the hounds and their master, in a steep-sided pass where there was barely enough room for one creature to pass. If the dogs wanted to get past him, they would trample him, perhaps even maul him...

The boxer was not about to let that happen!

He began running with all the speed of which he was capable.

Fortunately, he had a clear lead on his canine pursuers.

He soon reached the end of the path—a flat area that made up a small promontory encircled by the sea.

However, still sensing the dogs at his heels, he didn't stop running.

After progressing another 100 yards, he made a bewildering discovery that left him transfixed with amazement.

From his vantage point, Jupiter could see almost the entire cove.

He had been convinced that he was finally going to catch up with the prankster, but a quick glance showed him that there was no one there... Instead, there was something else which he had not expected to find.

With a cautious step, Jupiter approached a lit lantern that had been mysteriously set on the ground.

He wasn't more than a few feet away from the mysterious light when he suddenly stopped. In its yellow, gleaming rays, he had seen a red wallet lying on the ground next to it.

He wondered what could be inside it and eagerly picked it up and opened it. The boxer stared in amazement as he pulled a large roll of banknotes from it! For several minutes,

Jupiter remained motionless, confused, trying to gather his thoughts.

The dogs, the prankster, the whistles, the lantern, the banknotes... It all whirled together in a bizarre haze. At last, he understood.

And then, his joy burst forth like the light of the summer Sun.

"This is the money that Lieutenant Dragg stole from me!" he shouted. "This is my money!"

Suddenly, he heard another man's voice.

"Stop! You're under arrest!"

"Who, me? Under arrest?"

"That's what I said."

"But why? I'm Jupiter, the boxer..."

"Right! You must be the man who's escaped from the steamer..."

"Me, escaped from a steamer?"

"Let's go! Don't act the fool! I'm warning you, if you try to run, my men will shoot you. Is that understood? You, go to it!"

It was undoubtedly written on the immutable stone tablets of Destiny that the unfortunate Jupiter wouldn't have a single moment of peace this night...

Worse, he didn't understand a thing about this new occurrence. Accused of escaping from a steamer? Arrested? It was really all too much!

However, even if he didn't understand what the officer was talking about, Jupiter understood the meaning of his words.

Jupiter was seized with understandable panic. He didn't ask for further explanations. Turning on his heels, he ran away.

A few seconds passed, then there was a tremendous explosion.

Frightened, Jupiter threw himself to the ground. He remained there for several minutes, not daring to move.

He turned his head and looked in the direction of the soldiers and his blood rushed from his face.

"They've blown up a boulder just to stop me! Next, they'll shoot me dead!"

Jupiter was now a prisoner.

Chapter XII
Love... Love!

Since Winnifred Elders had come out into society, the young woman had established the tradition of holding a garden party every Wednesday.

She very much enjoyed an uncommon degree of freedom due to the fact that, living alone with her father at Diamond House, she had been the head of the household since her adolescence. The busy diamond merchant had scarce time to deal with domestic concerns, and thus it fell to his daughter to take on those duties.

Winnie had instinctively known how to fulfill the responsibilities of mistress of the house. One of the more pleasant of these was playing hostess as often as possible to those who comprised the best of Durban's society. During the season, the small group of friends and intimates that she claimed as hers in the city and its vicinity met regularly once a week.

Hans Elders' property was famous amongst the most elegant of Durban's suburbs; its hosts were always pleasant and welcoming. And for that reason, Winnifred Elders' parties were always well attended.

This Wednesday, however, despite the perfect temperature and radiant Sun, Winnifred's guests were not as cheerful and lively as usual.

The attendance was satisfactory; the number of guests was large, perhaps larger than usual. Still, no one's mind was at ease, and important concerns were affecting all those who, by connection or habit, had become the accustomed guests of the Elders' fashionable receptions.

They particularly surrounded Colonel Morris, a middle-aged officer with an imposing presence, who commanded the Queen's company of lancers garrisoned in Durban.

The officer animatedly discussed the worrisome news in the middle of the group. They seemed satisfied with his comments, but still remained concerned and disturbed by what he said, and by what they feared he was going to say.

"Truly, do you believe this story, Colonel," questioned Miss Stowe, a high-ranking official's daughter, "and should we worry?"

"Unfortunately, Miss Stowe, and despite all the optimism that I'd like to show you, it's difficult for me not to be discouraging," replied the old soldier. "The situation is very serious indeed, and I'm afraid I must make things worse by informing you that the *British Queen*, the steamer that arrived yesterday from England, hasn't received permission from the port authorities to dock. This is because an epidemic has been declared on board, a very serious epidemic. Quarantine has been imposed."

There were calls for the Colonel to be more specific.

"An epidemic?" they asked. "What kind?"

"I can't conceal that the situation is very serious," the Colonel explained in a low voice. "It's the Plague, they say. It's already wreaked terrible havoc..."

The crowd murmured amongst themselves. However, Colonel Morris, with an anxious frown on his forehead, again interrupted the conversations.

"It's necessary to take the greatest sanitary precautions," he said. "Of course, we all hope that that grim disease won't touch Africa's soil. As a matter of fact, the customs officers on the coast have reported arresting a man who may have come from the *British Queen*."

This last declaration revived the guests' anxiety; they again pressed the officer, wanting to know what the authorities was planning to do about that man who might be infected with the deadly disease.

"I've received my orders, ladies," he declared. "He's not to leave the isolated cove where he landed. Troops are guarding him and watching from a distance."

"What kind of man is he?" asked his audience. "Where did he come from? Do you know his name? His social status?"

The Colonel shrugged and made a vague gesture.

"They don't know exactly... They only saw him from a distance... It seems that he's a colored man... Alas! He's most likely to be afflicted with the disease..."

Hans Elders arrived and took the officer aside; he led him to the small study where, some days before, the peculiar drama that had thrown confusion and despair into the hearts of Winnifred, Jupiter and Lieutenant Dragg had taken place.

It was the fate of the latter which the diamond merchant wanted to discuss with the older officer.

"Well, Colonel," he asked, "what did you decide about this unfortunate Lieutenant?"

Colonel Morris, given the recent tragic events of the National Club, could not avoid answering Hans Elders' question.

"Lieutenant Dragg," he replied, "is currently under arrest in the barracks. In a few days, a court-martial will be held to pass sentence. It's a very regrettable matter..."

Hans Elders hypocritically lowered his head.

"Indeed, Colonel—especially for me and my daughter... The poor child's quite unhappy... Will she ever recover from this blow, I wonder?"

Hans Elders indicated Winnifred to the Colonel through the big open window. She was walking down a distant path, accompanied by a young man with whom she was speaking.

Actually, the girl didn't seem to be overwhelmed by the misfortune that had occurred to the man that everyone took for her fiancé, but who, in reality, was her lover.

At least, if Winnifred felt an understandable grief, she was undoubtedly making a point not to show it.

The young girl had been walking cheerfully for about an hour with an elegant young man with distinguished manners whom she had recently met.

That young man was none other than Jérôme Fandor!

After the National Club incident, Teddy had introduced him to various society personalities as a wealthy French tourist, and he had been well received. Hans Elders even invited him to his parties.

Winnifred discussed the last remark that they had overheard when walking by Colonel Morris' group of listeners.

"This is a poor introduction to our country, Monsieur," she said, "coming here at a time when it's being threatened by the Plague."

"My word, Mademoiselle," replied Fandor, "my philosophy is to take things as they come. And I confess to admire your compatriots' composure and calm."

"You believe that we're too cold?"

She's a funny girl, thought Fandor, *for someone whose fiancé has just been arrested. She doesn't seem to act as if she's carrying the weight of the world on her shoulders...*

Her flirtation amused Fandor. He looked at her discreetly and couldn't help thinking how pretty she was.

Winnifred was, in fact, very beautiful, a pretty brunette with a smooth complexion, lovely and abundant black hair, a pleasantly curved waist and a regal profile.

They both continued to move away from the house, walking down a narrow, shady path, with sweet-smelling fragrances.

Fandor had just accomplished one of his dearest wishes by attending Winnifred's Wednesday party. Her invitation, received and accepted, was but the first act in his projected campaign.

Fandor was increasingly intrigued by the events and mysteries surrounding Hans Elders and his family. He wished to gain more knowledge of the rich diamond merchant.

Now, he was inside and had even begun to gain Elders' daughter's friendship. Of course, he wouldn't abuse it, being too honest and loyal for that.

Fandor and Winnifred were alone in the woods, in the midst of its troublesome silence, which is one of the charms of South Africa.

Fandor considered the lovely girl by his side with a peculiar emotion. The journalist was curious to know to what extent the girl would be faithful to her Lieutenant's memory.

With a sincere and passionate impulse, he took her hand.

"Monsieur, what are you doing?" reproached, Winnifred, in a choked voice. "Don't you know that I'm taken!"

Yet, she didn't withdraw her hand.

Suddenly, Winnifred screamed.

She pulled herself abruptly away from Fandor's grasp and ran away, leaving the journalist alone with a newcomer who had just emerged from the forest's thickest part.

It was Teddy.

The young rider seemed both worried and irritated.

"What's new?" Fandor asked.

"Jupiter's found his money, as I told you," Teddy replied, somberly. "You see, Fandor, I'm not a liar... The money I gambled the other evening wasn't his..."

Fandor, touched by Teddy's emotion, tried to comfort him.

"I'm sorry," he said. "I never really suspected you, Teddy. I see in your eyes that you're clearly an honest boy. If the boxer got his money back, so much the better; we don't have to worry about it anymore..."

"He found it through my efforts," interrupted Teddy. "On the coast... Have you seen him since then?"

"My faith, no," said Fandor. "But you should know, Colonel Morris spoke a few moments ago about a man whom they thought had escaped from the *British Queen* and whom they arrested near a cove on the coast. He said that man is black. Could he be poor Jupiter...?"

Teddy was struck by Fandor's news.

"You must be right," he said. "My Lord! It can't be a mere coincidence."

Teddy signaled his horse to advance.

"Where are you going?" questioned Fandor. "You're leaving already?"

"I'm going to see Jupiter. I've got to do it while it's still light."

"Heavens," cried Fandor. "Don't leave like this! Wait— I'll go with you!"

"You'll be better off here, Jérôme. Court Winnifred, have fun, amuse yourself!"

While Fandor returned to the tennis court where they were now serving tea, he thought: *My friend Teddy's definitely bothered about something, but what is it?...*

Chapter XIII
Is He *Dead?*

Hans Elders stood up and left his office, which was scattered with papers, documents and accounting books. He had been working on some managerial work related to his diamond cherchery. Once this task was finished, he proceeded to violently ring a small bell by the fireplace.

Everyone in the house knew about his impatient nature and they also knew that he could also be severe. A servant rushed in.

Hans Elders questioned him with a clipped tone and bored expression.

"Are there a lot of people here, Tom? Are many people waiting?"

"Four visitors, sir."

"Well, have them enter, one after another, and only when I ring. Is Jerry here?"

"Yes, sir, he is."

"Send him in immediately!"

After the servant had left, Elders finished preparing his study so he could receive his visitors more comfortably.

However, his preparations were rather odd.

He pulled one of the drawers of his desk wide open; it was entirely made of double-layered steel and looked like a strongbox. He spread out a black velvet cloth on the blotter on his desk, then carefully checked the condition of a long revolver that he placed to his right, well within easy reach of his hand. He hid it from sight by carelessly throwing an unfolded newspaper over it.

This done, Elders walked to the window, closed the shutters and drew the large curtains.

The room was barely lit by an electric lamp. The lampshade, long and low, let a mere sliver of light into the office. His workplace had taken on an intimate and discreet atmosphere.

Clearly, this was the effect desired by the master of Diamond House. He cast a wary, questioning look around the office, scanning its shadowy corners, its mysterious recesses and the enormous library whose shelves rose to the ceiling. He also looked at the fireplace, with its gigantic hearth where massive logs could be burned whole.

Obviously satisfied by his examination, Elders finally sat down behind his desk and rang the bell.

A few moments later, the first visitor appeared.

The man was above average in size. His tall, wide brow gave the impression that he was savage and willful. This was emphasized by his prominent, black eyebrows, which were set low and almost joined together. His features were all sharply carved, lending his whole appearance a tenacious air.

The visitor was dressed like the Boer peasants who are half-hunters, half-warriors. He wore a short jacket with the collar turned up, broad, baggy velvet pants, and high riding boots stained with mud. Crossing his body were two bandoliers covered in cartridge pouches that clattered and clanked.

Elders greeted the newcomer in a tone that he tried to make sound cordial.

"Hello, Jerry!"

"Hello, Hans! What the devil's up with your servant? He forced me to wait... When I go to one of my partners' houses, I don't like finding closed doors, having to wait, or using formal protocols! That kind of thing makes me angry..."

The master of Diamond House, usually so unbending, renowned by his workers for his authoritative way of giving orders, didn't seem to take exception to his visitor's attitude.

"And yet, Jerry, you know that it's been close to four months since I've seen you. Is there anything new?" he briefly asked after an instant's silence.

"That depends."

This time Elders shrugged his shoulders.

"Jerry, you disgust me," he said in a scornful tone. "Are we going to play tricks on each other? You're here, on the agreed upon day. If you're here, I imagine that you have business for me. Show me, and I'll quote you a price."

"I'll show you if I feel like it," the other replied, "and I'll make a deal with you only if it suits me..."

"What do you want to tell me then?"

"Only this, Hans: I've had enough. And if you don't know what I've had enough of, I'll tell you!"

"Tell me then!"

Elders had clearly understood that this man was more foe than friend. He imperceptibly trembled. He had begun talking to Jerry sitting across from him in his armchair, both hands in his pockets, in a very natural gesture. However, he had soon moved to leaning his elbows on the desk, his right hand resting on the edge of the piece of furniture, against the unfolded newspaper.

"You wonder what I've had too much of? Well, I've had enough of you playing the boss, of you giving orders, of you acting like a fool! You say it's been four months since you've seen me? It could've been a lot longer—I considered not coming here today. I wanted to forget you. You were a friend once, and it would bother me to see trouble happen to you, Hans Elders..."

"I don't want any trouble, Jerry."

"You don't know anything! Besides, don't you wonder where I've been, Hans? Far away. I traveled. I crossed the veldt, passed over the mountains. I gambled—I lost. I was in the city..."

"At the Cape?"

"And elsewhere. I read the newspapers... You've lied to me, Hans! Don't act surprised—*he* isn't dead!"

Elders shrugged his shoulders again.

"*He*'s not dead?" he continued in a tone that was at the same time both furious and ironic. "*He*'s not dead? You came back to tell me that, Jerry? And you imagine that I, who was once his lieutenant, his friend..."

"You betrayed him."

"You accuse me of betraying him, me who serves his interests? If he were alive, wouldn't I have heard from him? Listen, Jerry, let's move on. I've often spoken to you like I've never spoken to anyone else who works here. That's why I told you that I wondered if *he* was dead—or missing. I doubted then. Today, there's no doubt. What does it matter? What bothers you now, Jerry, and what irritates the others, is that I'm the master now. *He* was *he* and I'm me! *He* kept you in an iron yoke and you accepted it. I'm good to you, and you rebel. Are you trying to scare me? Act as if you don't need me? Come on, Jerry, let's take off the masks! You're here because you have diamonds—hand them over. I'll tell you my price, and you can leave them or take them back. You're free, but don't forget which of us has the stronger hand..."

It was clear that a silent anger was gradually taking over the giant named Jerry.

At first, he made an effort to control himself, but soon he looked as if he wanted to grab Elders by the throat. In the meantime, Elders' right hand had slipped completely under the unfolded newspaper.

"You're the master, Hans, like a valet is master over a stable groom!" he muttered again. "You've never been anything but Fantômas' servant, and you never will be anything else! Take care!"

Hans Elders smiled, and imperceptibly shook the newspaper.

"I am taking care."

Jerry stood up.

"You want to see my rocks?" he asked. "Here's what I have. Make your offer..."

The giant inserted his huge hairy hand into one of his jacket's pockets. He pulled out four or five small stones that he pressed for a second between his fingers in an automatic gesture, and then threw them on the black velvet stretched in front of Hans. They shone with a superb brightness.

The stones that Jerry had thrown with such a contemptuous hand were, of course, beautiful diamonds!

One after another, Hans took each stone and examined it thoroughly.

Curiously, and unlike what one would expect in diamond hunting country where one would expect to see stones in their natural state, these diamonds were all cut.

"Where do they come from?" asked Hans.

Jerry made a dismissive gesture.

"From here and there... Paris, Vienna, Berlin, Cairo..."

"You don't know?"

"No, I don't know."

"Is anyone... looking for them?"

"No."

"You know who cut them?"

"Me."

"Good!"

There was another long silence, then Hans pushed the precious stones back.

"Too bad," he said. "I imagine you'll be asking too much! I'm just a buyer. Unfortunately, a few days ago, I was robbed..."

"You! You were robbed? Of stones?"

"No, money."

"You know the thief?"

"Perhaps..."

Jerry laughed.

"Come on! No more jokes! Your theft doesn't worry me; it probably only happened in your imagination. You want me to feel sorry for you so you can pay me less!"

"You're wrong, I really was robbed."

"You'd better compensate Fantômas then!"

"I don't need Fantômas!"

"If you're saying this to haggle, then let's get on with it. Tell me what you're willing to pay or give me back my diamonds!"

"You'll have a lot of trouble selling these. Jewels like these are too nice, as you well know, to be easy to place... That's why you came to see me, because you've already talked to all the fences. You only came here after you were convinced that I was your last chance... What's your price?"

"Five thousand pounds."

Hans hesitated a second. However, he knew how stubborn the man facing him was. And he was very interested in the merchandise being offered to him.

"I'll give you your 5000 pounds," he said finally, "but only so that you don't accuse me, an old friend, of trying to take advantage of you!"

"Get on with it, then! Pay me! But don't treat me like a fool, Hans! We both know what those stones are worth and you're not losing a penny."

After pocketing his money, Jerry re-buttoned his jacket.

"Good night," he said. "I've got my eye on some other stones. I'll be back in maybe a fortnight. For what it's worth to you, I've heard a lot of things in the cities, Hans, and in my opinion, you should watch yourself!"

With those enigmatic words, the giant, who undoubtedly knew Diamond House well from having been there many times before, went right to a small door in the study, opened it and left.

Once he was again alone, Elders became thoughtful.

"What was he trying to tell me? Three times, he told me to watch out... For what? For who? Could he really have news of *him*?"

After arranging the diamonds that he had bought, Elders again shook the bell and the servant again opened the door.

"Master, should I introduce the other visitors first? Or Old Laetitia?"

In a single bound, Elders got up and ran to the servant.

"Laetitia? Is she here?"

"Yes, master, she's come. She wants to see you."

"She knows that I'm here?"

"She saw you returning, master, and she said to me: 'Go find Mr. Elders and tell him that he's got to see me.' "

Elders turned pale.

"Send her in," he ordered. "You're sure that Winnie's still in the greenhouse?"

"Yes, master."

"Good... Go... I'll wait..."

A few instants later, Laetitia stood in front of Elders. The old woman was pale, but the diamond merchant was paler. It also seemed that both looked at each other with hate-filled eyes.

"What do you want from me, Laetitia?" asked Elders in a voice filled with hate and fear. "You'd sworn..."

"Yes, Hans, I swore never to see you again, but you also swore..."

"I've kept my promises, Laetitia."

"You're lying!"

"Have I ever followed you? Have I ever bothered you?"

Laetitia collapsed into an armchair. She, who appeared to be weak and timid, incapable of clear will, unable to resist someone like Elders, suddenly seemed to be dictating orders to the master of Diamond House!

"You're lying!" she repeated. "And that's why I'm here. I'm only an old woman, Hans, but don't forget that I hold a powerful weapon against you..."

"Laetitia, what do you want? Tell me!"

Laetitia stood up.

"Hans, you made me swear to forget the child," she said. "You made me swear to make it as if he was dead to you. And, I promised you that the child wouldn't know anything until he was 20. That pact still holds, but under a single condition—and don't make any mistake about that, you know what my word's worth—accept it or you're lost. Return what you stole to me! Give me back the box!"

This time, it was Elders' turn to suddenly collapse in his chair.

"I didn't steal the box!"

"Yes, you did, and it was Teddy who realized it. He went to the docks to get it back. Oh! Don't try to deceive me, Hans, I'm well informed! It's because Teddy reclaimed it that you set fire to the warehouses. You thought the child would perish and that everything would disappear with him... Good Lord, Hans, you forgot fate! But I know, yes, old woman that I am, I know. I learned that the box had disappeared... It was stolen by a stranger, a man they took to the lunatic asylum..."

Hans grumbled indistinctly.

"Keep quiet!" said the old woman. "To the lunatic asylum. And there, you were able to steal the box back... Yes! I know it! Don't deny it! Well, give it back to me now, or—watch out! Yes, watch out, Hans Elders! Because, just as easily as I came here, tomorrow I'll go tell everything to the police!"

"Shut up! You're mistaken, Laetitia. You think I stole the box with a criminal intent? That's not it, I swear to you! Listen, the proof that I only have good intentions is that, right now, while you're threatening me, if I wanted, I could kill you! See this revolver..."

"I'm not afraid of your revolver, Hans, and I'm not afraid of you, because you can't kill me. You're afraid to kill me because you're afraid of *him*..."

"*Him*?"

"*Him*... and Teddy!"

"What do you want?"

"The box."

"I don't have it anymore!"

"You took it."

"Yes, Laetitia, I took it to destroy it, because, you see, I know what threatens us—or at least, threatens me... There are times when I wonder if *he* won't come back... And, like you, I wouldn't like it if, thanks to the contents of that box, that *monster* succeeded in finding out that—That's why I took the box, Laetitia, as God is my witness, but I don't have it anymore!"

At first, Laetitia didn't want to admit that Elder had actually lost the box to which she and Teddy attached such a great importance. But, gradually, the old woman, who had made an extraordinary effort to get to Diamond House, became exhausted and allowed herself to be persuaded.

She finally left the study.

Elders, alone again, stood near his desk and reflected. At first, he seemed hesitant, then decided, then satisfied.

"Bah!" he finally said in a low voice. "*Him*! *He*'s dead! The child's only a child... And as for Laetitia... She's old! She's bound to die soon!"

Then, he extinguished the lamp and left the room. It was late. Before receiving the other visitors that were still waiting, he wanted to go see his daughter Winnifred.

However, Elders had barely left the study when a strange, disturbing phenomenon happened in the darkened room.

If an observer had been in the park that surrounded Diamond House, he would have seen the study window slowly half open...

A shadow climbed over the safety bar... A man's silhouette stood out for an instant against the walls of the house. This man folded back the iron shutter, then, leaning, almost crawling, hid himself behind the huge trees. He crossed the entire garden and, at last, jumped over the fence...

Chapter XIV
No One Laughs At Him

Laetitia returned home to the isolated farm where she lived with Teddy. She was dreadfully tired and sad.

A few days before, Teddy had told her that Hans Elders had stolen the skull contained in the mysterious box. At first, she had feigned great surprise, then incredulity.

However, Laetitia had urgent reasons not to let Teddy guess her real thoughts. The very next day, she had decided to make the visit she had just finished, which had led to the despair she felt afterwards...

Elders hadn't denied that it was he who had stolen the precious skull first. On the other hand, he had asserted with much sincerity that it was no longer in his possession—and she believed him. But if he was telling the truth, then where was it?

Who had been able to seize the grim prize? Who was the thief who had robbed Elders of the prize he had first stolen himself?

There were clearly mysteries and powerful secrets between Laetitia and the diamond merchant. Laetitia had to have quite a considerable influence over Elders and know something about him from long in the past. Their final words to each other, when he hadn't dared lift a finger against her, proved it!

However, it wasn't any danger presented to her by Elders that caused Laetitia to feel flustered.

What upset the old woman as she sat sunken in her chair, eyes closed, looking despondent, lost in a dark daydream, was that she was frightened about Teddy's fate.

She claimed that the boy was nothing to her but a foundling orphan. Some unknown man had entrusted him to her, during the war, at a time when so many children became the innocent victims of the conflict between the British and the Boers.

Laetitia was so despondent that she almost forgot her anxiety about Teddy's current whereabouts. As was often the case, the boy hadn't yet returned to the farm that evening...

Suddenly, the old woman trembled.

She had heard a footstep in the courtyard.

It was a man's step, a precise, emphatic step, the step of someone returning to his own property, or at least to a property where he's certain of receiving a good welcome.

The door to the big room where the old woman waited was quickly opened. A man of about 40 entered. One could barely see his face. He was dressed in a long, dark coat, topped with a Boer hat, the excessively long edges of which were pulled down over his face.

At the man's appearance, Laetitia—who had no idea who the stranger might be—automatically stood up.

"What do you want?" she asked.

"Good evening! It's me!"

The stranger then repeated:

"Yes, it's me! Do you recognize me now?"

As Laetitia, her hands joined, remained silent, he insisted:

"Come along! Don't be foolish. Don't you want to welcome me? Or did you think that I was dead, too?"

Still silent, Laetitia shook her head negatively.

"In that case," resumed the stranger, "You were a better judge than Elders. I would have thought the opposite. Once, I would have trusted his insight more than yours, Laetitia... Bah! It doesn't much matter anymore. Still, we're not here to speak idle words. You recognize me now, right? Why won't you answer me?"

Laetitia's pale lips hissed a name, then she muttered another, that left her shivering and frightened—a name of horror, a name of blood, a name that seemed to invoke death.

"Fantômas! You're Fantômas!"

"Quite right! I'm Fantômas now! And he's someone, isn't he, Fantômas? Didn't I keep my word, Laetitia? Don't they know me all over the world?"

Was it really Fantômas, the elusive Fantômas, the outlaw who had so easily avoided, with incomparable daring and diabolical skills, the most energetic efforts of some of the world's best police forces?

Laetitia thought she would die of terror.

"What do you want?" she finally asked. "What do you want from me?"

Fantômas was overcome with laughter.

"I've come to reclaim my daughter," he finally said. "My little daughter whom I entrusted to you 14 years ago. Where is she, Laetitia? Return her to me! I no longer have any goal in my existence but to make her happy!"

It was undoubtedly this that old Laetitia had feared from the start.

In the past, Fantômas, who hadn't yet become a world-famous criminal, a terrifying monster, had entrusted a sweet little child to Laetitia. He had instructed her to look after her, to raise her carefully, to make her a pretty girl, endowed, if possible, with all of a woman's physical and moral charms. Laetitia hadn't considered the future... However, since then, she had been shaken by the discovery that the man whom she had met had become Fantômas, a creature whose very name the whole world feared and which evoked the most atrocious crimes!

Fantômas brutally reminded her of his predicament.

"Hurry up!" he ordered. "Do you think I'll simply wait for you to make up your mind? Can't you see I'm eager to be reunited with my daughter? Where's she?"

"Your daughter, Fantômas? I don't know where she is! I don't even know if she's dead or alive!"

No sooner had she uttered these words than Fantômas arose suddenly and threw himself upon her. He held her by the shoulders. He clutched her, shaking her.

"You don't know where my daughter is!" he shouted. "You're lying, old woman! You don't know if she's dead or alive? Ah! God damns me, Laetitia, take care! Don't say such things! You don't know what I do to people who try to deceive me!"

However, it seemed that the only result of Fantômas' brutal attack had been to give Laetitia time to regain perfect control of herself.

The old woman was again ready to fight. As she had fought Hans Elders, she would try to fight Fantômas!

"I didn't lie!" she said. "I don't know where your daughter is! Listen, Lord of Terror, or whatever they call you, I wouldn't dare lie to you! But if you ask me for something, for information, for a clue, a piece of information, there's only one man who can give it to you..."

"Who?"

"Hans Elders."

"Why?"

"Because isn't your former lieutenant the only one capable of betraying you? The only one capable of taking your child! Don't deny it, Fantômas! I swear to you that it's the truth!"

"When did he take her?"

"A long time ago! A very long time! I don't know anymore—many years!"

"Laetitia, you aren't lying to me now? You swear to me that you don't know what became of Hélène?"

"I swear it!"

"And you don't know who else, besides Elders, could tell me?"

"I swear it again."

"My daughter isn't Winnifred Elders?"

"Winnifred Elders?"

"Yes. Hélène didn't become Winnifred?"

"No! My God, no!"

"And what about your son? This child whom you raised? Teddy—he doesn't know what became of Hélène either?"

"Teddy came after Hélène had disappeared..."

"Laetitia! Laetitia! How do you think I'm going to punish you? How do you think I'm going to take revenge for your terrible lack of concern? How do you think Fantômas is going to make you pay for the pain that you've caused him?"

"I'm innocent!" protested Laetitia.

But Fantômas could not excuse the old woman.

"No!" he interrupted. "You're not innocent. Moreover, nothing could ever excuse your blunder, the consequences of which are likely to be irreparable... I entrusted my own daughter to you! My child! My little Hélène! And now, you're saying that, when I left Natal, when I left to conquer the world..."

Laetitia didn't reply—she felt more dead than alive.

"Once again, I ask you," resumed Fantômas, in an even more dramatic voice, weighting his words even more imperiously, "will you tell me where Hélène is?"

"I don't know!"

"Then you will die in the midst of the most abominable torments!"

"Kill me, Fantômas! Torture me, if you want, but I'm unaware of your daughter's whereabouts!"

What was the dark secret that connected Laetitia, Hans Elders and Fantômas?

The elusive monster had once lived in Transvaal during the war and had enlisted into the British ranks, betraying the Boers.

However, he was tied to the latter by an unbreakable bond. He had had a child, a girl whom he loved, with a woman from Pretoria—his wife.

Hunted by those he had deceived, Fantômas, who was then known only by the name of Gurn, had entrusted his child to Laetitia. He had hidden his family papers inside a skull which he had placed inside a locked box, then he had fled, thinking to return soon.

Circumstances had decided otherwise: Gurn had eventually become Fantômas, the murderer of his new master, Lord Beltham, and the lover of Lady Beltham.

Hans Elders, a gangster like Gurn, knew this. Having followed the adventures of his former accomplice from afar, he knew that Gurn, the father of the child entrusted to Laetitia, had become the formidable Fantômas.

Of course, Fantômas, having been without news from South Africa for ten years, shouldn't have been surprised by Laetitia's statement. Even less, because the old woman had learned from Elders that Fantômas and Gurn were one and the same.

He should have understood that it was quite possible that Laetitia hadn't lied to him when she stated that she was unaware of what had become of his daughter.

A child is such a small thing!

Especially in the immense plains of South Africa, a country infested with assassins, a land where every day, men fell under the claws and teeth of wild beasts teeth, or were killed by the assegai, the iron-tipped spear of the Zulu, or were struck down by an enemy's bullet, or destroyed by a malignant fever... All this was so frequent that a small child's disappearance should not have been the least surprising!

However, Fantômas, a man who, so far, had succeeded in everything he had undertaken, who had escaped from the worst perils imaginable using an amazing array of tricks, could not accept the terrible ordeal of his child's loss!

More than mere anger, a frightening rage overwhelmed him! Did Laetitia speak the truth? Or was she thwarting his will by refusing to tell him what had become of Gurn's daughter?

"Tell me!" shouted Fantômas. "Tell me which child bears the mark, the mark that will enable me to recognize my own daughter?"

"There was no mark!"

"Really? Then, you saw nothing!" exclaimed Fantômas. "Then," he added, mysteriously, "your eyes are useless, Laetitia."

"It wasn't my fault!" repeated the old woman.

"Well, since you don't know how to use your eyes, I'll make sure you no longer have them!"

Fantômas, not hurrying, certain that Laetitia couldn't make the least resistance, advanced towards the old woman. He grasped her by the arm and, with a single push, brutally threw her to the ground.

Laetitia fell to her knees in front of him. She moaned again.

"We'll see if you continue with your lying!" scoffed the outlaw.

While speaking, he had drawn a small revolver from his pocket. He brought the barrel down to the old woman's face.

"Speak!" he said. "Or I'll shoot out an eye!"

"Mercy!"

Fantômas fired.

"This is your own fault!" he said.

It was a terrible, horrible thing.

The monster's cruelty had reached new heights.

The weapon he had just fired was loaded with blanks. The igniting powder streamed out of the barrel in a burning jet that instantly destroyed the poor woman's eye.

Laetitia's face contorted in an appalling, painful grimace, then shrieking and bleeding, she collapsed to the ground.

"Monster! Monster! I told you that I don't know what became of your daughter!"

"You persist in taking me for a fool! You still maintain that you don't know what became of my Hélène? It won't be said that Fantômas could not break the will of an old woman!"

The revolver again approached Laetitia's face.

"Look well!" said Fantômas. "Look at me well! Because soon..."

A second detonation resounded in the room.

Jupiter was soaked.

Soon after the explosion, which had blasted a boulder and blocked his flight from the cove, he had realized that his predicament was difficult, but fortunately, not unsolvable. For he also knew how to swim...

Once he had thoroughly examined his surroundings, Jupiter came to the conclusion that it would be a simple matter for him to jump into the water and swim to a place not being carefully watched by the soldiers, who believed they had succeeded in blocking off their suspect...

The sea was calm, and his escape was mere child's play.

Unfortunately, he had barely made it back to firm ground when he had begun to shiver. Jupiter had made the rash decision to jump into the water fully dressed. Now, a cold wind was blowing and his soaked clothes caused him to tremble with cold.

He increased his speed, all the while holding in his right hand the wallet he had so mysteriously discovered and in which he had had the pleasure of recovering money that had been stolen from him.

He had hardly left the cove before he decided that he would go and tell all of his friends and acquaintances about the night's incidents.

Laetitia was a close friend; she had often helped him in the past. So, Jupiter though that she should be the first one to learn the news.

Alas, the ex-boxer didn't expect the horrible spectacle that he found at the old woman's farm!

No sooner had he opened the door than the wallet slipped from his hand. Shouting in grief, he sprang towards a corner of the room, where Laetitia lay, half dead and moaning, her body shaken by convulsive jerks.

"What's happened to you?" shouted Jupiter, half-crazed with terror, leaning over the old woman. "What's happened to you?"

He made such a din that everyone from the farm, and even someone from a neighboring farm, ran to see what had happened.

Jupiter, hearing that someone was coming, stood up and looked on the ground for the wallet that he had dropped in his shock at seeing his friend in such a state.

However, the wallet that Jupiter had seen clearly rolling against the wall was no longer there! It had completely disappeared!

And, Jupiter, also noticed another unlikely thing.

When he had entered the room, he was certain that he had closed the door behind him. Yet, it now stood wide open!

The poor man barely had time to burst into tears at this new loss, when once again events raced forward...

Jupiter had been grabbed by the crowd he had attracted with his cries. The newcomers quickly noticed Laetitia, covered with blood. They lifted the old woman and questioned her.

"What happened to you? Who did this to you?"

Half-mad with pain, not thinking about her words, Laetitia answered:

"There's the assassin! It's him! Stop him!"

The old woman didn't realize the horrible mistake that she had just made!

Eager to avoid a fate that he guessed too well, Jupiter leapt from the room and slammed the door behind him. He was running, gasping for breath, on the road to Durban.

Behind him came the farmers, mad with rage, terrified by the horror of the scene that they attributed to him, burning with the desire to avenge poor Laetitia. They were filled with hate for Jupiter.

"There's the assassin!" they screamed. "Stop him! Kill him!"

Chapter XV
The Mysterious Tree

It was only 8 p.m., but already everyone seemed to be asleep at Diamond House. No lights shone from its two large front windows. Complete silence reigned over the house and its garden.

However, what was the shadow that lurked by the foot of a large tree? Was it just a strange combination of leaves that formed that pattern of a human profile? No, it moved! It was a man!

The mysterious stranger stopped and grumbled under his breath.

"Is this an honest man's garden? Elders must be piling up money in his safe, while beautiful Winnifred dreams of her lover. How that girl intrigues me! If I believed her transparent glances and pleasant smile, I'd be the most carefree person in the world! But alas! She's also the daughter of a thief and the fruit doesn't fall far from the tree! Still, I don't know what to believe! At times, she has a mysterious allure that gives me much to think about! I need to know the truth! If I stay beneath her windows, I'll know how she spends the night... If I'm not mistaken, her room's here, on the first floor. If I climb up to this baobab tree's first branch, I'll be high enough to see inside..."

Suddenly he choked down an oath before it could escape his mouth. He dropped behind the gigantic trunk to completely hide himself.

He drew his revolver from his pocket; a slight click indicated that he had released the safety.

A shadow emerged from a nearby thicket.

"For heaven's sake, Fandor, don't shoot!"

"Teddy! Is that you? You startled me!"

It was indeed Teddy who had just appeared, and the nocturnal stalker was none other than Fandor.

Teddy seemed angry at Fandor's presence. A furious grimace contracted his face.

"What are you doing here?" he asked in a strained voice. "Don't you want to tell me the truth? Then, I'll answer for you. You came to see Winnie. I realized that you love her several days ago, but wasn't absolutely sure. Now, I no longer have any doubts. I'm certain she'll appear at her window soon! And you'll sing her a love song, like all you Frenchmen!"

"A love song! You're mad! A poor journalist like me can't love to a diamond king's daughter."

"Then, why were you getting ready to climb this tree when I got here? Go on! Don't deny the obvious, it's useless..."

Fandor smiled. He could only explain Teddy's presence in the garden at this hour by assuming that the young man was in love with Winnie himself. He had come to do exactly what he was accusing Fandor of doing.

However, when he saw that Teddy had become emotional, he ceased joking and answered in an affectionate tone, taking him by the hand.

"Teddy, you're completely mistaken. I'm not in love with Winnie. In addition, if she suspected my presence here, she'd be more likely to take me for a thief than a lover. Yes, I think she's very beautiful. I get great enjoyment talking with her, but I don't love her. In fact, I'm only here because of the investigation we're both conducting. Therefore, have no fear, I won't steal away your love."

"But I don't love her either!"

"What do you mean, you don't love her?"

"I swear to you that I don't."

"Come on, Teddy! I must tell you what you're always telling me: you aren't being honest with me. Admit it! I'm your friend. Hans Elders' daughter is quite pretty, and you're a little infatuated with her. There's no shame in admitting that!"

"I don't love Winnie."

"Really? Wasn't it jealousy that got you so excited a few minutes ago? Wasn't it because you thought I was flirting with Winnie that you became so angry?"

"I wasn't angry with you. I was a bit... unsettled... I don't know... It's the night, the Moon perhaps... Don't ask me about it any more, please... I can't answer you."

With Teddy present, Fandor abandoned his earlier plan and had no difficulty in changing the conversation.

"I have some very serious things to tell you. If you'd like, we could go to the far end of the park where the thicket is."

"Not necessary; we're completely safe here," said Teddy

"If you say so. Here's what's going on. You know that I watch Elders closely, and that I've taken to following him whenever I see him leaving his plant. Last Friday, I saw him leaving Diamond House rather mysteriously and behaving strangely. He wore boots and a jacket as if he were going hunting, but he didn't carry a gun. I started to follow him and he led me straight to the edge of the forest..."

"Which forest?"

"The one that stretches from here to the sea, and which is the least frequented of all the ones that surround Durban. I followed him at a considerable distance, so that he wouldn't suspect my presence. It was rather difficult, for he took the path that crosses the big tobacco plantation that's completely bare. But finally, by skimming over the neighbors' hedges and hiding behind rows of coffee trees, I arrived shortly after him at the forest's edge. There, much to my amazement, I saw him getting ready to climb a gigantic latanier."

"A palm tree? Why did he do that?"

"That's what I couldn't determine, unfortunately, because I accidentally stepped on a dry branch and he heard me."

"Did he see you?"

"No. He started to run in the direction of the noise, but by the time he arrived, I'd been able to get away and hide in the undergrowth. But, in order not to compromise the success of my investigation, I couldn't move until he left, which is why I don't know what he did..."

"Hasn't he returned to the forest since Friday?"

"Yes, every day!"

"Then, you only had to lie in wait at a favorable spot to watch what he did!"

"Don't get carried away, my dear Teddy. I did that, of course. I didn't have any more trouble following him on Saturday, when I saw him leave his home with the same equipment as the day before. Knowing where he was going, I was able to arrange to get there before him. I hid myself a few meters from the tree in a place where I believed that I could see everything without risking being seen... But—alas!—I was unable to discover his purpose. He climbed the tree, vanished for a few moments in the middle of some branches, and then came back down almost immediately."

"Why didn't you climb up the tree yourself? You'd have seen if there was anything odd about it. There must be something there that motivates Hans' visit."

"That's exactly what I told myself, and I did go up the tree. I saw leaves and branches, and nothing else than what would expect to find in any palm tree."

"That is strange," murmured Teddy.

Since it wasn't about Winnie anymore, the young man seemed to have regained his self-control, and he reflected deeply.

"Let's go over what we do know. You said he climbed a tree?"

"Yes."

"Did he carry anything in his hand?"

"No. Several times he had a cane with him, but he always left it at the foot of the tree"

"And when he left, did he take anything with him?"

"Nothing else."

"Good! Then he wasn't searching for anything, and he was only going to check on something that we can't yet determine. Do you know this latanier's exact position?"

"Absolutely, since I've followed in his footsteps several days in a row."

"Well, take me there. I want to go see it for myself. I'll climb up there and maybe I'll be more fortunate than you."

With extreme caution, Fandor and Teddy left the park. They crossed the gate, and soon, they were in the countryside.

However, despite the light, the walk was gloomy.

Teddy, who was used to it, wasn't bothered. He walked with an assured step as if he were on the streets of Durban in the middle of the day.

It wasn't the same for Fandor. Without feeling the least bit afraid, he couldn't help but be moved by the sinister aspect of the landscape that they crossed.

At night, the immense forests took on a fearsome air to cause decent people keep away and protect the sleep of outlaws and ferocious beasts!

"I'd just as soon be in my bed ," said Fandor, "but since the wine's been poured, it's got to be drunk. Anyway, we're here—there's the palm tree that that Elders came to visit every day."

The tree stood in a corner of a vast clearing filled with the smell of tamarinds. Its size was truly gigantic. Up to the first shoot's level, it had a smooth, perfectly straight trunk. Then, it divided into a number of big branches that headed in all directions, and whose broad leaves blended with those of other trees. Teddy quickly climbed to this first branching. There, he stopped to examine where he was. He was uncertain of the direction to take, and questioned Fandor.

"When you went up the tree, did you see any tracks on the branches? If Elders had on hunting boots, the nails would've scratched the bark."

"I admit I didn't think of that."

"I'll look for them."

The Moon had just hidden behind a thick cloud and the night was completely dark. However, Teddy took an automatic lighter from his pocket and started to inspect the branches in its wavering light.

All of a sudden, he called Fandor.

"I've just found nail marks on a big branch," he said. "I also see a bit of torn cloth that must have come from Elders' jacket."

The young man had quickly risen three or four meters on the branch in question. He balanced wonderfully, holding the lighter in one hand to plan his route and to see what motivated the diamond merchant's escapades.

Teddy had interrupted his ascent to speak with Fandor. He leaned forward and looked toward the ground so that his voice reached Fandor more distinctly.

At that point, the branch to which he was clinging became entangled with the branches and undergrowth of coconut trees and mangroves.

As he was about to resume his climbing, the Moon came out from behind the cloud that had hidden it and started to shine in all its brightness. One of its rays suddenly hit the trunk and illuminated it. Teddy leaned over abruptly. His lighter slipped from his hands and nearly fell. He rubbed his eyes repeatedly as if he were the victim of an illusion. Then, finally, not being able to doubt what he saw, he shouted a cry of triumph.

"The skull!"

An anxious voice answered him from below. Fandor had heard him.

"Is it possible?"

"Yes! I've found the skull!"

"You have it?"

134

"No, I don't have it yet, but I see it. It's at the far end of a hollow tree trunk just below me. If you can, go into that undergrowth of coconut trees and look for a mangrove struck by lightning. It's that one..."

Teddy hadn't even finished speaking before Fandor rushed off. He didn't feel the undergrowth that tore at his clothing, or the thorns that pierced his body. He ran across holes into which he risked falling and bushes that mangled him, but at last, he arrived at the foot of the mangrove and circled it.

Filled with joy at finally finding the object whose disappearance they so much regretted, he had no further thoughts of the difficulties that might arise. He saw only one thing: himself, climbing up along the trunk so that he could slip inside and seize the skull...

He was halfway up when he suddenly stopped and turned pale. A high-pitched hiss could be heard.

From every hole and crack in the old, half-rotted tree, an army of snakes woke with a start, slithering with a confused and continuous rustle, moving towards him.

Despite his fear, Fandor drew his revolver and got ready to defend his life by massacring the horrible beasts. However, from the top of the other tree, Teddy's anxious voice howled at him:

"Don't fire, in the name of Heaven, or you're dead! You don't fight with snakes—you'll kill ten of them, but a hundred will remain! And a single one of their bites is instantly lethal! Run! Run as fast as possible! I'll take care of getting the skull without the least danger!"

Fandor didn't hesitate to obey for an instant. He realized that Teddy knew the habits of all this country's wild animals, and he understood that, if Teddy ordered him to flee, it was really impossible to consider any other plan.

He was painstakingly controlling his emotions when Teddy, who had quickly climbed down the palm tree, landed at his feet.

"What do you intend to do?" Fandor immediately asked him. "You can't be thinking of entering the tree in the middle of all those snakes?"

"Absolutely! It's certain death for you—but not for me. Snakes and I are old friends! A long time ago, my nurse Laetitia taught me how to charm them... Now, I'm a master at it, and I'll use my talents."

Fandor moved away and Teddy advanced fearlessly toward the trunk struck by lightning. When they heard him coming, the snakes, that had been surprised by their first prey's abrupt disappearance, turned menacingly towards him, aiming their slimy fangs. But then, Teddy started to hiss in a soft, bizarre rhythm.

Oscillating their heads, the astonished reptiles slowly seemed overcome by an irresistible languor caused by the strange melody.

Teddy continuously hissed, while making no abrupt movements and walking in rhythm. He arrived at the tree's foot. He wasn't worried about the snakes that slithered up his body, trying to approach him, attracted by his strange melody. He slowly started to climb. He reached the summit and disappeared inside the tree trunk, a genuine mane of reptiles hanging from his body!

Meanwhile, Fandor stationed himself at the clearing's other end. He thought that each minute that passed seemed to last an eternity.

Suddenly, something attracted his attention. He heard the hoofbeats of a horse, some distance away.

He took a few steps in the direction of the noise, wanting to see who was approaching. He was amazed to come to a turning in the path and find himself face-to-face with Lieutenant Wilson Dragg!

"What a surprise to find you here, Monsieur Fandor—the man who insults people, then refuses to fight with them! I'm delighted to meet you. Maybe, I'll be more fortunate than I was the other day and will find satisfaction, late but complete..."

"Lieutenant, it seems to me that the reasons that justified my alleged insult still exist. As long as the identity of the man who stole Jupiter's money hasn't been ascertained, the accusation laid on you will prevent any man of honor from fighting you."

"Then, you continue to believe these stupid and ridiculous allegations, purely on the basis of your friend Teddy's evidence? I swear that I'll have my revenge on that young scatterbrain some day. But, before that day comes, I want retribution from you because of your even crueler affront. I'm going to kill you..."

"That would be murder, since a duel between us isn't possible. So you would add that to robbery?"

"That's one too many insults for any man to stand! How convenient for you to use such infamous slander when you doesn't have the courage to defend yourself! But if your cowardice needs a loophole, and you're afraid of my gun, I'll treat you like one treats any coward—I'll beat you like the dog you are!"

Wilson Dragg had arrived at a paroxysm of fury. Foaming with rage, he brandished his whip and advanced on Fandor with a terrible determination.

During the entire discussion, Fandor had remained calm. However, at this last threat, he, too, lost his self-control and, moving back a step, drew his revolver.

"Well, then, let's fight!" he shouted.

Dragg had a triumphant smile, as he entered the clearing.

"I'll stand in front of this tree," he said, "and you stand in front of that one. We'll each fire when we hear this stone that I'm going to throw into the air fall to Earth."

Fandor nodded in agreement and, without saying a word, went to the designated place. Wilson had already gone to his. With their eyes, both adversaries measured the distance that separated them.

Suddenly, an unexpected crash erupted into the forest's silence and stopped their half-raised arms.

"Stop him! Get the assassin! He killed an old woman!"

A crowd that they couldn't yet see was rushing towards the clearing, yelling and screaming. From time to time, huge flares of torch-lit faces convulsed with anger. People brandished bludgeons, threw rocks, and screamed continuously.

"Get the assassin! Kill the murderer!"

It was clear to both adversaries that the crowd was after a man who was between them and the mob, and who would soon appear.

"It's Jupiter!"

With a dumbfounded expression, the black man stopped in front of the two men who had unexpectedly appeared in front of him. Then, recognizing the Lieutenant, he shouted a wild cry and rushed him.

"Thief! Thief!"

Just like that, he sent the Lieutenant rolling on the ground with a single blow of his fist. He stepped over the body and continued his rapid race, while the unconscious officer remained still, like a corpse.

The scene had happened so rapidly that Fandor had not had time to intervene.

As soon as the black man had disappeared, he tried to rouse Wilson Dragg and help him. However, he didn't have time to do anything.

The roaring crowd had just emerged into the clearing.

"Death to the murderer! Death to the assassin!"

They surrounded Fandor and, seeing the sprawled body, they assumed that he was another of Jupiter's victims.

"Where did he go? Come with us! We'll hang him!"

Fandor was jostled. They pulled him along without his being able to make the least resistance. Understanding the danger that Teddy was running, and not wanting to awake suspicions about his presence in the clearing, he couldn't even try to reason the crowd.

He was swallowed up by the human flood, and, little by little, the clearing was again plunged into darkness and silence.

Meanwhile, the strange, slow, continuous hissing could still be heard.

Teddy emerged from the hollow tree.

The young man was extraordinarily pale, but a joyous light shone in his eyes.

His situation, however, was dreadful.

All the snakes that he had charmed were still coiled around him. Their heads were now leaning toward his mouth as if they were drinking the harmonious sounds that came out of it. Their venomous fangs almost touched his lips. However, Teddy didn't seem to notice. The skull that he held in his hand. and that seemed to shine with a phosphorescent gleam, held all his attention.

He managed to get out of the trunk with very slow gestures, like those he had made when he had entered it. He slid down to the ground and headed for the clearing's center.

Teddy walked very carefully.

He finally stopped and stood still, like a statue.

The hisses then changed, becoming an almost imperceptible murmur.

Little by little, the snakes unrolled from his limbs.

When Teddy finally fell silent, all the reptiles had returned to the ground and only the sound of their coils rustling on the dry grass could be heard as they returned to their dens.

The young man finally spoke. He was worried, for while he was inside the tree, he had heard an appalling din outside. However, he had not been able to figure out what had happened.

"Fandor!" he shouted. "Fandor, I've done it! I've got the skull! Fandor... My God... He's not here! What could've happened to him?"

Teddy believed himself to be alone in the clearing and didn't see the inanimate body of Lieutenant Dragg lying in the shadows.

Chapter XVI
The Theatrical Death

As Jupiter ran, he felt like a hunted beast.

He had no idea where he was going; he just ran.

With all the speed his legs could muster, he rushed straight ahead, without a goal, not even knowing in which direction he moved.

He looked back from time to time, hoping he had outdistanced his pursuers.

The roaring crowd of Laetitia's avengers naturally drew any the passers-by into the chase that rolled on mindlessly!

When Jupiter had left Laetitia's farm, there were, at most, 15 individuals on his trail. When he passed through Durban's gates, a quarter of an hour later, there were more than 100 so-called dispensers of justice on his tail!

He kept up a rapid pace, continuously urged on by the pursuers' howls, as he entered Durban's main street.

It was 11:30 p.m. The streets were almost deserted. There were no trolley cars, or trams; hardly anything moved but the lingering night birds.

Jupiter's insane race had brought him to a sidewalk where he saw a half-opened door.

Not thinking, he walked through it and entered the corridor upon which it opened.

A few seconds later, he came to a staircase, which he climbed, then turned into a narrow hall and entered a room which left him confused and astonished.

As Jupiter moved a few feet forward, he was suddenly forced to stop. He was dazed and blinded and, ahead of him, the floor seemed to be missing!

He felt as if a thousand points of light were shining into his eyes. To make matters worse, while he reeled, angry voices called out:

"Help!"

"He's a madman!"

When he could see again, he noticed a fiery cordon at his feet, and a raging crowd standing there shouting:

"Help! Help!"

"What's happening?"

Jupiter quickly realized where he was: he was in a theater, on the stage, facing an audience. Footlights burned at his feet and a spotlight dazzled him. The roaring crowd was the audience, and the cries were those of the panicking actors!

To make matters worse, he was in trapped in a dead end. He walked to the edge of the stage, thinking he might escape into the wings. But, alas, he hadn't gone two steps when he collided with a wall, a wall that had slowly moved into place from above.

Jupiter was truly captured now, as someone had thought to lower a metal curtain.

"What's happening? "

"Take your place! And the rest of you, get out!"

"But ,sir!"

"Help! Help!"

"He killed an old woman..."

"How did he get in?"

"We've been chasing him for nearly an hour!"

The audience had been impatiently awaiting the entrance of the diva when the unlucky Jupiter had made his appearance.

At first, no one had understood what the mysterious sweaty, breathless, haggard, gasping, was doing in front of the footlights.

Was it some sensational, unannounced number?

From the orchestra to the balcony, the audience instinctively rose to its feet. They had not yet recovered from the first shock of Jupiter's unexpected appearance when the theater was next invaded by a large crowd of individuals, crying and screaming angrily, who seemed as breathless and gasping as the man on stage.

These new arrivals rushed down the aisles, towards the orchestra, barely answering the questions with which the audience peppered them as they passed.

It was then that Jupiter turned around, headed toward the footlights, but the iron curtain descended, blocking his retreat.

Emotion was at its height. Panic overcame everyone, causing all those who were armed to instinctively draw their weapons.

In the auditorium, the cries redoubled:

"Kill him! Kill him!"

Bullets started to whistle through the air.

Jupiter was first hit in the hand, then in the arms. Gunshots continued to ring out and he was hit in both legs. He stumbled, took a few steps, then collapsed on the floor with a horrible moan.

Suddenly, as if his death had been a signal awaited by all, the shouting and clamor ceased.

Jérôme Fandor stood at the top of the center aisle, having helplessly watched the horrible scene. He gritted his teeth, shook his fists and screamed in a voice shrill with anger:

"Miserable wretches! Ah, you miserable murderers!"

He railed against the horrible murder that he had just witnessed. He was the first to dare call it so since Jupiter had died!

Fandor then bowed his head, horrified, livid with anger. No one had understood his rage. The spectators who had just behaved like butchers, assassins and torturers had not even realized that they were the objects of Fandor's wrath!

Chapter XVII
A Courageous Doctor

In Durban, where emotions were always intense, some worried that the authorities would eventually take pity on the passengers stranded on the plague-stricken ship and allow them to disembark. They feared this so much that, in an selfish but comprehensible fear of seeing the epidemic spread, they demanded to know the local government's intentions as soon as possible.

A soldier came out of the administration building and walked to the signal tower where the people had gathered; he began a proclamation.

Shouts of "Silence! Silence!" came from the crowd.

The soldier read a document to the population, which told them the current situation aboard the *British Queen.*

"There's no cause to worry about any contagion," he said. "Precautions have been carefully taken and rigorously observed. The ship has requested permission to dock. This request was made with only one goal in mind, to request one of the city's doctors to go aboard. This is because the Captain informed us that both ship doctors have died. They ask for our compassion in sending them vaccine and medical personnel..."

A frightened shiver spread through the crowd upon hearing this grim bit of news.

Sending vaccine was good; authorizing doctors to go aboard was even better. It was even essential. However, they also feared that anyone boarding the contaminated ship might return as a carrier of the terrible germs...

"What was the Port Authority's response?" someone in the crowd shouted, with growing irritation.

"The Port Authority is trying to find out whether there was, indeed, a doctor willing to board the *British Queen*," said the solder, "and this, under conditions that will ensure that this will not cause any danger for the city's population. The Port Authority believes that it is its duty to let it be known that there are immense risks in such a venture, and that only a man willing to face death should present himself..."

Anxiety reigned after the official statement's pessimistic conclusion. Feelings were divided.

On the one hand, the crowd felt pity for the poor people who were dying on board the *British Queen*, deprived of medical care and vaccine; they also felt pity for any doctor dedicated enough to undertake this perilous assignment.

Bit there was also a strong fear that any precautions taken to prevent the epidemic's spread would not be sufficient.

While the crowd wavered, a man stepped across the open space before the signal tower.

"It's a doctor! He's committing himself!" whispered the crowd.

The man entered the administration buildings and have the officials there take him to the Health Commission.

There, he briefly greeted those who received him.

"Gentlemen, I've just heard your proclamation," he said in a firm voice. "I'm a doctor, and I'm willing to go over there if the conditions are acceptable. What are they?"

The Health Commission had been assembled that morning to deal with the plague-infected ship; an older gentleman, known for his frankness, chaired it.

"Doctor," he responded to the stranger, "you know that going over there is courting death?"

"I do."

"Then, what drives you to do something that won't bring you any reward?"

"Simply the satisfaction of doing my duty, sir."

144

"Doctor, here are the conditions: We'll give you three cases of anti-plague vaccine. A steamboat will carry you to the *British Queen*. As soon as you're aboard, it will move away and position itself upwind... Fifteen minutes after your arrival, this boat will approach the ship again. You'll have two minutes to board it, no longer. Then, you'll be brought back here where you will submit to a rigorous quarantine. If you're unable to do so, remain on board the *British Queen* until the epidemic runs out. If you're still alive then, and there's no longer any danger of contagion, you may then resume your duties in the city without further obligations..."

Not without a certain irony, the Commission's president concluded:

"Do you still want to do this?"

"Yes, sir. I'll go to the *British Queen*. I'll remain there fifteen minutes, then I'll return here and submit myself to the quarantine. I'm ready to go aboard the ship immediately, because my conscience, as an honest man and as a doctor, won't allow me to know that there are people dying only a few yards away that might possibly be saved, and not attempt to do it!"

An hour later, the courageous doctor's departure was a distressing spectacle.

The crowd shouted enthusiastic, emotional cheers from the pier.

After a moment that felt like eternity because of the terrible anxiety that gripped their hearts, the steamboat finally slipped away.

They followed its race toward the *British Queen*, the desolate outline of which stuck out in the distance.

Soon, the steamboat was nothing more than a small, black point. The crowd, with their eager binoculars, could barely distinguish the white dot who was the extraordinarily daring doctor, standing at the craft's bow.

What did this man, who likely risked death solely to assist those in distress, feel?

145

They would certainly have been surprised if they had known his identity, if some secret artifice had allowed them to search this man's heart.

For this doctor, whose insane heroism had been acclaimed by the entire population, this brave man who, scorning the plague, was unafraid of visiting the desolate hell that the *British Queen* had become, was none other than Fantômas!

Yes, the same Fantômas who had been, in fact, responsible for this abominable crime: spreading the epidemic merely in order to trap Juve in the quarantine net that he knew would be inevitably cast around the infected ship.

Fantômas, already concerned when he had spied on Hans Elders in his study at Diamond House, had begun to panic after his visit to Laetitia. He had tortured the old woman in vain, since nothing she told him had helped him learn what had become of his daughter, Hélène, whom he had come to find in Natal. For, through one of those natural quirks that make even the worst monsters sometimes experience the most tender of feelings, Fantômas cherished his child.

The steamboat quickly passed between the rows of smaller ships which, at a good distance, blockaded the *British Queen*.

Terrified at being so close to the epidemic's hot spot, the sailors hastened their operations. The steamboat docked quickly and the one they all mistook for a doctor quickly disembarked. Faster yet, they unloaded the three cases of vaccine.

"Fifteen minutes, doctor, and we'll be back! No more!" shouted the boat's skipper.

Then, the steamboat moved off at top speed.

Fantômas was back on board the *British Queen*, face-to-face with death, near those who were dying murdered by his own villainy.

He slowly walked around the plague-infected ship.

Yet, he heard nothing; it was the silence of the grave that greeted him. It seemed that death reigned here as master...

"Will I have to search the entire ship?" thought the monster. "This morning, they made signals. Therefore, someone was still alive. In which case, I should be able to find them. And what about Juve? He's the one I want!"

Minutes passed. Suddenly remembering that he couldn't remain more than fifteen minute aboard the *British Queen*, under penalty of being forced to remain there, Fantômas shuddered.

"Juve! Juve!" he called.

However, only an echo answered him.

He advanced more quickly, still shouting:

"Juve! Juve!"

Suddenly he stopped.

Walking towards him were two men.

One of them, entirely wrapped in black, was unrecognizable. He was dressed in clothing that draped around him and a black veil hid his head; he almost didn't appear to be alive

But next to him was a man whom Fantômas recognized. It was Juve! Juve—or his ghost! For his face was livid and tormented, frightening to see.

Fantômas instinctively noticed that the two men had also stopped. Perhaps they were as surprised to see him as he had been alarmed at their appearance?

However, as he dashed forward, his hands, which were extended toward them, collided with a partition that barred his way. At the same time, he felt his shoulders brutally seized from behind!

A knee dug into his back. Two nervous hands clung to his arms. He lost his balance and fell.

Then, he felt someone wrap a cable around his ankles, while a thin cord tied his wrists.

"Help!" he cried, not quite sure if he wasn't the victim of a frightful hallucination.

But only Juve's mocking voice answered him.

"It's your turn to become prisoner of the Plague, Fantômas! Releasing your diseased rats to confine me here was devilishly clever, but now it's your turn to become the victim of your own plot! Now is my chance to triumph over you! You'll remain here! I will dress in your white coat and wear your surgical mask and will return ashore in your stead!"

Fantômas was pale with dread. Juve's plan was clever—and irrevocable. The villain knew that it would be useless to ask for any favors that the policeman would never grant.

Fantômas was going to remain imprisoned on board the plague-infected ship! But his fear of death was something with which he had dealt every day for many years.

"Juve," he finally said with a voice unbroken, "have you forgotten that if I die here, you'll never find Fandor?"

"If Fandor is still alive, and he's here, as you told to me, then I have no doubts that I'll be able to save him without your help. You've betrayed him just like you've betrayed me, Fantômas, when you tried to confine me on this ship by condemning all of its innocent passengers to death! I've no reason to spare you!"

A few minutes later, those watching from shore saw that the steamboat had again docked near the *British Queen*'s gangway. They saw the courageous doctor, recognizable by his white coat, jump on board.

At full steam, the boat moved away from the *British Queen* and returned to Durban.

Chapter XVIII
The Blind Woman

Laetitia lay moaning on her bed, where someone had finally had the sense to take her.

Jupiter had been widely assumed to be the old woman's attacker, without her even being aware of her mistake. He had fled, followed by a crazed mob, howling for his blood. While these angry madmen raged against what they believed to be Laetitia's torturer, someone calmer, older, who didn't care about revenge, slipped into the old woman's home. He had the wisdom to provide Laetitia with the first aid that her condition required.

He wasn't white and he wasn't black. He belonged to a mixed race, trusted neither by the natives nor by the white men. His name was Sosthene and he was a bonesetter.

His home was always well stocked with an extraordinary quantity of herbs with medicinal virtues. He knew magical words to make wounds heal and amazing concoctions to help fractures knit.

Sosthene had looked at the old woman's case with a certain delight.

"This is a good case!" he'd exclaimed. "A very good case!"

And, in mere minutes, he was already hesitating between two remedies.

Sosthene was so busy and preoccupied by his preparations, which he carried out with fanatical zeal, that he did not hear someone jumping over the hedge and enter the farm.

Teddy's sudden appearance made him frightened and anxious.

For Teddy didn't like him!

Teddy, who was well read and educated, didn't believe in local witchcraft and believed even less in bonesetters.

"What are you doing here?"

"I... I'm caring for someone..."

"Who?"

"I'm caring for Laetitia."

"Laetitia's sick? What's wrong with her? Hurry up! Answer! Say something! Where is she?"

However, pointing his finger toward Teddy, the bonesetter gasped in horror

"Oh, child! What is that you're carrying? It's terrifying!"

Teddy was, of course, still carrying the mysterious skull under his arm, the same enigmatic skull that he and Fandor had sought for such a long time and that, despite the snakes, he had been able to wrest from the hollow tree.

Unfortunately for Sosthene, Teddy didn't feel like chatting.

"Get out of here!" he shouted in a childish pique of anger. "Quickly! If Laetitia's sick, I'll care for her, you wretched witch-doctor. What's the matter with you? Go! Quickly! Just seeing you and your so-called remedies makes me want to strangle you!"

Sosthene didn't argue. With a brusque movement, he freed himself from Teddy's grasp and disappeared as quickly as he could.

Delivered from the amazing bonesetter whom he foolishly believed was dangerous, Teddy headed toward the farmhouse.

He rushed into the large room.

"Laetitia? Laetitia?" he called.

Laetitia, half-unconscious, remained motionless, but was no longer screaming.

Standing on the threshold, Teddy suddenly discovered her horrible wounds.

He let the skull that he had gone through so much trouble to recover roll onto the floor. Then he to his knees near the old woman's bed.

"Laetitia, do you hear me? It's Teddy, it's your poor Teddy speaking to you. Please tell me you hear me?" Then, grabbing the mysterious skull from where it had fallen, he shook it in front of the old woman.

"Please, Laetitia!" he said. "Look what I've found! Can you tell me the secret? You know it, don't you?"

"I can't see! I can't see anymore! I'm blind!" the old woman screamed.

Poor Teddy was at last seized by the full horror of the situation.

The old woman who, as far as he knew, was the only one who could tell him the secret of his birth was dying right in front of him. Only she could tell him how to open the skull and, once that was accomplished, how to decipher the message carved on its bones.

Two hours later, in the quiet peace of the morning, without having said a word, without having regained full consciousness, Laetitia died, murdered by Fantômas, taking to her grave both Fantômas' and Teddy's secret.

Chapter XIX
The Tragic Wake

"Winnifred! Winnifred!"

The call resounded in the dead of night.

It came a third time, uttered from beneath the windows of the house where Hans Elders' daughter lived with her father and their servants.

At the third call, a first floor window half-opened. Winnifred's gracious face appeared, lit only by the golden gleam of a lamp shining inside the room.

Winnifred's large eyes pierced the darkness. She strained her ears, moved by having heard her name.

She was gripped by a violent emotion, because she had recognized Lieutenant Wilson Dragg's voice.

At last, she heard the light rustle of crumpled leaves and turned her attention in that direction.

She saw the officer's silhouette at the foot of a large tree. She had not seen him since the disastrous evening when her father had driven him out of the house, accusing him of a theft of which he couldn't clear himself.

Winnifred, haughtily, finally called out in a nervous voice, choked by emotion.

"Flee, sir... I don't want to see you again!"

"Winnifred! I'm injured, dying perhaps. I want to speak with you. It's important, please..."

Winnifred still refused this extraordinary rendezvous requested by her former lover.

The Lieutenant begged again, putting his entire soul into his words.

"Winnifred, I beg you! Come down and talk to me!"

The girl left the window.

A few instants later, a light step was heard inside the house. The door that connected the veranda to the garden opened slowly and Winnifred, who had dressed in a great hurry, appeared on the threshold.

"Winnifred! Winnifred!" the Lieutenant stammered. "Thank you for coming. You don't know the good that you've done me!"

The officer's dreadfully pale face was covered with blood. A broad cut traced a red furrow on his forehead.

This alarmed Winnifred.

"What happened to you?" she asked.

The Lieutenant attached little importance to gaining pity by emphasizing his recent injury. What he sought was a different kind of mercy: redemption in the eyes of the one he loved. To reclaim his place in his mistress' heart!

"You've accused me, Winnifred," he spoke painfully. "You thought I was guilty, like your father, like everybody... I swear to you that you're mistaken. I'm innocent of that theft. By all that passes for honor and love, Winnifred, believe me. I'm the victim of a terrible plot..."

"Your wound," she said.

With a few words, Lieutenant Dragg related the aggression of which he had been the victim a few hours earlier, when Jupiter had thrown himself him before he had had time to guard himself.

"What were you doing at the forest's edge?" Winnifred asked.

"I was looking for Jérôme Fandor," replied the officer. "I wanted to kill him."

Winnifred shuddered.

Certainly, she felt a sincere and true love for Lieutenant Dragg in the depths of her impassioned heart. Still, the mention of Jérôme Fandor's name reminded her of the seductive French journalist with whom she had flirted, carefree, the day before at her party.

"I've discovered some abominable things," the officer continued, speaking with difficulty because of the head blow he had suffered, "The ambush of which I'm the victim was set up by that French journalist and Teddy."

"Impossible!" Winnifred exclaimed. "Wilson, that's nonsense!"

"I swear to you that I'm telling the truth," the Lieutenant repeated, raising a hand to the sky as if taking an oath. "This Fandor's a monster. Two weeks ago, I failed to have him shot as a suspect for setting fire to the docks. He was like a madman. I had the weakness of believing him, and especially believing Teddy, who supported him passionately. I sent him to the Lunatic Asylum. But he escaped, thanks to that horrible child's complicity..."

The officer then related the humiliating scene at the National Club, his arrest by the Colonel, the trial that they were bringing against him which would likely end with his court-martial.

"Wilson," asked Winnifred, "you were under arrest and you ran away?"

"Yes," acknowledged the officer somberly. "I've disobeyed my superiors' orders. But it was necessary. Was I wrong?"

Winnifred felt more and more pity. Her heart bled at the idea that her lover, to see her again, had made his situation worse.

She even began to believe Lieutenant Dragg's statements. She felt a deep anger rise in her breast.

Suddenly, she rose. She had reached a decision. She was sure of herself. It was her duty to save her lover since he was innocent, even if it meant compromising herself and revealing that she had been his mistress.

"Wilson," she offered, "if you're strong enough, we'll go together this very minute to ask for explanations from those whom you accuse."

"Winnifred, with your help, I'll go to the ends of the Earth," the officer exclaimed. He was unsteady, but willing, and stood again with a supreme effort.

"Let's go," she said.

The two lovers disappeared into the night.

However, they had been so preoccupied with themselves, so concerned with their fears, their hopes and their loves, that they had not noticed a shadow attaching itself to their steps and following them...

Even though it was the middle of the night, the interior of the farmhouse where Laetitia and Teddy lived was illuminated. Through the windows not hidden by shutters, one could see all that took place on the ground floor.

The entry door that connected the garden directly to the old woman's room was open.

Winnifred and Wilson Dragg stopped on the threshold, holding their breath, wondering what they should do next.

Resolutely, the Lieutenant entered the house, drawing his mistress behind him. They hoped to find Teddy. In fact, they did see him, but a strange, unexpected and funereal spectacle nailed them to the spot.

The young boy was on his knees in front of the bed where Laetitia's body lay. Teddy was shaken with violent sobs. Above the white sheets, the old woman's pale and wrinkled face stood out, hard, angular and still.

The officer and Winnifred immediately understood what had happened.

Teddy was crying over Laetitia's death!

However, at the noise made by the two lovers when they entered, Teddy got up. He looked at the newcomers, hastily drying his tears, suppressing his pain.

Misunderstanding the purpose if their visit, he thanked them with an imperceptible motion of his head.

"It was good of you to come," he said, "You knew her, then?"

He was even more surprised by Lieutenant Dragg's presence.

"And you were able to come as well?"

"I came," the officer said, "because I escaped, and I escaped because I'm innocent..."

The attack was direct. Winnifred trembled. What would be the result of the argument that was going to take place between these two men?

Winnifred had planned to mediate between them; however, she remained mute, stupefied, her eyes wide.

In a corner of the room, she had just noticed something extraordinary and terrifying.

It was a skull—a shining, polished skull that appeared to be looking at her. The shadows of its hollow orbits were like two immense holes which seemed to swallow the very light around it.

However, Teddy, unlike what they had assumed, addressed Wilson Dragg in a pitiful tone.

"My poor friend, I know for a fact that you're innocent! You poor man..."

Teddy stopped, for the officer, who had first been paralyzed with surprise by this declaration that he hadn't expected, had sprung forward. His tightened fists almost stuck the young man, forcing Teddy to recoil.

"You liar! You scoundrel!" he howled. "Since you knew I was innocent, why did you accuse me in such a cowardly way? Why? Answer me!"

"If I was did that, Lieutenant Dragg, it was to expose the real culprit."

"The culprit," the officer shouted, "is you—you and your accomplice, Jérôme Fandor. You're both responsible for the theft!"

"Lieutenant, as sure as you're innocent, I'm not guilty. The one responsible for the theft is—"

At that moment, Teddy looked at Winnifred with an air of profound commiseration.

"It's..." he stammered, "...is impossible to say."

However, his two questioners didn't want him stopping so abruptly on the path of revelations.

Winnifred and Dragg were convinced, from that moment on, that Teddy, who felt a strange sympathy for the mysterious French journalist, didn't want to reveal that he was the culprit!

Teddy, on the contrary, didn't think for a single instant of accusing Fandor. He didn't even suppose that the journalist needed to be defended.

Indeed, Teddy had Hans Elders' name on his lips and was ready to reveal it.

Despite his emotion, however, and the moral tortures that he felt, Teddy refused to do it, for the thief's own daughter, Winnifred, stood right in front of him.

Increasingly irritated, made furious by Teddy's silence, Wilson Dragg threw himself on the boy, seized him by the arm and shook him with a rage so brutal that the young man fell onto the ground.

Teddy's mood then took a turn! A dreadful anger mounted in him! The officer had taken the liberty of laying a hand on him! Armed with his riding crop, Teddy lashed at Wilson Dragg's face!

The officer howled in contempt and anger. He pulled himself from Winnifred's arms, which were trying to restrain him.

"Thief! Little thug!" he shouted.

The officer's eyes sought something to use as a weapon. Without realizing it, he touched a heavy, round, polished object and grabbed it.

Seeing his gesture, Winnifred gave a horrible cry. Wilson had seized the skull and his hand was wrapped around its jaw.

Teddy had also seen Dragg's gesture.

"No," he said, "don't touch it! Drop it!"

Involuntarily, Drag obeyed.

But the jaws that had separated themselves so that he could force his fingers into the maw contained a hidden spring, and they suddenly snapped shut on the officer's hand just as he seized the skull.

He screamed in horrible pain.

The skull, freed, rolled to the ground.

Dazed, Dragg took a few steps back, then fell to the ground without a word. His eyes were twitching, his limbs jerked with nervous spasms and his face was slowly turning red.

Winnifred rushed to her lover and, half-mad with terror and emotion, attempted to revive him.

Teddy pulled her away from him.

"Don't go near him, Winnifred," he said, also terrified. "He's been poisoned!"

It was too much for the unfortunate girl. She fainted.

A few minutes later, she regained her senses and worried about what had happened during her stupor.

She looked around, in a panic, and saw that Dragg's body was no longer lying sprawled near her feet.

A new day was dawning, accompanied by the tinkling bells of an ox pulling a cart outside.

Teddy, who' had lavished care on Winnifred, took the girl outside.

"This nice man has agreed to transport the Lieutenant," he said, indicating the cart's driver. "In an hour, he'll be in the city. Go with him, Winnifred, if you're not afraid of compromising yourself. Take him to the hospital. There may still be time to save him. Do you dare to accompany him?"

Superb in her arrogance, Winnifred stood up.

"Wilson Dragg is my lover," she shouted. "I'll follow him anywhere, even unto death!"

The cart slowly began to move. Winnifred took her place beside her lover, who no longer showed any signs of life.

As he reentered the empty house, Teddy remained stunned and dismayed, his eyes fixed on the center of the room.

The deadly skull, the mysterious skull that had somehow poisoned Wilson Dragg, had disappeared!

Who had come in during his absence?

Chapter XX
An Imposter Returns

When the crowd on the shore saw the doctor transfer from the *British Queen* to the steamboat, which was soon speeding towards them, there was a murmur of controlled excitement. They believed that this man had just proved his devotion to his duty by visiting the plague victims.

They had anxiously followed the drama of his departure, and had gone *en masse* to the harbor to await his return. Nevertheless, they took great pains to remain well back from the pier where the craft had to dock.

Cheers and huzzahs resounded; some waved their hats, others applauded wildly. It was truly an enthusiastic display of support.

This doctor, who had been daring enough to visit the *British Queen*, who had just confronted death, did deserve the warm-hearted reception that the crowd had in store for him.

None of the officers and members of the City Council, however, thought that it could possibly be their duty to officially congratulate this courageous citizen, this admirable philanthropist who had just risked his life!

Since they were all terrified of the least risk of contagion, not a single official was at the harbor to greet the returning doctor!

However, another doctor, the director of Durban's Civil Hospital, had come.

He was a 60-year-old man who didn't believe in modern medicine, but was an excellent general practitioner who did everything he could to save his patients. Sometimes, he even managed this, but as a rule, he denied all the generally accepted theories provided by modern science.

His name was Harbrock and he had barely awoken when he had learned of the morning's events. He profoundly regretted that he hadn't been told about the plague victims' request as he would have gladly gone to their aid.

During the course of the clinical lesson that he held every morning, Doctor Harbrock had told his interns, "Gentlemen! Look at how this hero is being treated! It's up to us to welcome him! It is we who must celebrate his achievement! I hope that you'll all attend the reception I propose to throw for him in our own hospital?"

As Durban prepared itself for the heroic doctor's return, a sudden drama unfolded aboard the steamboat.

Juve was not without strong emotion and concern as the boat that carried him approached the harbor.

The policeman thought, "What's going to happen to me now? This morning, when I saw the doctor arrive and recognized him as Fantômas, I knew that he wanted to learn if I was dead or alive. But I've got serious challenges awaiting me on land! If the people f Durban learn that the doctor, or rather the one that they took for a doctor, remained on board the *British Queen*, and that it's I, one of her passengers, who has taken his place, they'll be so afraid of the Plague that they're quite capable of throwing me straight into the sea! I'll have to play this very close to the vest..."

From a distance, he hadn't yet seen the immense enthusiasm that animated those watching the boat, but as it came closer, he began to see the jam-packed pier and hear the huzzahs and cheers.

Juve had switched places with Fantômas, not as much from a desire to escape the horrible, plague-infected ship, but to actively search for Fandor.

He was so absorbed in his thoughts that he didn't notice the crowd's behavior when they pulled into the harbor. He was, therefore, surprised when he raised his head to see an old man, dressed in black, bedecked with medals, wearing a courteous expression, make a welcoming gesture.

"Doctor!" shouted the old man. "I wanted to be the first to shake your hand! Let me introduce myself: I'm Doctor Harbrock, director of Durban's Civil Hospital. These gentlemen are my interns. We're here to pay you homage and offer our most sincere sympathy..."

Juve bowed, infinitely touched, but even more worried.

"My dear colleague," Doctor Harbrock continued, "I was hoping that you would accompany us to my establishment. First, you'll find all the disinfectants that might be necessary there. And you'll be able to get rid of your coat and mask..."

Juve made up his mind quickly. After all, since he had to take the risk, why not do it under such favorable conditions.

"I accept with all my heart, Doctor Harbrock," he replied. "Besides, I confess that I'm anxious to be rid of these clothes!"

Doctor Harbrock was brave. While his interns kept a prudent distance from Juve, he grabbed the new arrival familiarly by the arm and led him to his car.

"In three minutes, we'll be at the hospital," the physician said. "And, believe me, my dear colleague, you won't be bored... After having lunch, I'll take you with me on my rounds. I've got two or three very interesting cases..."

Provided they don't stick me into quarantine! thought Juve, increasingly anxious about his situation.

Doctor Harbrock's car rounded a curve and entered the hospital's courtyard, parking in front of a flight of stone steps.

"Follow me!" said the old physician. "I'll take you right to a room where you can disinfect yourself."

Doctor Harbrock graciously offered clean linens and uncontaminated clothing so that could remove his mask and strip off his clothes. The excellent practitioner left the lab where he had brought the policeman.

"Now is when things might go wrong!" Juve said. "Once I'm dressed, my host won't recognize me, or perhaps someone in his entourage will realize that it wasn't me who left for the *British Queen*."

Although everyone had hastened his passage on his arrival at the hospital, and Doctor Harbrock had been a great help to him, overwhelming him with attention, it now seemed as if they had totally forgotten Juve.

After more than 15 minutes, dressed and ready to leave, Juve wondered why no one had yet come to see him.

"Such neglect after such a warm reception is odd," he thought. "Have they already pierced my deception? Will I fall directly into a policeman's hands when I leave here? Will they send me back to the *British Queen*?"

Not without a certain trepidation, Juve turned the knob on the bathroom door. A large corridor opened in front of him. He followed it haphazardly.

"This is really bizarre," he thought. "What happened to the staff?"

Suddenly, a voice interrupted his soliloquy and made him jump.

"My dear colleague."

Juve turned around and saw the Doctor Harbrock standing there.

"Excuse me for not attending to you sooner," the old physician said. "Someone has just brought an extraordinarily injured man to the hospital, requiring all our care. Come and help us. I'm certain that you'll give excellent counsel..."

"An injured man? But I'm not a surgeon, I'm strictly a general practitioner, Doctor... What's the case?"

"Oh! It's a case that requires more medical knowledge than surgery, my dear colleague. It's a young officer whom they've just brought in, poisoned, half-delirious and almost purple..."

"What poisoned him?"

"I have no idea," said Doctor Harbrock. "He's delirious and his companion's saying some incomprehensible things. It would seem that he was bitten—by a skull!"

"By a skull?"

"Yes, by a skull—and following that bite, he appears to have turned purple! It's an amazing story..."

Juve shook his head without saying a word. The facts had immediately taken on an exceptional importance to the policeman's ears.

He followed Doctor Harbrock into one of the hospital's rooms where they'd laid poor Lieutenant Dragg onto a bed. He was delirious and the interns bustled around him.

While Juve reflected, Doctor Harbrock rushed to the injured man's bed and called to his presumed colleague.

"In my opinion," he said, "we're in the presence of an unknown poison... The symptoms are extraordinary. I'm in favor of administering an emetic... What do you think?"

Juve couldn't think of anything to say, and didn't want to take any responsibility.

He coughed a few times.

"Isn't there any witness to this poisoning that might enlighten us?" he asked.

"Yes!" replied Doctor Harbrock, who was now trying to deal with the raving officer. "You're right! Try to obtain some information from the young woman who accompanied him. I had her taken to the garden. Go find her."

A few instants later, in the garden, Juve questioned the forlorn Winnie. Because she was almost out of her head with worry, at first, her answers were confused. However, she soon proved able to give him some factual details.

Juve's interrogation, however, was soon interrupted by the arrival of an intern sent by Doctor Harbrock.

"The young man's better," he announced. "He's asked to see you, Miss."

"Then take me to him!"

Juve's curiosity was now so great that he no longer worried about the risk of being exposed as an imposter!

Chapter XXI
Prisoner Of The Machines!

The skull was gone again!

There had been a witness to the tragic incidents that had followed Laetitia's death.

Taking advantage of the confusion, and realizing that no one was in the farmhouse, a man, whose face was hidden by the raised collar of a large coat, had entered the home. This mysterious person had been following Winnifred and Wilson Dragg for some time.

The enigmatic stalker had remained in the shadows outside the house, keeping carefully hidden behind a clump of trees during the brawl between the officer and Teddy, that had ended so tragically for the serviceman.

Then, he had entered the darkened room with surprising agility. Without even casting a respectful eye on the dead woman lying on the bed, he had immediately gone for the skull that had rolled on the floor after having so severely wounded Lieutenant Dragg.

Smirking in satisfaction, the mysterious man had seized his mysterious booty and, hiding it under his coat, had hastily made his escape.

When Teddy returned to the room soon afterwards, he could no longer find the precious object which so consumed him.

The mysterious individual who had just committed this incomprehensible robbery was none other than Hans Elders, the diamond merchant!

Meanwhile, Jérôme Fandor was alone, lost in the diamond mine's maze of workshops. It was a Sunday afternoon, and the shops were empty. From Saturday evening until the next morning, this place which, during the week, was a humming beehive was in total silence.

Fandor was pushed by his inquisitive and ever-curious mind to know the why of things. He had told himself that the best way to do it was to enter the workshops when they were deserted.

The mines, the cherchery, the workshops and the innumerable machines constituted a true city that took several hours to explore, even for a casual visitor only interested in the industrial site; Fandor's research, on the other hand, was delicate, complicated and meticulous.

In one of the last workshops he visited, in the gem cutting section where rose quartz and diamonds were made ready for sale, the journalist stopped and sat down on a stool, his head between his hands, reflecting deeply.

"Elders isn't just a strange character, but he's also a sinister crook, a formidable gangster! He's far from stupid, and his 'discovery' seems very ingenious."

Indeed, during his investigations, Fandor had learned that the extracted earth that was screened daily to uncover the precious diamonds seemed to contain an unusual quantity of stones.

Without being an expert in the matter, Fandor realized that these diamonds, allegedly extracted from the soil, didn't have the true appearance of rough diamonds, like the ones normally found in nature.

It was as if this strange site gave refined diamonds rather than virgin diamonds.

This had surprised Fandor as he had been inside the plant where, they said, carefully selected personnel cut the stones.

By studying the machines supposedly required to cut the diamonds, Fandor had realized that these tools couldn't be used for their stated purpose.

"These machines," he thought, "are merely for show, and this gem cutter they claim is of the same type as the one found in Amsterdam, obviously doesn't cut anything at all. But why this *mise en scène*, what is its purpose?"

As he asked himself these questions, Fandor felt the answers slowly forming in his mind. He gradually remembered that Natal wasn't considered a prime diamond-producing country; one found some gold, platinum and silver there, but no precious stones. How, then, had it happened that, suddenly, within a few leagues of Durban, Elders had discovered such a priceless treasure that, until then, no one had suspected?

"When they acquire a certain number of precious stones," he continued, "thieves can't just get rid of them that easily. One could speculate on the risks that they run when they try to sell their illegally-acquired loot. The fences that buy from them would pay a miserable rate. I suppose that someone like Elders had the idea of making people believe in a genuine deposit of legitimate diamonds, sowing them in the ground first, then having them discovered by prospectors. He then sets up a factory where they're properly cut. And from that point on, any diamonds that come out of that factory have a genuine provenance, a honest virginity! Nothing's simpler than shipping the stones back as if they had really come from his cherchery!"

Fandor's exploration of Elders' factory had been far from useless. He now understood what a phenomenal criminal Elders was.

From there to believing that the man was himself a gang leader was only a small step! Perhaps the gang's most visible accomplice was a broker named Ribonnard, who bore a singular resemblance to a man named Ribonneau, formerly condemned by the Court of Assizes of Versailles.

Was it possible, then, that Elders was Fantômas?

But Fandor had to accept that he wasn't, for when he had asked himself this question before, he had always answered it negatively.

But if Elders wasn't Fantômas, maybe he was the elusive outlaw's accomplice?

Hadn't Fantômas once confessed that he had arrived in Europe from South Africa?

Hadn't it been Fantômas who, a few weeks earlier, had shipped Fandor from London to South Africa—where he had undoubtedly followed the journalist?

Consequently, Fandor asked himself another question.

What was, then, the purpose of the mysterious skull, the possession of which was undoubtedly valuable because of the secret it contained? Clearly, it was something that Elders seemed to be determined to keep from Teddy.

Fandor didn't have enough time to consider his latest conjecture as he heard a noise.

In order not to be trapped in the middle of a workshop where nothing would justify his presence, he was forced to hide.

Fandor spotted Hans Elders.

"I wouldn't mind asking him a question or two," he thought.

But Elders wasn't alone. He was with some fearful-looking characters whom the journalist realized were members of the local constabulary.

"Yes, officers," said Elders, "I'm sure our man's hidden somewhere in the workshops. You saw him entering the cherchery. What could he want here?"

"Undoubtedly," retorted a voice unknown to Fandor, "to steal your diamonds, Mr. Elders."

"Clearly," said Elders. "Still, that Monsieur Fandor is also trying to conceal himself from the authorities. He can't avoid the charges against him for long, and he must know that our laws aren't lenient towards criminals. He claims to be a French journalist, but he's certainly a thief, also possibly a dangerous lunatic. Well, gentlemen, you know the orders given by your governor. You must capture this Fandor 'dead or alive.' Those were Sir Houston's very words! Don't hesitate to shoot if he refuses to obey."

167

Fandor, who had heard the whole conversation, bit his lips. He felt a chill when he heard the dry click of pistols being armed.

He carefully scanned the room and saw that there appeared to be only one exit. But he couldn't use it because that was where the officers were headed.

So, Fandor cautiously moved back to the workshop's other end. There, he saw a handle and heaved a relieved sigh.

He pressed on it, but suddenly, he heard a violent sputtering. It wasn't a door handle at all, but an electric switch that had lit the arc lamps!

These were so bright that, despite the daylight, they did not go unnoticed.

Outside, Fandor heard his pursuers' astonished exclamations!

Instinctively, the journalist moved to put out the lights. But the moment he reached for the switch, his arm accidentally set off another switch. This time, a tremendous whirring sound suddenly filled the plant with a deafening noise.

The mighty machines had started up, the sturdy milling devices began their movements; the electric lathes faceted imaginary diamonds, and heavy pulleys began their action.

The workshop's door opened, and Fandor saw a multitude of bodies jostling through the narrow entrance.

"Hands up!" shouted one of them.

Fandor resignedly raised his hands above his head, awaiting his fate.

Just then, his fingers were brushed by something that caused him to look up. He saw that it was a large drive belt, started a few moments before by his own clumsiness.

Coupled to a pulley, the broad belt climbed to the top of the workshop and passed through the roof to who-knows-where.

The journalist immediately understood the advantage he could take of so simple a mechanism. The space around the belt was clear.

Before the policemen had time to understand his intention, Fandor had grasped the belt with both hands. He was instantly whisked away like a wisp of straw.

The belt brought him to the workshop's roof. There, Fandor was able to slip through a service shaft that allowed the belt to pass. However, as he was lifted away, the officers began to fire!

The journalist didn't have time to worry about the shots, as he was soon hurled into space when the belt came to the point where it returned to the workshop. For a second, Fandor felt that he was going to be smashed to the ground.

Luckily for him, he didn't fall but, instead, landed in the middle of a vat of oily muck that was being stirred by a large, stone grinding wheel.

The giant millstone violently pulled him onto the blades of an equally large paddlewheel, causing him to continue his unintentionally acrobatic journey.

The journalist was bruised, blinded, and half-choked from the combination of water, sand and muck in his eyes, ears, mouth and nostrils. He was incapable of making the least effort to fight against the unrelenting machines that held him prisoner.

Suddenly, Fandor found himself abruptly plunged into freezing cold water and carried by a new current of tumultuous streams.

Making an unimaginable effort, he succeeded in swimming back to the surface of the freezing whirlpool. Then, the mighty current pulled him forward. He saw that he was being drawn towards a great chasm, and he was powerless to escape.

It was all too much and Fandor lost consciousness.

Chapter XXII
In The Drift

Meanwhile, on the *British Queen*, the plague continued its ravages.

The many corpses that were rotting on the ship rendered the air practically unbreathable. The preserved food stores that had been the only available source of nourishment were now exhausted. The passengers' only recourse was to eat spoiled food of dubious quality. The situation was terrible!

This was the topic of conversation between four passengers sitting in the dining room.

Jordan Le Clain, a former medical student, was speaking. He had chosen to abandon medicine to become an explorer, something more in line with his adventurous tastes.

He had gone to Australia to chart its unexplored regions. But now, his earlier studies had qualified him to become the ship's latest doctor, following the deaths of the two doctors. before him. Richard Tower, a young biologist, already famous for his works on capillaries, André Raymond, a French professor, and the gracious and lively Miss Dorothea Smythe, assisted him in this impossible task.

"It's hopeless," said Le Clain. "There were 15 new cases this morning. Perhaps we should simply resign ourselves to death."

"Maybe there's still some hope," said Raymond.

The French professor had remained mute for the whole conversation as he reflected.

His eyes hadn't left another individual in the dining room, who stood in front of a porthole with his back turned to them. Raymond indicated the man with his finger.

"Do you know that man?" he asked his companions. "I'm convinced he has some vaccine."

"Vaccine!" they all exclaimed at the same time. "Impossible!"

"I'm sure of it. This morning, as I passed in front of his cabin, I saw a broken glass capsule on the threshold. I picked it up and became convinced that it had contained vaccine."

"Then, we're saved!" Tower exclaimed. "I'll ask him to share it with us. He certainly won't refuse, and then, we'll be able to successfully fight the Plague."

The unknown passenger had clearly understood, by watching the four pairs of eyes aimed in his direction, that they were talking about him.

He was thus on guard when Tower asked to speak with him.

"Sir," began the young biologist, "my approach may be forward, but the terrible situation in which we find ourselves raises us above such conventions, so you must excuse me. We understand that you may have a vaccine against the Plague. That vaccine is absolutely essential to safeguard some of the survivors. Since we four have assumed the task of volunteer doctors and nurses, we ask you to share it with us."

"Your strange request surprises me, sir. I've never had a single vial of vaccine in my possession."

"It's useless to deny it, sir," insisted Towtea, "vials were seen in your cabin..."

"Stop right there. I've already told you: I don't have any vaccine."

"Well, since that's how things are, we're sorry not to have your cooperation. But we'll search your cabin without it."

So saying, he gestured for Raymond and Le Clain to carry out the mission.

"Stop, or I'll blow out your brains!"

171

The stranger had pulled a high caliber Browning revolver from his pocket and pointed it threateningly at the two men.

"How dare you plan to enter my cabin without my permission—and on what authority?" he screamed. "As to the vaccine, well, yes, I do have some, but you'll all die without me giving you any of it..."

The passengers that were in the room when the argument had started had stood up, but now, under the gun's threat, they fled in disorder to a corner of the room. They remained there, terrified. Only Le Clain and Raymond still stood at the top of the stairs, while Tower was a few steps away from the mystery man.

Raymond and Le Clain suddenly jumped the stranger. Pushing back wildly, he sprang across the room, aimed his weapon and fired three times. His three adversaries suddenly lay dead at his feet.

The other passengers moved even further back and engaged in whispered conversations.

"He's a criminal!" suggested one of them.

"He's a lunatic!" said another.

Whatever the man was, the passengers were all of one mind; they only had one thought: to gain his good will so that he would share some vials of the vaccine with them.

After the incident, the man was able to walk the ship as he pleased, free from threats and supplications.

But it was all in vain. The stranger remained impassive to their pleas.

A few days later, they had all perished and the *British Queen* was no more than a vast, floating coffin.

During the last moments of their agonies, the mysterious stranger had withdrawn to his cabin, protected from the Plague by frequent injections of vaccine.

He came out only when he believed that all the other passengers had died, and methodically inspected the ship to be sure there were no survivors.

He had arrived at the foot of a mast and, mechanically, looked upwards.

"If I'm not mistaken, there's someone up there," he explained. "Who could it possibly be? Juve, perhaps? No, he's long gone. Hello, up there, come down at once or I'll put a bullet through you!"

He didn't have long to wait. A child of around 15, ragged, lean, his eyes filled with terror, quickly tumbled down the mast and fell at the stranger's feet.

"Who are you?" the man asked.

"I'm Topsy, the cabin boy."

"What were you doing up there?"

"I was waiting for the Plague to stop."

"How long were you up there?"

"Since the beginning. When I heard there was the Plague on board, I though that it wouldn't be a bad place to stay, and that the air up there had to be better than anywhere else. I made a package of supplies and carried it with me. I lived up there until the moment you called me..."

"And you never felt ill?"

"No."

"You're pretty thin though."

"That's because it's been two days since I've eaten anything. My supplies ran out and I didn't dare come down to look for more."

The stranger handed him a biscuit and a bottle.

"Eat and drink," he said. "I need you. You want to get away from here, don't you? Me too, but we're in quarantine. If we launch a lifeboat, the soldiers from Durban will see it and shoot at us. So, instead, this is what we'll do. Tell me when the next tide is due. Then, we'll release the mooring chains. The current will carry us toward the coast. When we run aground, we'll swim ashore."

"That's impossible! The chains are massive steel that don't break, even during the worst weather. I've only seen a ship lost that way once, and that was only because it was on fire. The chains had been wrapped around the capstan, which burned."

"Then we'll set fire to the *British Queen* and it will seem natural."

And they did just that.

Barely had the high tide begun to push the waves when they rushed to the capstans and set the ship on fire.

An immense flame rose into the air.

The *British Queen*, caught by the current, started to slowly move toward the coast.

The mystery man examined the shoreline carefully, trying to calculate approximately where they would run aground. Suddenly, he jumped with astonishment. In his binoculars, he saw some unusual activity along the shore. A crowd of people was rushing to the place where the ship was most likely headed.

Almost immediately, a shell passed over the ship's bridge with a loud whistle. They heard a detonation like a thunderclap, which reverberated on all the cliffs surrounding the coast.

When the stranger turned to his young companion to speak to him, the youth was gone. The shell had hit him squarely in the chest and thrown him overboard.

After that, the projectiles followed one another quickly.

The *British Queen* started to go down.

Impassive, Fantômas—for it was he!—his arms crossed, facing the shore, defying death, showing no concern about the water streaming into the ship, watched the incoming, incandescent projectiles.

Chapter XXIII
The Impossible Vision

Doctor Harbrock had just taken leave of the man he believed was a fellow physician.

"I'm sorry to have received you so poorly, my dear colleague," he said, "We certainly couldn't give up on that unfortunate officer..."

Then, Juve and Harbrock exchanged a series of salutations, congratulations and promises to see each other again. At last, Juve thought it was high time to leave his host, using the excuse that he had made up to get away quickly.

"It's urgent that I report my mission to the authorities..."

The hospital's large gate closed behind him. But Juve, instead of going to the authorities as he had said, hastened to cross the city's encumbered streets as fast as possible, in order to reach the countryside outside of Durban.

The policeman walked quickly, his head low, his mood somber and anxious.

Juve dropped down on a turf-covered slope as soon as he left Durban. He discovered a field where tall grass grew alongside a road and hoped, with any luck, that he would be able to remain there quietly while he planned his next move.

"This adventure's suddenly gotten more far complicated than I thought," he reflected. "Where do I go from here? How do I find Fandor?"

Juve was excited because, while questioning Winnifred Elders about Lieutenant Dragg's condition, he had learned news that delighted him. In passing, Winnie had spoken to him about Fandor! Fandor was alive! Fandor was nearby!

It was necessary to find Fandor as quickly as possible. And then, the two of them would finally capture that monster, Fantômas, and render him unable to carry on his series of crimes.

Fantômas had surely had an important reason to send Fandor to Natal. Some powerful motive had dictated the action. But what could that motive be?

For several moments, Juve, mad with rage, clenched his fists.

"Our fight will resume, Fantômas! Take care! Your time will come soon! Someday, you'll be made to pay! And your punishment will be terrible, for you were merciless, your crimes are without measure and you deserve the worst of fates!"

"...So, Ribonneau, you've earned yourself a small fortune? You have no complaints about your current job?"

"None at all."

"And you have no news of our friends?"

"What friends?"

Ribonnard, or as we now know, a former convict named Ribonneau, shrugged, signaling both his complete ignorance of and his total indifference to the matter.

Stoic by nature, Ribonnard restricted himself to answering with a special terseness that was particular to him in most circumstances.

"Who are you and where do you know me from?" he asked.

The man to whom he was speaking burst out laughing.

"I'm Pierre! *Gueule-d'Empeigne*! From the *Rendez-vous des Copains*?"

Briefly, Ribonnard told Pierre, whom he sincerely didn't remember, the complicated events that had taken him to Durban.

"So," he concluded, "I changed my name right from Ribonneau to Ribonnard, and got into the business of placing diamonds! You could say that I'm both salesman and dealer!

And all for a guy who doesn't quite have the guts to do it himself: Hans Elders..."

Ribonnard spoke candidly. He should have been more cautious, especially if he could have foreseen his questioner's reaction upon hearing Hans Elders' name!

Pierre was quite remarkable; he wore velvet trousers that disappeared into high boots, a leather belt gripped his waist, a red shirt floated across his chest and a linen jacket, the sleeves of which he hadn't slipped on, was thrown over his shoulders. His head was covered by a large maroon fedora.

In reality, this apache nicknamed *Gueule-d'Empeigne* was none other than Juve under one of his aliases!

After having lengthily rested and reflected in the field where he had gone to meditate, Juve had finally decided on a plan of action.

"I seem to be mixed up in two separate plots, and in order to remain true to my methods, I have to take care of both investigations at the same time. The first, however, is far more important: finding Fandor. As to the second, I must discover what Fantômas did after he escaped from the *British Queen*, upon our arrival in South Africa."

Ribonnard had pronounced a name that had immediately caught Juve's attention. The man knew Hans Elders; the policeman needed to learn more.

Juve now understood Ribonnard's "profession" and tried to be cagey in his questioning.

"I see you're not bored! You've been lucky to meet Elders. Have you heard from another of our friends? His name's Jérôme Fandor. I'm told he hasn't done too badly for himself here either."

Ribonnard nodded.

"It happens that I have. I heard it without trying to hear it. It's a bit shady—the kind of thing me and my pals try to keep out of..."

"Why is that?"

"Lots of reasons! He's a funny fellow, this Fandor. Guys like us, Pierre, we know everything. Now, Fandor, he got himself noticed fast. But, how did he get here? No one knows! At any rate, he made trouble for himself right off... You wanna know what he tried? He set fire to the docks, and I'm telling you, they burned! Oh how they burned!"

It seemed an unlikely thing for Fandor to do, but Juve thought the moment wrong to protest.

"Maybe he thought he could make off with something during the chaos?" he said

"Probably," agreed Ribonnard. "But it was a bad move. A kid named Teddy pinched him right off and handed him over to the soldiers. He played it like he was mad! He said he'd found some skull somewhere and waved it around and looked like such a lunatic that they locked him up at the Asylum..."

Once again, Juve acted as if he followed Ribonnard's narrative, but actually, he understood less and less.

"So he's been in the Asylum ever since?" he asked.

Ribonnard laughed loudly.

"Ever since? Hardly! I can't even begin to tell you what he's been doing since then! I don't know what's going on with your pal, but the other day, at a bash at Elders' house, I'm sure I saw him hanging around with the guests. You see, I'd seen him when the soldiers took him after the fire on the docks... That's why I'm positive it was him I saw at Elders' house—a little changed, a little disguised, and playing up to both Teddy and the boss' daughter!"

Juve wanted to learn more, for he now felt great concern. However, before he could ask for more details, Ribonnard banged his fist on the table.

"Well, who cares what becomes of him. Do you smoke?"

Juve was taken aback, as he was smoking a cigarette at that time. What could Ribonnard mean?

"Yes! Of course, I do," he replied.

"Then let's go, pal. I'll take you to my favorite den—the best in Durban."

Two hours later, Juve was no longer in control of himself, and he wasn't the least bit pleased about it!

But it really wasn't his fault.

After telling Ribonnard that he "smoked," Juve had accompanied him, not having the least idea as to where he was being taken.

Ribonnard led the policeman through the torturous and deserted streets of Durban until they came to a small, low house that seemed abandoned, located in one of the city's suburbs at the center of a large, uncultivated garden.

"This is my opium den!" said Ribonnard.

And then Juve understood.

In Natal, like in all British colonies, opium reigned as master. The dreaded poison, with its tragic effects, which causes dreadful ravages, was widely used.

Juve decided right away that he wouldn't smoke it. At the same time, however, he was pleased with the opportunity that he had been given to get information inside one of these hellholes.

He was sure that it was in a place like this, that he had the most chance of hearing news pertaining to either Fandor or Fantômas.

Following his guide, Juve entered the opium den.

Ribonnard had disrobed upon entering and had quietly stretched out on one of the cushioned beds, no longer appearing interested in Juve.

A young Chinese woman approached the policeman.

"Do you want me to make up your pipes, sir," she asked, "or do you make them yourself?"

Juve, who was less and less inclined to smoke, answered with calm and nonchalance.

"Leave! I'll make them myself!"

Then, just as he was cooking his first opium pellet, he heard a voice in the hall outside the room. It immediately grabbed his attention.

"It's me, Teddy," a young and well-timbered voice said, "and I've come to smoke because I'm very sad today!"

Teddy! Juve had heard that name mentioned several times in connection with both Hans Elders and Fandor!

Just then, a young man dressed as a horseman slipped into the opium den and stretched out on the cushioned bed to Juve's right.

Was this Teddy?

Right away, Juve made a decision: not only wouldn't he smoke, but he would also do his best to resist the strange numbness that he had begin to feel since he had entered the opium den.

Juve knew that, during their drug-induced dreams, the opium smokers often spoke. If by chance this Teddy was the same Teddy of whom he had heard, it was an extraordinary chance to have him as his neighbor. He would have to try to spy on him and lay in wait for his words.

He watched as the smoker turned over on the cushions, his face pale and eyes twitching.

The young man's dreams had begun.

After that, Juve was certain that his neighbor wouldn't notice the way that he looked at him, and he took fewer precautions. He turned on his own bed to lie on his side.

Only a single table separated him from the young man, a low table on which were laid out Teddy's smoking accessories, and a large crystal flower vase, which Teddy looked at fixedly, his eyes dilated, as he abandoned himself to his opium dreams.

Juve had been looking at Teddy for a while when he suddenly felt a bead of cold sweat run down his temples. He could clearly see a skull sitting between the flower vase and Teddy! A skull of which he could distinguish every detail!

He wanted to examine it more closely.

Juve rose up, sat on his cushion and leaned over to see the skull.

But, amazingly, there wasn't any skull!

Juve lay down again.

When he had regained his initial position, there it was again, clearly visible through the flower vase: the sinister skull!

This time, Juve stood up in a single bound.

No! He wasn't the victim of a hallucination; he had seen it clearly; a skull was there!

But leaning over the vase, Juve again had to be convinced of the reality of things: there was no skull!

The policeman suddenly heard the sound of a cannon firing.

While the opium smokers remained impassive and indifferent to the succeeding explosions, Juve got up, ran to the door, left the opium den and, guided by the cannon's noise, rushed towards the harbor from where it seemed to originate.

In the open sea, one could see a large ship—the policeman recognized it immediately as the *British Queen*— and she was ablaze.

"Curses!" thought Juve. "I left Fantômas on board. Did he set that fire? Has he escaped?"

Chapter XXIV
The Torments Of New Love

Jérôme Fandor opened his eyes.

He was lying on some kind of thick foam and seemed to be surrounded by reeds, which were giving off a cloud of moisture.

The journalist was stiff, numb and shuddering with cold.

He felt hot breath caressing his face. He had seen the monster's immense and frightening mouth when he opened his eyes.

What was this new horror?

Fandor moved back, then immediately breathed a sigh of relief. The mouth that had terrified him was that of a large dog that had approached and appeared to be watching him compassionately.

Still shaken, Fandor felt something soft and warm on his frozen hands.

He found that there was another dog licking him!

Finally, Fandor saw a third dog, lying on the ground, staring at him with his large, gentle eyes.

The journalist was more and more stunned.

Where was he? What had happened to him?

Fandor had discovered that his clothes were bunched up, hard, stiff and uncomfortable, as if they had been in the water a long time.

Looking around him, on the far horizon, he saw a rectangular silhouette, broken up by roofs and chimneys. In the foreground was an immense pipe—perhaps six feet high—that looked like a giant reptile curving along the ground.

The journalist remembered the phenomenal escape he had just made, when he had fled from Elders and the policemen looking for him in the workshops of the diamond factory. He had been carried by the conveyor belt, then thrown into a big siphon which carried the water supplying the machines. He realized that he had been tossed around in the current like a debris until the pipe had spit him out into the river.

However, Fandor wondered how he came to be lying on the riverbank itself? And where did the dogs fit in?

The journalist slowly turned around and discovered a new surprise: a saddled horse seemed to be awaiting its rider. It was tied to a tree branch by the bridle, quietly nibbling the leaves.

Fandor immediately recognized the horse.

"Teddy's horse!" he cried.

But why had the boy left the animal, and why wasn't he there as well?

Fighting his tiredness, Fandor stood up.

He took a few random steps, not really knowing which way to go, when he tripped over an inert body.

It was, of course Teddy's.

The young man was lying pale, muddy and unconscious!

Fandor assumed he had fallen and noticed a slight wound on his temple.

Comparing Teddy's position to his own a few moments earlier, and looking at his surroundings, the journalist realized that he must have been deposited on the riverbank by a favorable current, and then someone using considerable power, had hoisted him through the undergrowth and the swampy reeds onto dry land.

It must have been Teddy, who had then passed out from the exhaustion.

While considering this hypothesis, Fandor leaned over the brave friend who had so valiantly saved his life.

Teddy was breathing slowly, very weakly, and was clearly experiencing some trouble regaining consciousness!

He seemed to breathe with jerking movements.

Fandor, observing this, noticed a strange detail.

Teddy breathed unnaturally from the top of his chest.

His jacket, tightly closed, constricted his throat and squeezed his neck.

Fandor, to ease his friend's lungs, didn't hesitate to undo his clothing and bare his chest.

By so doing, he discovered pure lines, delicate, fine, white skin, and, finally, the surprising, unexpected, shape of Teddy's chest.

His surprise was intense!

Fandor turned red at this unexpected revelation and didn't dare touch Teddy further, fearing to be disrespectful.

For he had just discovered that Teddy wasn't a boy at all—instead, *she* was a *woman*!

Gradually, Teddy regained consciousness. Without suspecting Fandor's presence, she noticed that her clothing had been loosened and, instinctively, she closed it again while blushing.

Then, Teddy noticed the journalist and gave him a sympathetic look.

Fandor approached, not daring to say anything, waiting to be questioned and wondering if this enigmatic person whose sex he had just discovered knew that he had just discovered her secret.

"Teddy!" murmured Fandor, "I'm sure that it was you who saved me yet again. But how did you know that I was there?"

"I am always wherever you are!"

Fandor hesitated to speak. Teddy's face displayed such a natural surprise and her clear glance was so truthful that the journalist wondered at first whether it was necessary to acknowledge the secret that he had uncovered.

But in the end, Fandor decided that his anguish was too great.

"Is Teddy really your name?" he asked.

"Of course, it's my name," the young woman replied. "Why do you ask me that?"

"Because..." stammered the journalist. "Because Teddy is usually the diminutive of Edward or Theodore... And those are... boy's names!"

Teddy placed her hand on her throat to assure herself that her clothing was well closed again. She lowered her eyes.

"Teddy," asked Fandor, "I've several things to ask you. They concern me. They go back to the first day we met. Tell me, when you met me on the docks, the night of the fire, why didn't you let Lieutenant Dragg shoot me? It looked as if I was guilty, but you convinced him that I was a madman to save my life. Why? And at the National Club, when the same Lieutenant Dragg provoked me, and we were about to fight a duel, you accused him of being dishonored—even though you knew he was innocent—and thus stopped the duel. Why? Finally," he added even more gently, "when I was with Winnifred, when I had the opportunity to flirt with her and you believed that I had found her charming, you lost your temper, you got angry, you almost hated me—but you said you had no feelings for her yourself. So, why was it hard for you to watch me court her?"

Teddy sobbed passionately and stammered through her tears.

"Oh! Fandor, Fandor, forgive me for having deceived you for so long! But if I acted like that, it's only because I love you!"

The young man and the young girl remained a long time in one another's arms, tenderly embracing. And, as joyful tears ran down the girl's cheeks, Fandor also felt his eyelids moisten. It seemed to him that a new era of happiness was opening for him.

Admittedly, until then, Fandor hadn't thought about the nature of the affectionate feelings that he felt for the mysterious teenager whom he had believed to be his own sex.

Fandor roused himself from these reflections.

"Teddy," he began.

Then, he stopped and smiled.

"That's not your name; I can't keep calling you that..."

"Fandor, my dear friend, I don't have another name—for the time being at least—than the one by which you know me, by which everyone knows me! What is my real name? Alas, I don't know! Poor Laetitia could've told me... But she didn't think she had to, and now she's dead, and I don't know anything... The secret of my birth does exist however, and the one who holds it is that monster, Hans Elders. He's doing his best to hide it from me for some reason that I don't know."

Without knowing why he did so, the journalist knew that this had to be some plot conceived by Fantômas and those who were his accomplices.

"Call me Teddy again... Always..." the young woman suggested. "No one else needs suspect my gender. You're the only one to know since Laetitia's death. We'll both be brave and discover the secret of my birth. Elders holds the truth. I'm sure that he was the one who took the skull that contains the papers that will reveal my true identity... But what did he do with it?"

Fandor boiled with impatience.

"We'll find that skull," he swore. "I'll make it my duty. Come on, Teddy, let's go!"

"Wait, Fandor, not so fast! You're being hunted. The police want to capture you; you were nearly taken..."

"Good Lord," he uttered, irritated, "the charge against me is idiotic. Maybe I should just go to the authorities and explain the whole thing?"

Alarmed, the young girl threw herself in front of him, as if she wanted to use her graceful body to protect him from some imminent danger.

"No, Fandor!" she cried. "Don't do that! Like me, you have an enemy, a formidable, fearsome enemy, Hans Elders. He's a very powerful man, without conscience, who doesn't back down for anything... He's capable of anything. He persuaded the police that it was you that stirred up the crowd against Jupiter. Lieutenant Dragg fingered you as the man that set fire to the docks... If you're taken, Fandor, you're lost for good! We need to hide you, then you have to leave, flee the country..."

Suppressing her huge emotion, she added:

"...And leave me..."

But the journalist wouldn't consider such an idea.

"Leave you?" he swore, clutching her tightly to his chest. "I'll never leave you, I'd rather die..."

"For the next few days," said Teddy, "until we get the skull back from Elders, we'll need to keep you safe from the police. I know the perfect place... Let's go!"

Chapter XXV
The Ossuary's Secret

Juve woke up in an extremely bad mood.

He hesitated a few seconds before getting up—he had wound up in one of Durban's least luxurious hotels—then suddenly leapt up and got dressed while cursing and jostling everything in the room.

Where was Fandor? What was he doing? And why was he hiding? Juve had begun to have a vague idea of what was going on...

From Ribonnard's statements, the policeman had had retained only one thing: the public and the authorities blamed Fandor for the dock fire. Juve hadn't understood until later, after he had left the opium den, that Fandor was also somehow connected to the boxer Jupiter's terrible death.

It wasn't without a retrospective dread and a frightened shiver that Juve now thought of the opium den! What had happened there?

Of what tragic illusion had he been the victim?

"I know I saw a skull sitting there! Yet there wasn't one!" he said angrily. "But I didn't smoke any opium, so I wasn't intoxicated! And it wasn't the heat of the room that made me imagine things either; I was in total control of myself. I was completely conscious of my actions when I rushed out toward the harbor to witness the bombardment of the *British Queen*..."

Juve wondered if Fantômas had been able to escape the plague-stricken, burning ship that the authorities had sunk to avoid the spread of disease?

The policeman was suddenly gripped by his need for action. He hurriedly finished washing and dressing, paid for his room, left the hotel and went to a gunshop where, as a precaution, he purchased a good revolver. Then, he left Durban to head into the countryside.

"It seems to me that there's only one way of solving all these mysteries," he mused. "Somehow, there's one person whose name crops up over and over again: Hans Elders. He is the one who has, or wants the skull. He is the one Fandor is after, or else he's after Fandor. In either case, there's only one course of action: to investigate this man!"

Juve had left Durban with the intention of going to Diamond City to inquire about Elders as unobtrusively as possible. It took him two hours to arrive there without attracting undue attention.

It was still Sunday and the workshops were deserted. Juve entered through a half-open window and didn't see a living soul.

After a long walk through the cherchery, Juve decided to leave to go and spy on the inhabitants of Diamond House. However, when he crossed the large sandblasted court that separated the buildings, his attention was attracted by a small steeple located behind one of the hangars where earth was deposited before it was sifted for diamonds

Juve considered the steeple.

"I suppose," he told himself, "that whenever one is on British soil, one can't take two steps without running into a Protestant church!"

Walking behind a big shed that hid the church from him, Juve tried to reach the steeple. Suddenly he was struck by a thought. "It's Sunday, and it's still early... I bet they're all be inside that church, praying!"

But, as he turned the corner, he stood transfixed and amazed, for it wasn't a church at all that he saw, it was a cemetery. The steeple was only a part of a small monument, the purpose of which Juve didn't initially understand.

He entered the enclosure, where thin, black crosses, engraved with white letters, stood; he headed for the funeral monument.

Juve pushed the door. It opened.

As the policeman took a step forward, he again stopped in surprise!

This building wasn't a commemorative monument, as he had first believed. Instead, it was an ossuary, with skeletons piled up negligently, arranged one on top of another. In a corner, there were piles of skulls.

As Juve reflected on the whole affair, he began to think that, if Elders really wanted to hide a mysterious skull, such a place would be the most likely spot in which to do so.

Juve leaned over a pile of bones and, without any particular reason, started to take the skulls and examine them one by one. One of the skulls rolled; under it, the policeman saw another skull that seemed to cast a light into the sepulchral darkness!

"That's it!" he said. "This glowing skull has to be the mysterious skull that I'm looking for! Its phosphorescence proves it! The fact that it glows while the others don't means that, before being hidden here, it was hidden elsewhere."

He examined it attentively, but found nothing unusual about it. Nevertheless, once more, Juve felt a sense of extraordinary dread.

Then, his sharp eyes found a very small, almost imperceptible, spot that was devoid of phosphorescence.

He suddenly understood!

It also served to clarify in his mind the mystery that had intrigued him the day before at the opium den, when he had seen the phantom skull!

Another observation soon drew his attention.

"This skull is so heavy! Why is that?" he asked himself. And immediately, he found the answer. "It's because there's something hidden inside!"

Still, Juve hesitated to break the skull. He also realized that he needed to handle it with extreme caution, for he knew now that the skull he was holding was the one that had bitten Lieutenant Wilson Dragg!

As he carefully slipped his hands under the jaw, and then pressed on one of its teeth, the skull opened with a dry snap, the snap of a spring-loaded box.

Several lead balls, obviously the reason the skull had been so heavy, rolled on the ground at his feet. In their midst was a parchment scroll.

Abandoning the skull, Juve seized the precious papers and rushed towards the light, where he hurriedly studied what was written on them.

The parchment revealed the most amazing of secrets!

It was the birth certificate of a child, a girl named Hélène Gurn!

Juve couldn't doubt the documents he had before him; the details that he eagerly read unquestionably established that Fantômas had a daughter named Hélène!

Initially overwhelmed by the extraordinary discovery that he had made in the first parchment, Juve hastily deciphered the other documents that he held in his hands.

He found that there were property deeds that proved that Hélène, Fantômas' daughter, was enormously rich, that it was undoubtedly for her that Fantômas had, for years, been committing his crimes...

He further learned that Fantômas had abandoned this infant and entrusted her to the care of an old woman whose name, however, was not written...

In addition, there was a detail that caused Juve to pale: he learned that Fantômas, to be certain of finding his daughter when he wanted to, had used an ingenious trick. On the delicate flesh of the baby that he had abandoned, on the nape of her neck, he had had a tattoo of a tiny skull created by an extraordinary artist, whom he had then killed so that he wouldn't be able to reveal the secret!

It was, said the document, a "tattoo so fine, so small, that it was almost impossible to see it with the naked eye."

Nevertheless, under a magnifying glass' examination, it could immediately be recognized as the contours of a skull.

Moreover, this mysterious tattoo was reproduced and enlarged by half, while still remaining invisible, on the very skull that contained the parchment.

Juve now understood the entire extraordinary adventure!

The black spot that he had examined earlier on the skull's top was the tattoo, and the phantom skull that he had believed he had seen the day before in the opium den, between himself and Teddy, was quite simply the tattooed skull on the nape of Teddy's neck. The flower vase, filled with water, had formed a magnifying glass that had shown him the mark each time he looked through it.

Juve reeled in the face of this unexpected, formidable revelation.

If Teddy, the young teenager who had been his neighbor in the opium den, had a skull tattooed on the nape of the neck, then she was a young woman and not a boy! Teddy was therefore Hélène—Fantômas' own daughter!

Two hours later, the ossuary had regained its gloomy stillness.

The skulls that Juve had thrown around had been carefully put back into their places. The mysterious skull itself had been returned to rest under the pile of other skulls.

Elders could return to the ossuary to reclaim the bones of which he was so fond.

The master of Diamond City wouldn't be aware that Juve was lying in wait for him, hidden under a pile of skeletons, controlling his breath holding a revolver in one hand, while the other clutched his jacket pocket, which now contained the parchments he had so extraordinarily discovered.

The policeman was ready to spring at anyone who came to take the skull in which Fantômas had entrusted his daughter's secrets.

Chapter XXVI
The Past Never Dies

Hans Elders had only been settled in his study for a few minutes.

The diamond merchant was absorbed in the delicate work of accounting, and his eyes were glued to the page on which, in his firm and forceful hand, he inscribed figures, one after another.

Suddenly, he jumped up with such a brusque movement that he overturned the armchair on which he had been sitting.

A haughty voice, shaded with irony and scorn, had uttered a single word.

"Hello!" The voice continued in the same sarcastic tone. "Hello, Elders, how are you?"

Elders then saw a man emerge from a shadow-filled recess in the far end of the office and walk towards him.

The diamond merchant stretched his arms towards the apparition in a terrified gesture, as if warding off a ghost.

"You!" he said.

"You seem more surprised than pleased by my visit, my friend. Weren't you waiting for me? Aren't you glad to see me again after such a long absence?"

Then, a word slipped from Elders' bloodless lips, a word that he hardly dared pronounce, that he said with hesitation, as if insane with fear.

"Fantômas!"

Indeed, it was Fantômas who stood before him. The elusive outlaw had slipped into Elders' office, unobserved by the servants, had waited for him and now, had callously revealed himself.

Fantômas seemed to be greatly amused by the extraordinary fright that had overcome Elders.

"Fantômas!" he repeated, imitating the diamond merchant's trembling voice. "How you say that, my friend! It almost seems as if you're afraid to recognize me. What confusion has taken over your mind? Why are you trembling so? Why are you showing such inexplicable fear? Didn't I swear to you, as we stood surrounded by burning, devastated farms, that I would return? Did you doubt my word? Were you so absorbed with your own affairs that my name, the name that I made famous, frightening and respected, never came to your notice? Hadn't I promised that would be so?"

Elders once again uttered only a single sentence, but it was one that seemed to contain within it all the terror that had apparently taken over his soul.

"Fantômas, it's you! Why?"

Fantômas took note of the speaker's last word.

"You ask why I came back, Hans?" he replied in a quiet voice. "Have you lost your memory? Do I have to remind you of the deal we made?"

"No! No!"

"Then, I'll repeat my question: why are you so surprised to see me?"

"I heard you were dead. I believed..."

However, before he could even complete his sentence, Fantômas interrupted him with a burst of laughter.

"Dead!" declared the outlaw, who seemed to find the idea enormously amusing. "Dead! Can Fantômas die? Is Fantômas mortal?" Then, dropping his mocking tone, the outlaw continued: "We were partners once, Hans, extraordinary companions in adventure. During the war, we did it all: we plundered, we raided, we murdered. Was there any horror that made us pause? No! We were the greatest of friends! We would have had similar destinies, Hans, if your spirit hadn't been, at its core, weak and timid. For while I knew, even then, that I was destined for great things, you, with your weaker spirit and lesser ambition, felt satisfied with your fate!

"That was when I made a proposal to you and when we signed the agreement that made you my main lieutenant and me, the architect of your fortune. It was I, Fantômas, who gave you the brilliant idea of the false diamond cherchery. I committed myself to finding you suppliers. I promised that gems would flow into your coffers. Was I lax in my duties? Did I betray my promises? Did I not perform the task that I'd set myself? Answer me!"

The unfortunate Elders was pale and could not stop trembling. He found it difficult to marshal his thoughts.

Fantômas noticed this and shifted his attitude to show a mix of compassion and challenge. He moved a chair next to his old accomplice.

"Sit down and calm down, Hans," he said. "If you really did believe that I was dead, I understand why you'd be surprised at my reappearance, and I don't blame you. But now, it's time for you to get control of yourself. We've got work to do..."

"Work to do?" Elders repeated, like a weak echo.

"Yes, work to do," Fantômas restated, "But before that, answer me: was I the faithful associate that I promised you I'd be? Did your diamond cherchery thrive? Did I make the millions that I'd guaranteed you, all in perfect impunity?"

Hans Elders could barely nod his head.

"Yes," he said.

"Then, my friend, in that case, it seems to me that it's time you kept your side of the deal" resumed Fantômas in the same mocking voice. "Give me an accounting and tell me the size of my share."

The size of his share!

Gurn and Elders had once been nothing more than common looters in the wild veldt, following in the wake of the armies driving across the countryside. Elders had been happy to accept his partner's proposal. He had seen an easy way to make a fortune in Fantômas' offer to regularly provide him with precious stones, and starting the false cherchery...

Then, after the war, Hans had begun to receive visits from shady individuals that Fantômas had sent to him. These so-called "brokers" who were in fact merely fences, such as Ribonnard and many others. His cherchery had prospered beyond belief.

And, as Fantômas remained out of touch with his partner, as he became ever more legendary a figure, as his death was reported time and again, Elders had begun to believe that his formidable associate would never come to settle his accounts and claim his due!

Now, the moment that Elders had eventually stopped dreading had arrived. All of a sudden, Fantômas stood before him and, in a voice filled with contempt, said, "Let's divide the spoils!"

Hans Elders was panicking! But he wasn't yet at the end of his troubles, for suddenly Fantômas changed his tone. Now, he was no longer a mere man mocking Elders, he was instead the Lord of Terror. He was a master, a master who threatened, a master now had turned angry...

Yes, suddenly, Fantômas, expert actor that he was, dropped his bantering tone for one of deadly menace. He shook with rage as he advanced towards Elders, hands outstretched, eyes bloodshot.

"Miserable wretch!" he howled. "Traitor! Despicable worm! Backbiting jackal! Do you think I'm ignorant of your treason? Listen! I've been spying on you for months! For six months, I've known, day by day, your every move and your cowardice... You've told our men I was dead because you intended to steal from me, your benefactor, your master... from the Master of Everything, from Fantômas! You intended to steal my share, that rightfully belongs to me, from this cherchery that my efforts alone created, that only my hard work has supported!"

"It's not true! It's not true!"

Fantômas recovered his temper. He controlled his anger and his voice became once again cold and implacable.

"But you did worse, you dared worse! Your thefts, your cowardice, your treachery, your duplicity—I'd forgive it all! What I won't forgive, Hans Elders, is that you tried to steal the box that I'd entrusted to Laetitia, the box where my daughter's papers were hidden!"

Elders was beside himself, dazed, haggard and terrified before the anger of his lord and master. He knew that Fantômas would grant him no mercy.

However, as cowardly as Elders was, he was even more miserly and greedy for gold. At that very moment, even when it was a question of begging for Fantômas' forgiveness, he still felt the need to lie.

"I didn't steal the box!" he swore.

He was quickly silenced.

Such a flash of anger shone in Fantômas' eyes that the diamond merchant no longer dared to lie.

He was cowardly to the end. Getting up from the armchair where he had collapsed, he threw himself to the floor, on his knees, and crawled towards Fantômas.

"Master! Pity! Pity!" he moaned. "I thought you were dead! That's why..."

Fantômas interrupted him.

"Even if I had died," he said, "my daughter was undoubtedly still alive, wasn't she? You tried to steal her fortune by stealing the box. She was the one you were trying to rob?"

The words that Fantômas pronounced were a small gleam of hope for Elders.

Fantômas had said: "My daughter was undoubtedly still alive..." He was therefore unsure of her fate!

Terrified, yet still maintaining a vague hope of escape, Elders solemnly launched his ultimate gamble.

"You're mistaken, Fantômas. I've shuddered myself while thinking of the horrible news that you're going to hear, since you seem to be unaware of it..."

Fantômas turned pale

"My daughter?" he asked, clearly worried.

Elders stood up and seemed once again to be in control of himself.

"Your daughter is dead!" he said.

As Fantômas didn't even appear startled, Elders gambled everything he could.

"Yes, your daughter's dead, Fantômas, and I thought you were too. That's why I stole the box, to get hold of the documents that made her rich. But since you've returned, the situation's changed. I no longer have any reason to hide anything from you..."

While he spoke, Elders watched Fantômas' face for a reaction. However, the master criminal remained impassive. Did he truly believe his daughter to be dead or not? It was impossible to guess from his expression.

The outlaw smiled enigmatically, then drew a revolver from his pocket and aimed it squarely at Elders' chest.

"There are both lies and truth in your claims, Hans," he said coldly. "Understand, however, that Fantômas will never be your dupe. I know how to read your words and your heart. I'm armed and ready for anything! You know that I never miss my target and, if it pleases me to kill you, I'll shoot you like a dog—and there will be no escape. Now, take me to the place where you've hidden the skull that contains the parchments that I came to reclaim from you. I must get them at any cost!"

And such was the absolute will of Fantômas that Elders, not daring to resist him, not daring to try a new lie, nodded and said he was ready to take Fantômas to the ossuary where he had hidden the fateful skull a few days earlier.

Chapter XXVII
I'm The Murderer!

Fantômas and Elders had entered the mysterious ossuary in the center of the graveyard that was surrounded by the diamond factory's buildings.

As aware as he was of the terrible adventure in which he was mixed, Elders, pale and trembling, didn't dare make a gesture or say a word. He acted automatically, without feeling anything.

As for Fantômas, he wore a somber expression, but his eyes flashed with unholy energy; he appeared to be in the grip of a furious anger, ready at the least suspicious movement to get rid of the wretch whom he had accused of having betrayed him.

"It's here that you hid the skull?" he asked.

"Yes, but I don't know if I can find it easily..."

This final attempt by Elders to try and fool Fantômas would have been ridiculous were it not so tragic.

"You have five minutes to return what belongs to me, Elders, that which you had the insane conceit to steal!" And Fantômas laconically added, "Or your life is forfeited."

Elders could no longer hesitate. He threw himself on his knees to the ossuary's ground.

His hands shaking with a convulsive tremor, he began, with jerky movements, to overturn the piles of skulls that were arranged in sinister pyramids around the small building's walls.

Soon, in the dim, ambient light, the glowing skull appeared, terrible to see with its grimace, its sardonic rictus framed by the shadowy orbits and the jutting jawbone.

"You see, master!" whimpered Elders. "I haven't lied to you! Here's the skull that you used as your hiding place."

Fantômas didn't waited for his accomplice's explanations. He roughly pushed Elders aside, almost knocking him over onto the flagstones, then greedily seized the skull.

Fantômas almost seemed to forget Elders' presence, while the diamond merchant now stared at the outlaw with haggard eyes.

Nervously, the King of Crime turned the sinister skull over in his hands.

Yes, he recognized it, it was definitely the skull he had been seeking, the one which contained the papers of his daughter, Hélène.

Although he did not want to open it where Elders could watch, Fantômas was incapable of repressing his impatience. He sought the mysterious spring, pressed it and the skull opened.

But although Fantômas thought that he was at last achieving the goal that he had been pursuing, a cry of rage escaped from him instead!

There was nothing inside the skull! The parchments that he sought were gone. Someone had stolen them. He'd been betrayed... He'd been duped!

Mad with rage, Fantômas seized Elders. He grabbed the diamond merchant's collar and shouted at him.

"Miserable wretch! Where are the documents? Traitor, vile traitor! What did you do with them?"

Elders, who had never been able to discover the secret of the skull's spring opening, couldn't understand how the papers Fantômas sought had disappeared. He hardly had time to reply.

"I don't know!" he stammered.

Fantômas was unable to control himself. With an instinctive movement, he violently pushed Elders back, causing him to whirl around, dazed, stumbling, ready to collapse.

It was also instinctively that Fantômas drew his revolver. Without even taking the time to let his former speak, he fired almost point blank at the man he had accused of treason!

"Miserable wretch!" he yelled. "You'll pay for this with your life!"

Hans Elders, shot squarely in the heart, fell dead, without a sound, onto the vault's ground.

The gunshot set off muted echoes.

Then, a dreadful silence returned, where the only sound that could be heard was that of Fantômas' husky breathing. He was so indifferent to Elders' fate that he had already forgotten his dead accomplice. He was despairing over the disappearance of the precious parchments and had to lean against the wall.

A couple of minutes passed. Suddenly, Fantômas raised his head. A cold sweat broke out on his forehead. A convulsive tremor agitated his whole being. What was happening?

Fantômas thought that he had heard a step.

It was at the far end of the vault, where there was only one door. Would he be trapped in this small building like a mouse?

A young, fresh, clear voice cried in the silence:

"Don't move or you're dead!"

Fantômas leaped toward the door, ready to force his way out.

He stopped when he saw the slender silhouette of a young man in the doorframe. The new arrival had a rifle pointed at him, ready to fire at the slightest movement!

"Who are you?" growled Fantômas. "What do you want from me? Get out of my way! Don't interfere in things that don't concern you!"

However, the young man repeated again, in an unmistakably serious tone:

"Don't move, or you're dead!"

Fantômas stood still for an interminable second then wondered, what should he do and who was this unknown boy?

Then, ready to risk everything, as was his habit, he decided to leap on the young stranger, risking a gunshot if need be, to clear a passage at any cost.

However, the outlaw had no time to execute his escape plan. A crowd of workers and servants rushed towards the ossuary.

The sound of Fantômas' revolver when he had shot Elders had made a tremendous din, resonating under the small building's arch. Everyone had heard it and rushed to see what had happened.

Fantômas realized that he was lost.

The newcomers had seen Elders' corpse at his feet, and the young man holding him in check, ready to accuse him. It was 50 against one. There was no way he could fight them all.

But the evil genius that was Fantômas abruptly found a final trick.

As the workers neared the ossuary, Fantômas shouted.

"Help! Murderer! Someone's trying to kill me!"

After killing Elders, Fantômas had thrown his gun as far away as he could; therefore he was unarmed. He stood next to the victim. There was always the chance that they would believe he was a victim too!

He didn't hesitate. He decided to accuse the mysterious young man of Elders' murder!

The new arrivals were almost stopped by his yell. None of them understood why this man, whom no one knew, was in the ossuary, shouting for help, standing next to Elders' corpse. What exactly had happened?

A giant of a man abruptly seized the boy who was holding Fantômas in check.

"Teddy!" he yelled. "What have you done?"

"I've stopped the man who murdered Hans Elders!" the youth replied.

However, at the same time, Fantômas shouted.

"He's lying! He's just killed Hans! Now he's trying to kill me! He's crazy! Keep hold of him!"

The crowd continued to hesitate. They kept Fantômas trapped inside the ossuary, but disarmed Teddy, taking the rifle with which he was still threatening his enemy.

Trying to figure out what had really taken place, everyone began shouting at the same time.

"Are you accusing Teddy of killing Mr. Elders?"

"Who are you?"

"Why would Teddy want to kill you?"

"What are you doing here?"

With a gesture from his hand, Fantômas imposed silence on those who questioned him. The outlaw had recovered his self-control.

"Yes, I accuse this young man, whom you call Teddy, of killing Hans Elders!" he said, calmly. "And further, I accuse him of wanting to kill me too! Take him away and I'll be happy to explain everything."

The presumptions were in Fantômas' favor. The men had found Teddy armed and seemingly ready to fire; also, he didn't defend himself, and just stood there with a fiery, contemptuous glare, scorning the charges leveled against him!

Instinctively, the workers had taken him in custody.

"Why did you kill Hans, Teddy? Why?" those who held him asked

"Lies! It's not me, it's this man who is the murderer!" replied the young man.

But Fantômas had an answer against which nothing could prevail.

"I who killed him? Then, look! I don't have any gun and you've clearly seen that this boy had a gun aimed at me!"

With this statement, the truth of which no one could deny, and which seemed a definitive proof, a brutal sense of anger overcame those at the tragic scene.

With a rush of excitement, without reasoning or trying to learn the truth, they rushed Teddy, ready to take him away, possibly to do him harm, leaving Fantômas to flee.

Then, something unbelievable happened, which left them all immobile and terrified!

At the far end of the ossuary, from within the impenetrable darkness, they heard a noise.

There were only skeletons there, lying one beside the other, but now, it seemed that they were moving!

They appeared to stand up, then collapsed.

A sound of terror came from the crowd as if they were one.

From beneath the pile of bones, a man emerged, his expression calm mocking and yet commanding.

"Release Teddy, he's innocent!" he shouted. "The murderer is this man! And his name is—Fantômas!"

Juve could no longer avoid intervening.

Hidden under his pile of skeletons, he had not had time to rush Fantômas when the outlaw had killed Elders. The villain's gesture had been so sudden that it had taken the policeman by surprise.

Teddy's abrupt appearance at the door had again paralyzed Juve for some instants. Then, the policeman had chosen to remained still to learn if Fantômas knew that he was in the presence of his daughter... But the murderer's accusation launched at Teddy proved the opposite. So Juve no longer hesitated to intervene.

If those who had seized Teddy almost released the young man at the policeman's timely appearance, they were not quite ready to throw themselves on Fantômas.

No one knew Juve. They conferred, hesitating to trust him.

"Don't believe this man," shouted Fantômas. "He just wants to save his accomplice! You can see that I've been led into an ambush!"

With his usual mental clarity, Juve immediately understood the danger of Fantômas' maneuver.

The outlaw's assertions appeared likely, in fact. By hiding inside the ossuary, Juve appeared to have been lying in ambush...

Were they going to attack him now? And try to take him as well as Teddy?

Without hesitating, Juve shouted to Fantômas:

"Be silent, you miserable liar!"

Then, indicating Teddy with a finger, he added:

"Haven't you seen the tattoo that she carries on the nape of her neck?"

No one understood his words, or paid them the least attention, except Fantômas!

The outlaw seemed appalled and turned abominably pale at the policeman's declaration.

"Damned!" he said quietly.

Then, inventing a new ruse, finding a supreme resource deep within his fertile mind, before Juve had time to intervene again, he crossed his arms on his chest and advanced toward the ossuary's door, toward those that blocked his passage.

"I can't go through with it," he shouted. "I can't have an innocent condemned in my place! You want to know who murdered Hans Elders? It was I! I'm the murderer! But I defy you to stop me! I've also escaped from the *British Queen* and I have the Plague! Get out of my way! Anyone who touches me is condemned to death!"

Events then moved very quickly.

Fantômas hadn't even finished his amazing declaration when he dashed forward, bolting through the crowd, laughing sardonically.

"Out of my way!" he shouted.

And they all moved away.

Juve sprang towards Fantômas, intending to stop him, come what may.

However, Fantômas outran his adversary and had enough time to leave the ossuary and cross the few yards that separated him from the graveyard's surrounding wall.

"Thank you, Juve!" he cried. "You saved my daughter! I'll save Fandor for you!"

Then, the outlaw jumped on the horse that Teddy had left behind when he had entered the ossuary. He spurred it on both sides and took off.

"Curses!" Juve shouted. "Fantômas is escaping!"

The policeman rummaged in his pocket and took out his revolver.

He was on the point of firing when a tremendous blow stunned him.

Juve hardly had time to recognize his aggressor.

It was Teddy who had just saved Fantômas' life!

Chapter XXVIII
A Saber Duel

"My god! Am I to be deprived of sleep now? Listen to that devilish racket they're making outside! What's going on? Are they after me, or don't they suspect I'm here? It's dangerous for me to show myself... but on the other hand, I've got to know... It's been ten minutes since I first heard that racket. I'm fed up!"

The speaker clearly exaggerated.

There were indeed whispers that accompanied a few quiet and careful steps in the courtyard of Teddy's farm.

Nevertheless, although the noises were light, they were still too loud for the complaining sleeper.

The buildings that made up Teddy's farm included a series of stables and sheds grouped around the main house. Further along, a little out of the way, was a bigger shed, the ground floor of which was used to store agricultural machines, while the first floor had been turned into a loft for fodder.

And it was in this shed, from deep inside a pile of hay, that the sleeper had voiced his complaint. At last, he emerged from the fodder, his hair in disorder, covered with yellow twigs, his clothing all crumpled.

It was, of course, Jérôme Fandor!

When they had left the riverbank where the journalist would have met a tragic death without Teddy's timely intervention, the pair had gone to the farm. There, Teddy had persuaded Fandor to keep quiet, at least for a while, and to remain hidden in the loft.

"I beg you, listen to me" Teddy had said, "Do what I tell you. Just avoid the searchers for a few days and you'll be safe, cleared of the matter! As long as they hold you responsible for poor Jupiter's death, no one will think I would have anything to do with you. But if they were to find you now…"

It did not suit Fandor's character to hide. Brave as he was, the journalist would have preferred to fight his adversaries face to face, but it was obvious that Teddy was right.

That accusation, as well as all the other accusations that weighed on him, however idiotic they might be, was serious. It was impossible for him to ignore them, and he needed to be careful and not take them lightly.

Fandor, resigned, had listened to Teddy's advice, and had hidden himself.

"After all," the journalist had thought, "if I'm to continue my investigation, it's important that I'm not stopped so stupidly! Better to gain time before deciding how to act next."

Teddy had told him that she was leaving to find out where the pursuit of Fandor stood. Trusting in her word, he had let her go and, keeping his promise to her, had buried himself in a bundle of hay to sleep, as in the quietest of hiding places.

It was during his nap that the noise that he heard in the courtyard had awoken Fandor.

Thinking that it couldn't possibly be his pursuers, and believing that he was adequately sheltered from any searchers, the journalist committed a major indiscretion. He crossed the loft and, hoping to discover the reason for the noise, poked his head out of one of one of the windows.

It was a poor decision, which he realized immediately, as he had hardly appeared at the window when he was greeted by furious exclamations.

"There he is! We've got him now! Cheeky fellow! Lock the shed!"

Fandor now knew exactly who had caused the noise and was thus foolishly and stupidly captured.

Undoubtedly, some neighbor had seen him arriving with Teddy and must have informed the soldiers—who also acted as policemen—that he was hiding in the feed shed.

They had quietly surrounded the building and it was now impossible for Fandor to escape.

Surprisingly, the journalist wasn't too upset. For a long time, he had felt that his adventures would finish badly; he thought that the hour had finally rung for him to pay the piper. Fatalistically, he told himself, "This is it! I'm caught!"

Nevertheless, while the soldiers were yelling in the farmyard, Fandor had instinctively thrown himself back into the loft and was looking around for an exit like an animal taken in a trap.

Alas, there was none. Running to another window, Fandor quickly realized that the entire loft was surrounded.

There was no way to flee. They would lock him in irons and take him to Pietermaritzburg, where he would be tried and, in all likelihood, condemned to be shot or hung.

"Blast!" Fandor told himself. "If I've got to go, then I might as well get it over with!"

What he couldn't acknowledge to himself was that, in the furthest depths of his heart, the one regret that made him tremble and moved him, was the thought of losing Teddy. He really didn't know what to call the feelings he had for this strange girl he had so mysteriously met, and of whom he was so fond.

Fandor returned to the window where he had made his first appearance.

"Are you looking for me?" he asked impertinently.

More cries answered him.

"Get the murderer!"

Then a man who was clearly in charge rushed up.

"Give yourself up!" he shouted.

Fandor would have liked to resist, but how could he?

"Fine! I'll come down!" he answered. Still joking, he added, "Only there's no stairs to get down from this loft, and I don't want to break my legs by jumping. I'd be terribly obliged to you if you could bring me a ladder."

"Fine. We'll do that," the officer replied, "but don't try to escape! We're armed, and at the least movement..."

Fandor cut off the sentence with an amused exclamation.

"Why, is that you, Lieutenant Dragg? So glad to run into you again!"

The Lieutenant didn't answer. He regarded Fandor with a scornful, contemptuous look that was enough evidence of his hatred for the Frenchman.

Of course, Fandor returned it, glance for glance.

"He thinks he's going to frighten me," he fumed. "Bah! It's time to be philosophical!"

With a good-natured smile, Fandor rapidly descended the ladder that had been leaned against his window.

He reached the courtyard where the soldiers, rifles at the ready, threatened him.

"And now, what's going to be done with me?" he asked Wilson Dragg. "Are you to kill me immediately? No? Well, that's a bit of good luck!!"

As always, Fandor tried his best to joke. A true Parisian, a firebrand, it was when his situation was the most dire that he affected an amused indifference.

Nevertheless, he was soon silent.

Initially, no one had responded to him.

The soldiers, respectful of the rigorous discipline imposed on them by their leader, had seemed not to hear him.

As for Dragg, he pretended not to take account of the journalist's words. As Fandor waited, hands in his pockets, with the same impatient expression, the Lieutenant finally spoke.

"Keep this man in sight!" he ordered, turning toward his men. "Five of you will hold your guns at the ready. At his first movement, fire! The rest of you, come with me. We need to search this farm, which has all the appearance of being the lair of the worst riffraff in the country!"

Dragg led them off solemnly.

"The swine!" thought Fandor, who found it difficult to contain himself. "He's making fun of me! One should never make fun of a prisoner, and I'm his prisoner!"

Fandor chafed at the bit. He wouldn't have admitted it for the world, even to himself, but he was concerned.

How would all this end?

Fandor watched Dragg move towards the farm buildings, escorted by about 20 soldiers.

Suddenly, a new arrival appeared, one who, Fandor realized, might improve his situation.

The vague silhouette of a rider galloping at a lively pace was still far away, but Fandor had already identified that it was Teddy.

After the extraordinary scene that had just taken place at the ossuary, escaping those who pressed her with questions, Teddy had jumped on a horse.

She had vainly given chase to the fugitive. Then, abandoning her pursuit, she had headed for home to bring Fandor up to date on the latest events.

Seeing the uniformed soldiers on the farm, led by Wilson Dragg, Teddy had spurred her mount and arrived at a breathless gallop.

She stopped directly in front of the Lieutenant.

Then, roughly reining in her beast, she jumped out of her saddle and confronted the officer.

"What are you doing here?" she gasped.

Dragg took Teddy's measure.

"It's required of me," he replied, "to ask you by what right you've harbored a murderer here?"

"A murderer? He's not a murderer!"

"Yes, he is."

"You're lying!"

At the insult, Wilson turned pale.

"Teddy," he said in a quiet voice, "you've called me a thief; now, you accuse me of lying. My duty as an officer would be to scorn your insults, but my duty as a man doesn't allow me that luxury! You say that I've lied? Very well. I answer that you are a coward! For whenever I've endured your intrusive presence, you've escaped me by trickery!"

A coward!

No sooner had the shameful word been uttered than Teddy, becoming pale in her turn, raised her riding crop and lashed at Wilson Dragg, hitting him on the face!

"Miserable wretch!" shouted the officer, trembling with rage. He reached instinctively for his saber. "You'll give me satisfaction!"

"With pleasure!" Teddy retorted without hesitation. "Whenever you want it!"

"Here and now!"

"Yes."

However, just then, a voice yelled from behind.

"No, Lieutenant! If you want to cross steel, it's with me you'll cross it!"

It was Fandor who hurried to prevent a duel between Lieutenant Dragg and Teddy!

Kept in sight by the soldiers, manacled, Fandor had witnessed the quarrel between the officer and Teddy.

At first, the journalist had contained himself so as not to aggravate Teddy's situation. However, Dragg had gone too far and Fandor could no longer control his anger!

Let Teddy cross swords with Dragg? Never!

Fandor couldn't allow it. It was monstrous. He had to prevent it.

Teddy was a girl!

Whatever her physical training, she was obviously not of a size to go against an experienced officer such as Wilson Dragg!

To let this duel take place was to be made an accomplice to a murder!

For a few minutes, Fandor had feigned indifference to better fool his guards. Then, as Dragg drew his sword, as Teddy rushed to one of the soldiers to ask for his, to be able to fight with the Lieutenant with the same type of weapon, Fandor had sprung forward.

And so vigorous had been his movement, so quick had been his escape, that it had been impossible for the soldiers to fire on him, especially as Dragg stood directly in their path.

"Coward!" continued Fandor. "You're the worst of cowards to dare to provoke a lad! If you want to fight, you should fight against a man! Fight with me!"

Fandor phrased it like this because for nothing in the world would he have wanted to reveal to the Lieutenant that Teddy was a woman!

Fandor was persuaded that challenging Dragg and offering to duel him was an opportunity that the officer would be delighted to accept.

However, Fandor had misunderstood his opponent.

Dragg brusquely turned toward him and gestured at the soldiers. The men sprang forward and seized Fandor.

"Me, fight with you, Jérôme Fandor?" the Lieutenant said mockingly. "Don't even think about it!"

"You refuse?"

"I don't have to refuse."

"You dishonor yourself, Lieutenant!"

"I would disgrace myself," asserted Dragg calmly, "if I crossed steel with you!"

At this, Fandor remained mute with stupefaction.

What was the officer trying to say? Why would he dishonor himself by fighting with the journalist?

Fandor didn't have to ask.

"I imagine that you've never, even for the slightest instant, considered that I wouldn't agree to fight you," Dragg continued. "Good Lord, think about it, Fandor! Remember when I challenged you to a duel at the National Club? Your friend Teddy here chose that moment to state that one didn't fight with a man accused of theft, as I was then. Well, the same goes for you now. I've just arrested you. You're accused of murder and worse. I won't fight with a murderer!"

Pale, gritting his teeth, Fandor still pressed Dragg.

"You're a coward! You can't fight with Teddy..."

However, Teddy herself interrupted him.

213

She had turned pale seeing Fandor intervene.

She had an energetic soul and a valiant heart. Dragg had just insulted her and she didn't accept that anyone had that right!

Moreover, Teddy would never have allowed Fandor to fight in her place.

"This is too much, Lieutenant," she shouted, interrupting Fandor. "Is it because you're afraid of me that you keep talking? I'm right in front of you! Come on! I'm capable of defending myself and making you take back your contemptible words!"

Once again, Fandor tried to prevent the duel. He threw himself between the combatants.

"No! Teddy! Not that!" he pleaded.

But Teddy rudely shoved him aside.

"Let's go, Lieutenant," she said. "What are you waiting for to get this man out of our way?"

The girl's remark seemed to sting Dragg into action. He freed himself from Fandor, who had grabbed him by the arm, wanting to draw him away.

"Soldiers!" he shouted. "Take the prisoner to Durban! I'll join you as soon as I cut down this kid who's insulted me!!"

Then the soldiers threw themselves on Fandor.

What could the journalist do?

There were 20 against him. He felt himself dragged away as blows half-stunned him. However, he managed to turn his head for a second as he was dragged beyond the hedge that enclosed the farm.

He saw Teddy, alone, opposite Wilson Dragg, sword high, her face impassive, waiting for the Lieutenant's attack.

It was a horrible duel.

Dragg must have lost his sense of decency to agree to fight the young "man." Before, he had been a decent officer and a gentleman. His appalling conduct was caused by the series of unfortunate incidents that had recently happened to him.

Dragg was big, powerful and muscular, accustomed to handling a saber. Opposite him, Teddy appeared thin and small. The weapon that she held was obviously too heavy for her wrist.

"*En garde!*" the Lieutenant shouted.

"May God keep you," responded Teddy.

The swords glinted and collided with a crash. But while the Lieutenant bore Teddy's blows without bending, the girl was half-shaken by her adversary's violent attack.

Dragg took advantage of her weakness and, disdaining the back blow, he led with the point.

However, that proved fortunate for Teddy!

The girl clearly didn't have the size to withstand a great blow, where Wilson Drag's muscular superiority provided an unquestionable advantage.

On the other the hand, she was agile, nimble and quick.

As Dragg jabbed, cleaving broadly, Teddy had time to parry.

The Lieutenant's blade met Teddy's and slid. So widely had the officer swung that the two hilts met.

They were now shoulder-to-shoulder, body-to-body.

The Lieutenant freed himself and forced Teddy to drop her weapon. He then raised his sword, preparing to skewer his opponent with its point.

Teddy was about to pay with her life for the temerity that had pushed her to accept a battle of swords. Joining her hands together, a desperate cry escaped from her lips.

Suddenly, with the speed of light, a horrible drama occurred which both saved and confused her!

As Dragg raised his weapon, ready to deliver a lethal blow to Teddy, a man sprung up behind him!

In the newcomer's hand, something glittered for a mere second. The man's arm rose, and then dropped with lightning speed.

Before Dragg could strike, a mortal blow fell between his shoulders!

Teddy had not had time to intervene, had not been able to warn the officer about this cowardly assassination. She would have preferred death a hundred times over the dishonorable end that the newcomer had imposed on the duel.

"Murderer!" she stammered

In a gesture of proud revolt, she already had her hand on her revolver and she was ready to kill Wilson Dragg's assassin without mercy.

But Teddy didn't finish her gesture.

She left her revolver in her belt while a sob filled her throat. She fell to her knees.

"You!" she said. "Fantômas!"

"Yes, me! Your father!" the man who had just saved her life wearily answered.

It was the most anguishing scene possible.

Teddy had finally divined the horrible secret of her birth when Fantômas had escaped the ossuary while shouting at Juve, "You saved my daughter, thank you!"

She had often wondered why Laetitia had made her pass for a man and feared her discovering her father's name. Laetitia had often trembled at the name Fantômas.

Now, she had learned that she was Fantômas' daughter!

In addition, she had learned this just as she had witnessed her father murdering Hans Elders. She had learned this just as she herself had been on the point of firing at him, not suspecting that he was her father. Just as he had accused her of a crime without suspecting she was his daughter!

At that moment, when so many tragic mysteries were resolved, Teddy had been so frightened and confused that she had stood silent, even though she was herself in jeopardy.

Still, she had rushed to action when Juve had aimed his gun at Fantômas. She had shoved the policeman in a spontaneous and natural impulse to prevent him from shooting.

She couldn't let anyone kill her father.

And now, suddenly, this father was again in front of her. She was in Fantômas' presence, and again, she had seen him commit another murder!

She could shoot him, but she realized that such an act on her part would be the most abominable of crimes.

The whole world had the right—the duty even—to kill Fantômas, but for her, he was sacred because he was her father!

Collapsed on the ground, kneeling close to Lieutenant Dragg's body, Teddy repeated, as if she were hallucinating:

"Fantômas!"

The unfortunate girl was enduring the most terrible agony in the world. She would have died to escape it.

As for Fantômas himself, standing still in front of his daughter, he remained silent, overwhelmed and stunned.

The hour of his atonement had arrived!

However, the villain quickly pulled himself together and quickly took control of the situation.

He gave his daughter a hasty kiss, which made the unfortunate Teddy shiver with horror.

"Listen! Everything I've done, I've done for you!" he said in a harsh voice. "Yes, I owe you an explanation. I promise I will give you one. Once you know everything, you'll forgive me and love me."

A single word hissed from Teddy's white lips:

"Never!"

But Fantômas was already shaking his head. He was sure of his deeds. He believed no one could withstand him. He felt certain of winning over his daughter, just as he had won over Lady Beltham and gained every the treasure he had ever wanted.

"You will love me," he repeated. "You will love me when you know the truth—Hélène. And you'll know it soon. Tomorrow. Perhaps in two days. Now, I need to disappear. Someone is following me. Farewell!"

Teddy—or rather Hélène—remained motionless, rooted to the spot, while Fantômas fled with great strides.

It was a clear day.

In the pure sky, the Sun lit the faerie-like scene with its scintillating rays. The birds sang, the breeze was gently caressing, intoxicating with its scents!

Teddy stood up.

But it was no longer Fantômas, the father who loved her but whom she could not love, that she thought about.

She also did not reflect on the horrible drama that seemed to surround her. No, her thoughts were for another.

"Fandor! Where is he?" she murmured. "On my soul! I'll find him and save him!"

Chapter XXIX
Juve's Escape Plan

Exhausted after the events at Diamond House, Juve was also considerably troubled. Despite his fatigue, he feverishly crossed the flowered countryside and headed back into Durban.

After having identified Fantômas and avoided the irreparable misfortune of the monster having his own daughter killed, the policeman couldn't wait to leave factory and wanted to return to his hotel, near the city's center.

Events had moved with such lightning speed, and Elders' death had been so unexpected, that the policeman still wasn't completely sure of the motive behind Fantômas' decision to get rid of the diamond merchant.

Nevertheless, despite not knowing the details of what had occurred between the two villains, Juve had reasoned out the situation and felt that he understood at least part of it.

From the few words he had heard, the policeman realized that a powerful and mysterious connection already existed between Fantômas and the man who had launched a thriving diamond business in the peaceful region of Natal, but had likely also committed many crimes elsewhere prior to his transformation.

Clearly, something had caused a dispute between Fantômas and Elders.

This being the case, as usual, the weakest party had lost. And, when Fantômas faced an adversary, that man, whoever he might be, was always the weaker of the two.

However, the drama had unfolded so quickly that Juve had not had the time to undertake an immediate investigation, nor to capture his arch-enemy. With Fantômas' usual daring and his perfect self-control, the villain had been able to escape yet again.

But now Juve was less concerned with catching Fantômas than with finding Fandor. In fact, he felt the most dreadful anxiety regarding his friend.

Juve knew through his local inquiries that Fandor was known in Durban. Maybe too well known—for he was the object of terrible accusations and was being actively sought by the police.

Of course, Juve knew that Fandor was innocent of the charges against him, but he dreaded them with a legitimate concern. He certainly couldn't ignore them, and he suspected that the elusive Fantômas, in accordance with his usual tactics, had somehow provoked them.

He would find Fandor, for the journalist was probably unaware that his friend, answering his calls, had finally arrived at Durban!

As Juve entered the city, a large crowd hastening toward a group of soldiers drew his attention.

Clamors of hate and threats resounded from all sides.

Instinctively, Juve mingled with the crowd and cleverly managed to catch up with the squadron of soldiers which were crossing the city, bayonets on their guns, with a heavy and rhythmical step.

What did this deployment of armed force mean?

The soldiers were frequently forced to use their sticks to push back the aggressive population that crowded in on them.

Juve heard the crowd make threats.

"Prison's not good enough for him!"

"Hang him now!"

The policeman couldn't help but wonder about whom they were talking. Finally, he caught up with the soldiers and saw that a man, whose legs were chained, and whose hands were shackled, was their prisoner.

The cries became increasingly worse. Some in the crowd threw stones at the prisoner; others seemed to content themselves with shouting and showing their fists to the poor wretch who was undoubtedly being led to prison.

Juve approached a sergeant and questioned him politely.

"This is rather difficult, isn't it? All these people swarming about around you..."

"Yes," replied the sergeant, "they're very annoying, but still, one can understand their reasons and even support them..."

"Certainly," said Juve, who agreed without actually understanding. "You're holding your prisoner well; he won't escape."

"No," said the sergeant, with a fierce smile, "he won't escape, not this one. We've been looking for him for days. There's no one like a foreigner for knowing how to do an evil deed..."

At the word "foreigner," Juve pricked up his ears. He was suspicious and afraid of being right. His entire body shuddered.

His anxiety was transformed into panic when a slight disturbance of the soldiers' ranks, caused by the crowd's movements, enabled him to see the prisoner's face.

The man being protected against the multitude's attacks was Jérôme Fandor.

"My God!" said Juve. "Poor Fandor! I've arrived too late to save him."

Juve kept his emotions in check and returned to the sergeant to question him further, being careful to appear indifferent enough to not arouse any suspicions.

"What did this man do? Why are they taking him to prison?"

"Fifteen days ago," replied the officer, "after stealing money from Jupiter, the great boxing champion, he framed him for the murder of an old woman; then, he stirred up the crowd against him. Later, he shot Jupiter inside a theater full of people. They also say that he set fire to the docks before that."

Gasping, Juve continued his questioning.

"And what will happen to him now?"

The sergeant smiled.

"Oh, that's easy enough. We'll take him to prison. In two or three days, he'll be transferred to the central jail in Pietmaritzburg, then he'll be judged by the High Court."

"And doubtless found guilty?" observed Juve.

"Surely found guilty," retorted the sergeant, "and sentenced to death! The people are very worked up, so the magistrates will be severe, to make an example! There are crimes, murders and thefts all over the place these days. Ever since some foreigners started prowling around, life here has been completely disrupted. Excuse me, sir, but the lieutenant is calling me..."

The sergeant left Juve and, with athletic strides, gained the column's head.

Drawn away by a movement of the crowd, the policeman lost sight of the procession surrounding his unfortunate friend.

"It won't be said," exclaimed Juve, "that I let him perish! I'll save Fandor, even if it takes a show of force. I'm not certain yet of how, but as I live and breathe, they won't touch a single hair on his head..."

"Excuse me."

"Sir?"

"May I speak to the Chief Mechanical Engineer?"

"To which Chief Mechanical Engineer, sir? There are several..."

"Then, to the chief of the Chief Mechanical Engineers."

"There isn't one, sir. Each Chief Mechanical Engineer is his own boss."

"Well, the one I'd like to see is the Chief Mechanical Engineer in charge of locomotives."

"Very good, sir. Second floor, corridor B, room 27."

"Thank you."

"You're welcome, sir."

This brief conversation took place between a visitor and an employee of the Great Central Railway, the most important of the railway lines serving Natal and linking the country's principal cities. They were exchanged in the Company's main office in Pietermaritzburg.

Following the instructions, the visitor arrived at room 27 at the far end of corridor B on the second floor.

He knocked on a counter window and began repeating his question, this time being more specific.

"May I see the Chief Mechanical Engineer in charge of locomotives?"

"That would be Mr. Mullerstein," declared the clerk.

"May I see him?"

"No, sir, he's away."

"For a long time?"

"One never knows, sir, but it's probable that he won't resume his service for a few days, for they say he's distressed."

The visitor stood for a few instants in silence; he evidently didn't know what to say.

The clerk, obviously overloaded with work, or at least not eager to wait for this idler to decide what to do next, started to close his window. However, the visitor stopped him.

"I understood," he said, "that Mr. Mullerstein was going to Durban tomorrow to inspect the locomotive depot?"

The clerk, intrigued that a stranger was so-up-to-date on the details of the company's business, responded in a friendly manner. The man may be some kind of inspector from the Head Office, or a high-ranking civil servant. So he was careful to reply with a smile.

"Well, sir, the fact is that the Chief Engineer's inspection visits aren't ever cancelled—even when, as is the case in this instance, the gentleman can't make them. It keeps the staff alert, as they never know when there will actually be an inspection. And, of course, it's always possible that Mr.

Mullerstein might actually be well enough tomorrow to go to Durban anyway."

"I'd like to know exactly what Mr. Mullerstein is doing?" asked the visitor.

This time, the clerk made a vague gesture.

"That, sir, I'm afraid I can't tell you," he said. "And I don't see any way for you to find out unless your title authorizes you to visit the Chief Engineer himself. He'll be able to inform you better than anyone here."

The advice was good. The visitor obtained the senior official's address from a directory that an office boy obligingly lent him.

A few instants later, he jumped into a car and drove himself to the Chief Mechanical Engineer's residence.

Mr. Mullerstein lived on the west side of Pietermaritzburg, the most elegant part. His house was a beautiful property surrounded by a garden.

The visitor rang the gate and entered, after a long conversation with a servant, from whom he had extracted information by means of a generous tip.

He learned that a doctor had just left the house and that Mr. Mullerstein still needed to stay in bed for a good week.

The visitor then immediately left, drove to the railway station and took the first train for Durban.

The following morning, there was considerable excitement at the locomotive depot of Durban, where everyone was awaiting the inspection visit of the Chief Mechanical Engineer that had been announced a week earlier.

Firemen and drivers, superior employees, junior subordinates, were all checking that nothing in the depot was out of order, so that the Chief Engineer would be satisfied with his examination.

This visit was important to the company's employees, for at its end, the Chief Mechanical Engineer was to issue their performance reviews. These would be used to decide salary increases, merit promotions and retirement placement.

The immense hall was built in the shape of a fan. The huge locomotives within it vibrated and smoked while the operations team, made up of firemen and drivers, frantically polished them and attentively and cautiously checked their powerful wheels.

So great was the activity and the concern that each one had correctly accomplished his work, that no one noticed the presence in the depot of a person unknown to all.

He was a man dressed entirely in black, wearing a large slouch hat. He paced, hands in his pockets, speaking to no one. However, he watched closely, perpetually inquisitive and curious. Certainly, to any observer, he appeared to be acting as someone with a right to be there.

This was the same visitor who had, the day before, in Pietermaritzburg, inquired so carefully about the health of Mr. Mullerstein, the Chief Mechanical Engineer in charge locomotives.

He approached a superb engine of the Pacific type, which was taking water into the tender, and approached one of the men on board.

"Which of you is the fireman?"

"That's me, sir," said one of them. "How can I help you?"

"I'm the new mechanical engineer from Pietermaritzburg. I'm replacing Mr. Mullerstein, who's ill today."

The fireman respectfully bowed. The driver, who hadn't missed a single word of the conversation, worked with manic activity to clean his machine's ashpan, while supervising the bubbling water that filled the reservoir, intended to supply the boiler.

"Aren't you supposed to transfer to the express train to Pietermaritzburg when it arrives from Verulam in two hours?" asked the man.

"That's right, Chief Engineer."

"Our trip today, sir, is a little different than usual," the driver explained, "because we have an extra car to take with us and that will cause a bit of an overload. So, we'll have to use extra coal. But I don't think the schedule will be affected. Our Pacific is in great shape—I pride myself on that. She's powerful enough to get to 90 miles an hour, no matter what."

"What's this special car that you're to transport?"

The fireman indicated a vehicle on a remote siding.

"It's a penitentiary car we're taking to Pietermaritzburg. They're transferring a prisoner. He's scheduled to appear in Court to be tried tomorrow. He's a pretty famous prisoner, too! You've probably heard about him—Jérôme Fandor. He's the one who set up the attack that ended up with the murder of the boxer Jupiter, after he'd already set the docks ablaze."

The alleged Chief Engineer appeared to only take a passing interest in the fireman's story; instead, he leaned over the locomotive as if he was checking something. However this was just to hide his distress.

"I see that this is latest model of Pacifics," he continued. "Tell me, do you have any trouble with the drain-cocks?"

The fireman swelled with conceit.

"No sir, never! Not the least problem! Although, I know that the drain-cock is delicate, and can be difficult in unskilled hands..."

"True enough," declared the mysterious engineer curtly. Then, changing the subject, he asked, "At what time do you leave?"

"At exactly 1:12 p.m., sir. Usually, it's at 1:18 p.m., but they've advanced us six minutes today because of the penitentiary car."

"Explain your movements to me."

"We leave the depot and move onto the shunting line. We then attach the penitentiary car at the front of the train. After that, we move onto the main line and stop at the forward signal. There, we'll wait the arrival of the express train. The engine that brought it will detach and return to Verulam. When it's shunted clear, we'll get the signal to move forward. We'll then pick up the regular cars that will be waiting for us at the station..."

"Very good," interrupted the alleged Chief Engineer dryly. "I'll be back at 1:10 p.m. I'll be traveling with you to Pietermaritzburg as I want to make sure the drain-cocks are in good shape..."

The man looked at his watch.

"A quarter to noon," he said. Saluting the fireman with his hand, he added while leaving, "I'll have my lunch while I'm waiting."

Rather than returning to the city, the man who had passed himself as Mr. Mullerstein's replacement prowled around the penitentiary car for a few minutes.

Then, he retraced his steps, passed behind the depot and, climbing over a railing, lost himself in the wasteland that encircled the service buildings.

He was certain that no one was watching him. He advanced with long steps, his arms crossed behind him, and appeared to be thinking, as if he was worried about the scheme he was considering.

He had reason to be concerned, for with prodigious audacity, he had claimed a title to which he had no right.

For this so-called engineer who had said that he was replacing Mr. Mullerstein was, of course, none other than Juve!

Why was the policeman playing this dangerous game?

What was his goal?

He had but a single thought, a single desire: to save Jérôme Fandor at all costs!

It had been 48 hours since he had seen his unfortunate friend arrested and taken to prison. Juve had put together plan after plan and had increasingly given way to despair at the idea that none of them could succeed. The unfortunate Fandor would be dragged before the Court in Pietermaritzburg, be condemned and, afterwards executed, without anyone being able to help him.

The approach of danger is sometimes responsible for extraordinary inspiration. Juve suddenly came up with a daring plan: they were going to transfer Fandor from Durban's

227

prison to Pietermaritzburg, where the High Court sat, by train. So, he would have to arrange his escape during that trip

Juve had gone to the railway company's main office, trusting in his lucky star and swearing to himself that he would do whatever was necessary to travel on the same train. By what pretext, he had no idea, but he was convinced that he would succeed!

Luck had indeed been with him! The Chief Engineer whom he had hoped to approach had been taken sick and forced to abandon an inspection visit scheduled for the same day Fandor was scheduled to be moved.

Juve had immediately decided to take advantage of the situation and was audacious enough to replace the engineer. And now, he would be on the very locomotive that would pull the car in which Fandor would be transported.

After what he had just learned from the fireman, Juve thought that his task had been made relatively easy. The locomotive would first attach the penitentiary car on its tender. Then, with only this single wagon, it would stay on the shunt line, until the moment came to back up and pick up the other passenger cars waiting at Durban's station.

Thus, for perhaps a dozen minutes, a train consisting only of the locomotive and the penitentiary car would be traveling across the open countryside for at least a mile without any habitation or witnesses!

Juve planned to take it over by force, coerce the fireman, perhaps using a revolver as a threat, to drive the machine a little farther still. Then, he would have only to free Fandor and they could run off into the countryside.

They would have to find kindly people to hide them, perhaps for money, but no matter what happened, Juve would rescue Fandor or die trying!

As extraordinary and impossible as this plan appeared at first glance, as the moment approached to carry it out, Juve became increasingly calm, gaining the certainty that it was going to succeed.

Certainly, the most delicate part would be to force the fireman to drive a few miles further, when he was supposed to wait until it was time to back up to the station.

However, Juve told himself that the engine crew, despite the surprise that they would feel, would likely obey the order of the superior whom they believed him to be.

When they were in the open countryside, they would understand, but by then it would be too late.

At a crossroad, Juve entered a modest inn and had a frugal meal. He ate quickly, impatient to begin the task ahead of him.

Feeling terribly anxious, he returned to prowl in the vicinity of the depot, waiting until it was time to present himself.

At 12:58 p.m., Juve stepped across the barrier; he was again in the train station's enclosure.

From that moment, things would have to go off like clockwork.

"My plan," thought Juve, "is undoubtedly audacious, but not impossible. Will I be able to rescue Fandor?" And, tightening his fists, staring down an invisible enemy he concluded, "Yes, despite the whole world, despite Fantômas himself, I will rescue Fandor!"

Chapter XXX
The Hijacking Of The Pacific

The engine of the powerful Pacific locomotive sounded unhurried and deep, but inside its flanks thundered the white-hot combustion of half-a-ton of coal.

By another extraordinary piece of luck, Juve found himself alone on the machine whose engine crew had successively abandoned her. The driver had been lavishing attention on the locomotive for the past two hours, supplying the firebox and reservoirs, carefully greasing and oiling the smallest moving parts. Yet, contrary to protocol, he had left his post a few minutes before the operation was set to start.

In fact, the engine had left the depot. Its shunting crew had driven it onto the siding and driven back to the penitentiary car, to which it would soon be coupled.

It was 1:13 p.m. The express from Verulam had already signaled its imminent arrival.

Eager to play his role as a mechanical engineer with unruffled self-control, Juve had arrived a few instants earlier. He had climbed onto the locomotive and had found only the fireman aboard. He questioned him about the driver's disappearance.

Juve applauded himself for having taken this role. It enabled him to question everyone without his requests appearing suspect.

The fireman understood his surprise, for the driver's disappearance, at the hour of impending departure, had greatly surprised him as well.

What had become of him?

A few minutes earlier, he had said that he was going to look for a hammer that he had left near the coal pile, but his absence was too long to be justified by such a simple errand.

"Listen," said Juve, who had called the fireman into the cab after looking at his watch, "do me the favor of going to look for him right away."

The fireman looked surprised.

"Don't ask me to do that, sir," he answered. "You know that the regulations prohibit me from abandoning my machine once it's under pressure!"

Juve made a gesture that was both protective and authoritative.

"That's true," he said, "but don't forget you have one of your superiors on board. I'll take full responsibility for the order I'm giving you."

The fireman did not argue, although he was clearly upset by this breach of the rules. But after all, the engineer had made it clear who was in charge.

So the fireman went in search of his companion.

Remaining alone, Juve breathed a sigh of relief.

The circumstances had decidedly favored him, and the gods of luck were on his side. The driver's unexpected absence had allowed him to get rid of the fireman.

If the driver returned in the meantime, Juve could send him after the fireman, whom he would hopefully not find right away!

Juve wanted to remain alone on the locomotive for as long as possible.

Good policeman that he was, he had observed everything, and handling the powerful machine did not worry him. Juve had traveled frequently on trains, and knew the principal elements of the engine controls.

In fact, what the policeman mostly felt was considerable impatience.

A quarter of an hour earlier, he had watched as the unfortunate Jérôme Fandor had been taken to the penitentiary car, closely guarded by four jailers. However, the men had withdrawn after installing their prisoner in the wagon, leaving his hands and feet bound. He was under the supervision of a single soldier, whose job it was to escort Fandor to Pietermaritzburg.

If the wagon had been hitched to the locomotive's tender at that moment, Juve would certainly not have hesitated to start moving. He would have been able to flee into the countryside, putting a good ten miles of uninhabited space between himself and civilization, after which nothing would have been easier than helping Fandor escape!

But—alas!—the shunters were in no hurry to come and make the coupling. As the seconds passed, Juve felt beads of anguished sweat appear on his forehead.

He feared there would not again be such a perfect opportunity for fleeing without witnesses or adversaries.

To keep himself occupied while he waited, Juve charged the firebox. Soon, coal roared in the boiler. When its valves became too full, this released a burning vapor that issued a raucous whistle while escaping.

"Good God!" swore Juve. "I wish the shunters arrive before the driver and fireman return! If only this cursed wagon were hitched, we'd already be underway!"

The din that the locomotive made under pressure was so great, and Juve was so absorbed in his reflections, that he barely heard the last note of a strange siren that went off next to him.

However, a gunshot fired a few yards away from the locomotive caught the policeman's attention!

Not understanding what was happening, anxious, Juve leaned on the safety rail to see if he could learn anything.

Suddenly, he felt the floor vibrating under his feet and sensed that the locomotive was slowly starting, billowing out huge puffs of vapor, releasing black, ash-filled smoke from its chimney.

Juve turned to look around the engine room.

A man had climbed inside when his back was turned and had pulled the regulator that controlled the steam flow to the pistons. This man appeared to have collapsed in front of the coal-crammed firebox and now rested on the floor inert.

Juve noticed that the powerful Pacific was actually moving away from the penitentiary car rather than towards it!

Every turn of the wheel took them farther and farther from the prison in which Fandor was confined, and which, for the last 48 hours, Juve had so carefully planned to drag into the countryside.

The policeman howled in frustration.

"In God's name! Curse it!"

With an impulsive gesture, he grabbed the shoulders of the man whom he believed was the driver, and who had had the unfortunate idea of starting up the locomotive.

Juve turned the man over and stood back, amazed, for he recognized the face before him.

The two men remained motionless for an instant, as if each thought he was hallucinating. They were so astonished that they could not believe what their eyes were telling them!

This shock lasted a second and they threw their arms around one another.

"Juve!"

"Fandor!"

Indeed, by the most bewildering circumstances, the two had been reunited on this engine which presently hurtled down the rails at full speed, in a mad rush across the countryside.

These two names had been uttered with the greatest satisfaction and the most vibrant compassion.

The friends were together at last! After having run after one another for weeks, they were finally in each other's presence.

But how had it happened?

While Juve had been impatiently pacing alone in the locomotive, waiting for the shunters to come and couple the penitentiary car carrying Fandor to the engine, a tragic and poignant drama composed had brusquely unfolded in the space of a few minutes.

First, the unfortunate driver, whose absence had seemed unexplainable, had suddenly passed from life to death.

The unfortunate man had indeed gone to look for the hammer he had left in the coal reserve. He found the tool that was so indispensable for him, and was prepared to return to his post.

However, instead, he had been cravenly stabbed from behind with a dagger.

He had vomited streams of blood from his mouth and nostrils, sagged to the ground, sprinkled with coal dust, and died on the spot, without a word or gesture.

The crime had been committed with incredible skill and dexterity. And, it had been carried out with no witnesses.

Once this evil deed was accomplished, the murderer had quickly fled, leaving his weapon planted between his victim's shoulderblades.

The murderer immediately ran in the direction of the penitentiary car. He passed the engine and cast a mocking glance at Juve, who was still on the footplate and did not see him.

He entered the car where Fandor was alone with his young guard. The latter, surprised by the brusque appearance of the unknown man, was immediately on the defensive.

"Who are you? What do you want?" he asked.

The soldier's hand already moved towards his revolver.

The movement proved fatal for him and he never completed it.

The newcomer, with surprising speed, had thrown himself on the guard, squeezing his neck between two wiry and robust hands.

The unfortunate guard had quickly fallen and, a few instants later, he succumbed to strangulation.

The murderer then stood up, his eyes shining with a strange light. Anyone looking at him at that moment, his face contracted, his evil mouth twisted in a murderous grimace, could not have failed to recognize the legendary Lord of Terror whose very name made all humanity tremble.

For it was none other than Fantômas who had just committed the double murder in the space of a few minutes!

However, if the driver's murder had been accomplished without witnesses, someone had seen Fantômas strangle the guard!

The witness of the horrible drama had become pale, for he suspected that he would be the monster's next victim, and that nothing could help him. He was unable to defend himself; his hands and his ankles were shackled!

Fandor was seeing Fantômas again for the first time since the beginning of his sinister South African odyssey, and under circumstances that would have made the bravest man quiver.

Fantômas threw himself onto the journalist; yet, instead of striking him down, he returned his liberty.

In the wink of an eye, the extraordinary villain released the shackles and detached the chain that tied the journalist's legs.

"Fandor!" said Fantômas. "I'm giving you back your freedom. Now run!"

The monster seized the young man by the shoulders. Stunned, the journalist obeyed, yielding to the brusque shoving that propelled him out of the wagon and onto the railway track.

"Run!" insisted Fantômas.

Haggard, the journalist looked at the outlaw without understanding.

"That locomotive is waiting for you," Fantômas continued. "Climb up, release the steam regulator... The first handle on your left... The locomotive will leave. All is prepared."

"What? Who?" stammered Fandor.

The outlaw, laugh sardonically.

"Obey, and remember, Fandor, that you owe your life—to Fantômas!"

These bewildering words were said in the middle of an infernal din, in the ruckus that the puffing engine made at the moment that its cylinders were purged.

Fandor could barely see the man speaking to him, who was now enveloped in a cloud of thick black smoke.

He retained only two thoughts: one that he was free, but also that he owed his liberty to a new crime committed by Fantômas.

Fandor couldn't accept that!

Certainly, the journalist felt an inexpressible joy at the idea that he was rid of his bonds. And, in addition, by avoiding being tried by the High Court, he would likely escape a terrible judgment and an ignominious death.

However, Fandor was, above all else honest.

"Fantômas, I can't accept this!" he shouted.

"Accept," ordered Fantômas, "or die."

"I cannot," insisted Fandor.

Fantômas sprang out of the wagon. He seized Fandor, who had been stranding next to the track, unwilling to move.

With Herculean force, Fantômas dragged him onto the Pacific, and pulled the regulator bar to start it.

Fandor, stunned, unable to resist, dropped on the footplate next to the firebox.

Even though the locomotive was now on its way, Fantômas remained on the tracks.

He approached the penitentiary car and discharged his revolver. But before so doing, he had greeted the Pacific's departure with these cruel, enigmatic words:

"I'd promised to reunite you, Juve and Fandor, but only because I've vowed to kill you together!"

The gunshot attracted everyone nearby; people ran up and were surprised to see the locomotive leaving.

Fantômas, with brazen assurance and admirable aplomb, began to shout.

"Help! The prisoner's murdered his guard and escaped from his railcar!"

Meanwhile, the locomotive was rushing down the tracks, launching across the countryside, its signal lights burning, passing the small stations of Durban's outskirts like lightning.

Juve and Fandor were so surprised and happy to be together that they paid no attention to its journey.

Both spoke at once, asking questions at random, not listening to the other's answers.

It was more than disconcerting: Juve had found Fandor free and miraculously saved!

Fandor found himself in Juve's presence, after not having had the least news, and believing his friend to still be in Europe.

"How did you come to be here?" he asked.

While Juve was being pressed with questions, he also asked his own.

"Fandor, who was it who freed you?"

The journalist spoke Fantômas' name.

But hardly had he pronounced it than he fell silent.

Both men were suddenly concerned.

Of course, their fortuitous encounter could have been the result of a fortunate coincidence, but if they were together by the will of Fantômas, it was certain that their meeting had been worked out to allow the sinister criminal to accomplish some new plan, perhaps to drop his two adversaries into a new trap!

"If Fantômas has intervened," exclaimed Juve, "we must be wary!"

The policeman didn't know how wisely he had spoken.

For the last few minutes, the powerful locomotive had been making worrying jumps and was chugging with an abnormal fervor.

Fandor was close to the boiler's pressure gauge. He looked at it with an increasingly anxious air.

"It's climbing, Juve, it's climbing!" he exclaimed.

The two men looked at each other, terrified.

237

Obviously, by some evil means devised by Fantômas, the safety valves had been closed. The pressure was increasing dangerously, and an explosion was likely.

Juve and Fandor looked at their surroundings. They were in an isolated spot, but it seemed impossible to abandon the Pacific, which was hurtling at a speed of more than 70 miles an hour!

At that speed, jumping, especially given that the tracks were bordered with rocks and large trees, was to face certain death.

Nevertheless, the two friends didn't lose their strength of will.

Both men knew how to handle locomotives. They ran to the tender and to the lever activating the hand brake.

"Let's slow her down," Juve suggested, "and as soon as we can, we'll jump!"

However, a new discovery made them shudder!

The brake didn't work. It had been sabotaged!

There was nothing they could do!

Fantômas had definitely kept to his sinister promise. He had returned them to each other, true, but he was also sending them to their deaths together!

"Juve!"

"Fandor!"

"What can we do?"

"Alas, I don't see an answer!"

Then, they fell silent.

Boiling with rage, they considered their impending death and wondered how long it would take for the engine to explode.

The massive locomotive was practically flying as it achieved a breathtaking speed. At each curve, at each turn, they felt it oscillate on its powerful springs.

At each instant, it seemed that it was going to tear itself off its rails and fall into a chasm or climb some mountain slope's steep side.

It was a mad and macabre race, a race to the abyss, a race to the death!

Nevertheless, after the first instants of legitimate terror, Juve and Fandor had a resurgence of courage while awaiting the fatal instant of their demise.

"We shouldn't give up!" shouted Juve.

"Yes," cried Fandor, "let's try something—but what?"

Juve leaned over the platform that joined the tender and the engine; it was a removable plate, which he raised.

While Juve was engaged in this activity, Fandor cried out triumphantly, for he understood the policeman's intention.

Under the platform were located the chains and the powerful clamping screws that kept the tender and the engine attached to each other. If they succeeded in getting to these, and if they were able to unhook the chains and unscrew the bolts, the engine, released from the tender's weight, would spring ahead and go even faster. It would then explode far in the distance, without the tender being affected. The tender itself would slowly decelerate and would eventually stop on its own.

Animated by a gleam of hope, Juve and Fandor undid the retaining screws with feverish haste.

They finally succeeded in their endeavor and took refuge on the tender.

They felt two or three jolts, then the engine made a prodigious bound forward, suddenly relieved of the load that it had dragged behind it.

The locomotive separated itself from them. They were saved!

However, their triumphant cries abruptly changed into ones of despair.

A new, horrible spectacle had just appeared!

On the locomotive's small roof, intended to protect the fireman and driver from bad weather, someone had just stood up, and hands joined, arms extended toward them, seemed to be imploring them to help.

Juve and Fandor recognized the soft face, the large clear eyes. Together, they shouted her name:

"Teddy!"

"Hélène!"

The locomotive, now free from any control, was carrying the daughter of Fantômas away to a certain death!

Why was she there?

The daring and bold girl had learned of Fandor's transfer to the Pietermaritzburg prison. Just like Juve, she had had the irresistible desire to help the unfortunate captive, discounting the risk that would mean for her.

"God in heaven!" Fandor exclaimed.

Juve's eyes were wild with fear.

"She's lost!" he murmured.

Their words were wasted in the din of the overheated engine as it spat out smoke and vapor through all its cracks and openings.

As the seconds passed, the tender was slowing down while the Pacific was going ever faster.

A hundred yards separated them in the space of two seconds!

They heard one last terrible cry. The unfortunate girl being drawn away by the iron monster called in a heart-rending voice:

"Fandor, help me!"

The journalist, unable to bear the pain of seeing her rushing towards her doom, fell into Juve's arms. And, the stalwart policeman swore:

"I'll save her! I swear it! Juve won't let the daughter of Fantômas perish!"

THE END

Epilogue [12]

How did Juve and Fandor return to Paris? How, after the astounding adventures they had lived through in Natal, had they managed to cheat death once more, just as they were about to catch Fantômas, to uncover his secrets and rescue his daughter? How?

Here is what had happened:

Juve and Fandor, miraculously reunited on the locomotive that carried them at breakneck speed towards a terrible fate, had succeeded, after much labor, to unhook the tender from the engine.

After inertia had caused it to continue rolling for a few minutes, the tender and the empty penitentiary car had finally come to a stop.

They had found themselves stranded in the middle of nowhere, abandoned by all, isolated, condemned to face the perils of the veldt; lost, weaponless and without supplies.

Juve and Fandor, fortunately, were too resourceful to surrender to panic. Ignoring their fears and mustering their wills, they made the right decisions when anyone else in their predicament might have given up in apathy. They had barely escaped the terrible fate that Fantômas had had in store for them; but they were already prepared to take arms again, to continue their pursuit of their formidable enemy, that dreaded criminal, the elusive Lord of Terror!

"Juve!" shouted Fandor. "Fantômas may have won this battle, but we will have our revenge."

"Yes, Fandor, we will have our revenge."

---

[12] Excerpt from Volume 9: *Le Fiacre de Nuit* (*The Night Cab*), Chapter III.

These two brave men had shouted their defiance and their hopes before even beginning to think about the ways to extricate themselves from the perilous situation into which Fantômas' criminal genius had thrown them.

Soon, however, Juve, who was gifted with a methodical, precise and practical mind, had come up with a plan. In a fatherly fashion, he had placed his hand on Fandor's shoulder when the young man was thinking, resting his head on the thick grass of the railway embankment.

"Listen, Fandor, I know what's bothering you right now. It's Teddy's fate, or rather, Hélène's. You're not really in love with her, you know. It would be a terrible thing, a dreadful misfortune for you if you'd fallen for her. But you have some concern for her. That's understandable. You'd like to know what happened to her. So, get up, Fandor! Let's go and find out!"

Juve and the journalist had then managed, after almost superhuman efforts, to reach the nearest station. There, they were surprised to learn that a locomotive had indeed derailed at a turn in the line, but that there were no victims because there was no one on board. At least, the station master affirmed, they had found no bodies near the site of the accident.

What, then, was their conclusion? It was obvious: Teddy—Hélène—had managed, thanks to some unfathomable miracle, to escape safely from the terrible trap into which she had fallen.

Reassured as to the young girl's fate—and finding no more information about her—Juve and Fandor, penniless, had gathered their wits. As always, it was Juve who had decided on their next course of action:

"Natal isn't healthy for us," he said. "They think you're a murderer and, if they catch you, you might be condemned to death. As for me, Fandor, I have no more means than you to ask the authorities for help. We've been pursuing Fantômas for a while, sparing no effort, taking every risk, fighting every battle to capture him. A hundred times, we've been on the verge of triumph! A hundred times, he's barely managed to escape! Well, listen to me, Fandor—upon my soul, I swear that Fantômas is finally closer to our grasp, more exposed to our blows then ever…"

Juve paused and Fandor interrupted him, "What the Devil do you mean?"

"Just this: yesterday, Fantômas was a mysterious being, unknown to us. Today, we know whom he loves, for whom he kidnaps and murders, we have learned his *raison d'être*. Fandor, in every man there is a weakness, a love, a passion! Nothing has ever stopped Fantômas. Until now, we haven't found a single means of thwarting him; no plan has been good enough. But it was only because we didn't know how to fight him. Believe me, we're better armed now. Fantômas cares little for his lover, Lady Beltham, who worships him, and that's why we were ineffective when we tried to use her against him. But now, we've discovered that the Devil has a daughter: Teddy, Hélène, a daughter whom he loves, whom he wants to make rich and happy. Don't doubt it, Fandor, he is much weaker because of the affection he feels for her, virtually at our mercy…"

Juve then outlined a battle plan. They had to return to France immediately and wait.

Juve still had the papers he had taken from that strange skull. He had been able to decipher some of them, but others remained a mystery. These papers would be the bait he would dangle before Fantômas after they returned to Paris, the bait that would force him out in the open and make him fall into their trap.

"Let's go back to France," said Juve. "If we look like we're retreating, Fantômas will come after us, and rest assured that we shall emerge victorious from our next battle!"

Fandor agreed.

After a thousand sufferings and displaying superhuman energy, Juve and Fandor managed to reach the coast and secretly board a ship for England. And from there, they eventually made their way back to Paris.

Bibliography [13]

By Marcel Allain & Pierre Souvestre:
1. *Fantômas* (1911; translated as *Fantômas*, 1915; retranslated, 1986)
2. *Juve contre Fantômas* [*Juve vs. Fantômas*] (1911; translated as *The Exploits of Juve*, 1916; retranslated as *The Silent Executioner*, 1987)
3. *Le Mort qui Tue* [*The Dead Man Who Kills*] (1911; translated as *Messengers of Evil*, 1917)
4. *L'Agent Secret* [*The Secret Agent*] (1911; translated as *A Nest of Spies*, 1917)
5. *Un Roi Prisonnier de Fantômas* [*A King Prisoner of Fantômas*] (1911; translated as *A Royal Prisoner*, 1919)
6. *Le Policier Apache* [*The Apache Policeman*] (1911; translated as *The Long Arm of Fantômas*, 1924)
7. *Le Pendu de Londres* [*The Hanged Man of London*] (1911; translated as *Slippery as Sin*, 1920)
8. *La Fille de Fantômas* [*The Daughter of Fantômas*] (1911)
9. *Le Fiacre de Nuit* [*The Night Cab*] (1911)
10. *La Main Coupée* [*The Severed Hand*] (1911; translated as *The Limb of Satan*, 1924)
11. *L'Arrestation de Fantômas* [*The Capture of Fantômas*] (1911)
12. *Le Magistrat Cambrioleur* [*The Burglar Judge*] (1912)
13. *La Livrée du Crime* [*The Livery of Crime*] (1912)
14. *La Mort de Juve* [*The Death of Juve*] (1912)
15. *L'Evadée de Saint-Lazare* [*The Escapee From Saint-Lazare*] (1912)
16. *La Disparition de Fandor* [*The Disappearance of Fandor*] (1912)
17. *Le Mariage de Fantômas* [*The Wedding of Fantômas*] (1912)

---

[13] A more detailed bibliography can be found in *Shadowmen: Heroes and Villains of French Pulp Fiction*, q.v.

18. *L'Assassin de Lady Beltham* [*The Assassin of Lady Beltham*] (1912)
19. *La Guêpe Rouge* [*The Red Wasp*] (1912)
20. *Les Souliers du Mort* [*The Dead Man's Shoes*] (1912)
21. *Le Train Perdu* [*The Lost Train*] (1912)
22. *Les Amours d'un Prince* [*The Love of a Prince*] (1912)
23. *Le Bouquet Tragique* [*The Tragic Bouquet*] (1912)
24. *Le Jockey Masqué* [*The Masked Jockey*] (1913)
25. *Le Cercueil Vide* [*The Empty Coffin*] (1913)
26. *Le Faiseur de Reines* [*The Queen Maker*] (1913)
27. *Le Cadavre Géant* [*The Giant Corpse*] (1913)
28. *Le Voleur d'Or* [*The Gold Thief*] (1913)
29. *La Série Rouge* [*The Red Series*] (1913)
30. *L'Hôtel du Crime* [*The Crime Hotel*] (1913)
31. *La Cravate de Chanvre* [*The Hemp Necktie*] (1913)
32. *La Fin de Fantômas* [*The End of Fantômas*] (1913)

By Marcel Allain:
33. *Fantômas est-il ressuscité?* [*Is Fantômas Resurrected?*] (1925; translated as *The Lord of Terror*, 1925)
34. *Fantômas, Roi des Recéleurs* [*Fantômas, King of the Fences*] (1926; translated as *Juve in the Dock*, 1926)
35. *Fantômas en Danger* [*Fantômas in Danger*] (1926; translated as *Fantômas Captured*, 1926)
36. *Fantômas Prend sa Revanche* [*Fantômas Takes His Revenge*] (1926; translated as *The Revenge of Fantômas*, 1927)
37. *Fantômas Attaque Fandor* [*Fantômas Attacks Fandor*] (1926; translated as *Bulldog and Rats*, 1928)
38. *Si c'était Fantômas?* [*If It Was Fantômas?*] (1933)
39. *Oui, c'est Fantômas!* [*Yes, It Is Fantômas!*] (1934)
40. *Fantômas Joue et Gagne* [*Fantômas Plays and Wins*] (1935)
41. *Fantômas Rencontre l'Amour* [*Fantômas Meets Love*] (1946)

42. *Fantômas Vole des Blondes* [*Fantômas Steals Blondes*] (1948)
43. *Fantômas Mène le Bal* [*Fantômas Leads the Dance*] (1963)

About the Translator

Mark P. Steele has been a student of popular, fantastic and heroic literature for most of his life. He has four issues of a comics adaptation of Shea and Wilson's *Illuminatus!* to his credit: one self-published and three from Rip Off Press. He has also had art published in Kalamazoo Comics, a nationally distributed comics magazine.

Mark's current projects under development include *Age of Heroes,*® a series set in the pre-WW II era featuring a great many of the forgotten heroes of the time; the aforementioned *Don Juan Unbound*; a series of biographical sketches of various members of the Wold Newton Family and other literary greats; *Gloom and Doom,*™ a series set in modern Midwestern America starring a young teenage vampire and the corporate machinations of her mysterious uncle; *The Society of Protectors,* ™ about the greatest heroes of the 1920s; forthcoming fanfic art and stories; and many other projects, some of which might be seen on the Eye-n-Apple web site.

Mark is also working on: a new edition of the *Principia Discordia*, to be used to raise funds for the Katrina Relief Effort in conjunction with the Officers of Avalon; and Lord Omar Khayyan Ravenhurst's *The Honest Book of Truth*, having been a Discordian Episkopos for many years.